Book Writer

ALAN HINES

www.trafford.com
North America & international
toll-free: 1 888 232 4444 (USA & Canada)
fax: 812 355 4082

Acknowledgements

Special thanks to the creator of the Heavens, and the Earth for blessing me with life to live, and the power to write diverse genre on different levels; and I thank the creator for all his many blessings. Special thanks to my grandmother Jean Hines whom are in Heaven; the seeds she planted within me as a youth finally grew, and developed to something so beautiful. Special thanks to my mom, and dad for getting together, and creating me. Special thanks to my sister Alicia for inviting me to this wonderful world of book writing, and I appreciate all her love, and support. Special thanks to Julie Hull (attorney), John Fitzgerald Lyke (attorney), and to Mr. Marasa (English Teacher). And to anybody else that showed me any love, and support throughout life.

Thanks to the entire Hines, and Laughlin family, Ricardo Sanchez, Roscell Hines(Cel), Alan White(Block), I pray daily that your situations will soon come to an end. Thanks to my co-workers I appreciate all the help, and interest in wanting to see me prosper.....

Books of poetry already published by Alan Hines,

1. Reflections of Love
2. Thug Poetry Volume 1
3. The Words I Spoke
4. Joyce
5. Constant Visions
6. Red Ink of Blood
7. Beauty of Love
8. Reflections of Love Volume 2
9. Reflections of Love Volume 3

Urban Novel already published by Alan Hines,

1. Book Writer
2. Queen of Queens

Upcoming books of poetry by Alan Hines,

1. Reflections of Love (Volume 2, and 3)
2. This is Love (Volume 1, 2, and 3)
3. Founded Love (Volume 1,2, and 3)
4. True Love (Volume 1,2, and 3)
5. Love (Endless Volumes)
6. Tormented Tears (Volume 1,2, and 3)
7. A Inner Soul That Cried (Volume 1,2, and 3)
8. Visionary (Endless Volumes)
9. In My Eyes To See (Volume 1,2, and 3)
10. A Seed That Grew (Volume 1,2, and, 3)
11. The Words I Spoke (Volume 2, and 3)
12. Scriptures (Volume 1,2, and 3)
13. Revelations (volume 1,2, and 3)
14. Destiny (Volume 1,2, and 3)
15. Trials and Tribulations (Volume 1,2, and 3)
16. IMMORTALITY (Volume 1,2, and 3)
17. My Low Spoken Words (Volume 1,2, and 3)
18. Beauty Within (Volume 1,2, and 3)
19. Red Ink of Blood (Volume 1,2, and 3)

20. Destiny of Light (Jean Hines) (Volume 1,2, and 3)
21. Deep Within (Volume 1, 2, and 3)
22. Literature (Volume 1, 2, and 3)
23. Silent Mind (Volume 1,2, and 3)
24. Amor (Volume 1,2, and 3)
25. Joyce (Volume 1,2, and 3)
26. Lovely Joyce (Volume 1,2, and 3)
27. Pink Lady (Volume 1,2, and 3)
28. Mockingbird Lady (Volume 1,2, and 3)
29. Godly tendicies (Volume 1,2, and 3)
30. Enchanting Arrays (Volume 1,2, and 3)
31. Harmony (Volume 1,2, and 3)
32. Realism (Volume 1,2, and 3)
33. Manifested Deep Thoughts (Volume 1,2, and 3)
34. Poectic Lines of Scrimage (Volume 1,2, and 3)
35. Garden of Love (Volume 1,2, and 3)
36. Reflection In The Mirror. (Volume 1,2, and 3)

Upcoming non-fiction books by Alan Hines,

1. Time Versus Life
2. Timeless Jewels
3. The Essence of Time
4. Memoirs of My Life
5. In my Eyes To See
6. A Prisoner's Black History

Upcoming Urban Novels by Alan Hines,

1. Black Kings
2. Playerlistic
3. The Police
4. Scandalous
5. The West Side Rapist
6. Shattered Dreams
7. She Wrote Murder
8. Black Fonz
9. A Slow Form of Suicide

Chapter 1

Suzie and Carl sat at the table using dope.

"How many more bags of dope we got left," Carl asked Suzie while scratching and nodding all at the same time. "We got five mo bags of dope, why you didn't bring no rocks back so I can smoke me some primos," Suzie asked? "I couldn't the joint got hot the nigga who was working the rock packs disappeared, the only reason I brought some dope home is because every time I sold a blow jab, I kept me a couple blows for myself instead of selling them, I'm glad I did cuz the nigga who was working the blow jab disappeared to when the police came through. I know they wondering where the fuck I'm at I was supposed to work for the rest of the day, I'm just gone tell them I left cuz some police came through that had locked me up before," Carl said.

Carl continued scratching and nodding as if he was sleep for a few seconds. He slightly opened his eyes and looked up at Suzie . . . .

"This dope a bomb, this dope better than the dope they had yesterday," Carl said. "Yeah I know I think they put some new shit on the dope, whatever they putting on it they need to keep putting it on it," Suzie said.

Carl upped his dick . . . .

"Bitch suck this dick," Carl said. "I told you about calling me out my name, put your dick up before Latisha come in," Suzie said. "Aw yeah I forget she was in there, I'm glad she didn't walk in here while I had my dick out," Carl said . . . .

Ten seconds later in comes Latisha . . . .

1

"Mom I'm hungry give me some money so I can get me something to eat," Latisha said. "Girl I brought you something to eat yesterday," Suzie said. "But that was yesterday, what I only supposed to eat once a week," Latisha said. "Girl don't be getting smart at the mouth. I wish I would've listen to my momma and got an abortion when I was pregnant with you," Suzie said.

"Here girl here go ten dollars, and bring me some candy back," Suzie said.

Every time this bitch get high she always want to suck on some candy, Latisha thought to herself.

On her way to the store she ran into one of her little friends Jennifer . . . .

"Where are you going Latisha," Jennifer asked? "I'm on my way to the store to get my dope fiend ass momma some candy," Latisha said. "Why do dope fiends always gotta have candy when they get high off dope," Jennifer asked? "I don't know, I be wondering the same thing," Latisha said.

"My birthday is tomorrow," Jennifer said. "My birthday is in a couple of weeks," Latisha said. "Fo real," Jennifer said. "Fo real, I'll be eleven," Latisha said. "I'll be twelve," Jennifer said.

"Let me go get my momma this candy, cuz this bitch gone be tripping if it take me to long to come back with her candy," Latisha said. "Stop by here when you come back," Jennifer said. "A'ight," Latisha said . . . .

As Latisha made it within the store she noticed that all three lines were long as hell.

She went into the section where the candy was . . . .

What should I get candy bars, or jolly ranchers, fuck it I'll get one of each, Latisha thought to herself.

She went to get in a long ass line to pay for the candy . . . .

While waiting in line she begin to think about what was she going to order from the restaurant next door . . . .

I'mma order me a cheese burger, fries, and a slurpy, she thought to herself . . . .

The line continued to move slow . . . .

I'm tired of waiting in this line, Latisha thought to herself . . . .

Without no hesitation she put the candy bar, and jolly rancher in her pocket. She figured she'd steal the candy and keep all the money for herself.

She stepped outta line and begin walking towards the door . . . .

"Hey little girl wait, wait," the Arab lady said.

Latisha got nervous and tried to run outta the store.

A shot came from a .357 hit Latisha in the back.

Little Latisha never seen the gun, she just heard the shot, and felt the bullet. Her body couldn't take it she shook, and drop as the sound of the gun was like an echo as everyone in the store begin yelling, and screaming and running outta the store . . . .

The Arab man grabbed the gun from his wife.

"What made you do that," he asked? "I didn't do it purpose it was a mistake I pointed the gun at her just to scare her and it went off," the Arab lady said . . . .

The Arab man walked over and looked at the little girl lying there in her own blood. In his own silent mind he prayed to Allah that she wasn't dead. Swiftly visions of his very own little girl lying there shot and bleeding raced through his head . . . .

"I hope she aint dead," he said. "Go, go, get in the car and drive away," he said. "Where to," she asked? "Go to my friends Whola's house he got a private jet tell him to take you back to Saudia Arabia. Here take this gun to, and give it to Whola's and tell him I said dispose of it, he'll know what to do with it," he said . . . .

As she ran out the back door to her car, he ran to lock the front doors, and the back door behind her. He went to get all the surveillance videos, ran out the back door up the alley to throw the DVD's in the garbage, ran back into the store locked the back door swiftly.

Dialed 911 and told the police a little girl just got shot, and that he needed an ambulance right now. Little did he know someone had already called the police, they were already on their way.

Once the police and the paramedics arrived one paramedic checked Latisha's pulse and seen that she was still living.

Abdula felt a momentary sign of relief knowing that, that little girl was alive.

The ambulance rushed Latisha to the hospital.

He told the police his version of the story. Then they asked for the surveillance videos. He told them that he didn't have any because his surveillance system was broke.

The police continued to search for shell casings or any other type of physical evidence, none was found.

Some of the officer went outside across the street to the crowd, and got a statement for someone that was actually in the store when the incident occurred . . . .

After many hours searching for evidence the police escorted Abdula to the police station so he could file a police report. As they walked out the store once Abdula finished properly locking the front door they walked towards the police car as one female out of the crowd from across the street yelled out, "bitch I hope you die."

One black detective paused looked over at her curiously wondering why did she make that outburst.

So they continued on to the police station once they made it there it was seven other people there that was in the store when the shooting occurred getting reports filed.

The police surrounded Abdula and escorted him to the interrogation room way in the back. All the officers left him in the room by himself. Through the glass Abdula seen all the officers talking amongst themselves he couldn't hear what they were saying through the door that was closed and that had real thick glass.

Abdula noticed how the big black officer face was in shock as the other officers talked.

Majority of the officers left the hallway and went to various areas in police station as the big black officer and a little short fat white officer stayed in the hallway talking.

Eventually the white officer spent off as the black officer entered the room smiling . . . .

"So you say three men was robbing your store, as the little girl tried to run out the door one of the men shot her in the back, correct," the black officer said. "Yes, that's correct," Abdula said. "Three black guys right," the black officer said. "Right," Abdula said.

The black officer started to smile harder than before . . . .

"We got eight people, one by the store, and seven people in station right now as we speak saying that your wife shot that lil girl," the black officer said. "That's a lie, why would my wife shoot a little girl," Abdula said . . . .

The black officer gave no reply but handcuffed Abdula . . . .

For hours different officers tried to get Abdula to tell the truth about what had happen but Abdula stuck to his story . . . .

Abdula was placed in a holding cell, as they went on a manhunt for his wife . . . .

Somebody went back and told everybody from the hood that Abdula told the police a lie that a nigga shot Latisha instead his wife. People from the hood begin to uproar . . . .

Later that night Latisha's auntie walk up with her heavy make-up damaged from a over flow of tears. She walked up to some the guys standing on the corner felt to her knees and begin crying loudly . . . .

"She didn't make it, God took my baby away from me," Latisha's aunt said . . . .

A lot of people from the hood including Latisha's family just blanked out. First they went to Abdula's store and set fire to it. Then they went to each every Arab business in the hood, and fucked them up, damn near killed two Arabs. Burning down all their businesses to the ground; they pour gasoline on one Arab and set him on fire, damn near killed him to, but he saved his own life by using the stop, drop, and roll method once they left . . . .

It was hard for the police to contain the violence that night . . . .

For a couple of days to follow people from the hood, as well as homicide would search for Abdula's wife, she was nowhere to be found . . . .

Three days after Latisha was shot, and killed Abdula was charged with conspiracy to commit murder. Homicide rigged it up as if he told his wife to do it . . . .

Abdula was sent to the county jail, and given a high bond because he was a flight risk. His bond was set at a hundred thousand to walk. A hundred thousand wasn't shit to him he owned other stores and a few apartment buildings. He bonded out the same day . . . .

About a week after Latisha was killed, and buried niggas from the hood was tired of looking for Abdula's wife, but became even thirstier to find Abdula's wife to take her life away as she did Latisha . . . .

It was this young nigga that was sixteen named Twon whom inner soul had been crying out since Latisha's death; he cried out feeling like why, why this little girl Latisha had to die . . . .

Unexpectedly Twon had heard that Abdula had a store on the other side of town . . . .

The next morning Twon, and two of his guys got strapped, and went to the store early in the morning before it even opened looking for Abdula's wife or one of Abdula's family members. To his surprise there Abdula was opening up his store, he couldn't believe it he thought Abdula was still in jail. They pulled up the block and parked . . . .

"Man let's just rush up on him, and make him show us where his wife is," Twon said. "Be for real you think he just gone tell us where his wife is at," Q said. "People tend to do a lot of things that they wouldn't normally do once they got a big ass gun in their face," Twon said. "He aint gonna tell you where his wife at," John, John said with confidence. "We still gotta try," Twon said. "Fam, it's broad daylight man, you just wanna walk up and up guns on him," Q said. "What the fuck did we get strapped and come over here for," Twon ask? "We need to stake out the store first," John, John said. "You sound like a nerdy college motherfucker, one of them white boys, we need to stake out the store first. You niggas is stupid, we come all the way over here to gets down and you niggas act like ya'll scared. This nigga wife done killed this little girl, shot her to death for no reason. That's one thing about death aint no coming back from that shit once you die it's over. You know what, fuck ya'll niggas, on my life," Twon said . . . .

Twon bailed out of the car walked up to Abdula upped on him made him finish opening up the store walked him in made him get on his knees, slid his throat with a razor then shot him in the head once execution style and left the store.

Twon came running out the store with the razor in his left hand, and the gun in his right hand, bailed in the car pulled off . . . .

As they rode, destination to the hood Q and John, John remained silent as Twon talked and kicked it like nothing never happen . . . .

In reality Twon was going to walk Abdula into the store to force him to tell him where his wife was at, and for him to take him to his wife; but once he got in the store visions of Latisha laying in a casket begin flashing in his head which provoked him to take away Abdula's life . . . .

A couple of weeks later Twon was having a small birthday party for his seventeen birthday at a tavern in the hood. Outta nowhere homicide rushed in placed him under arrest Twon had no idea of what was going on, and he wondered to himself which murder were they grabbing him for cuz he had been doing so much dirt. He would've never guessed that it was the murder of Abdula . . . .

Homicide probably would've never grabbed or even suspected him over that murder if Q and John, John wouldn't never went back to hood and told people. Q and John, John only told a few people, but those few people told a few more people, and those few more people told a few more people and word of mouth slowly spreaded . . . .

Some nigga from the hood was getting hassled from the police for some other shit, and gave up information about Twon killing Abdula so they would let him free. The police didn't ask the nigga about any unsolved murders, but he knew that if he gave them that lead that they'd definitely let him go and forget about the petty shit they was harassing him for, and it worked . . . .

Once they made it to the police station Twon came to find out they had a witness whom lived across the street from the store seen him and that they had surveillance from the store that showed him killing Abdula.

What Twon didn't know was that by him having his hoody on with the strings slightly tied around his mouth, and had his head down majority of the time during the incident that the witness nor the surveillance really couldn't actually say, or show it was him . . . .

They put Twon in a line up in order for the one witness to positively I.D. him, and she did point him out that was only because he was a real short guy, everybody else in the lineup was tall.

Twon always thought line ups were only in movies but he came to see that the police do that for real . . . .

They shipped Twon to the county and charged him with Abdula's murder. Gave him a high ass bond so Twon knew he wasn't going to bond out . . . .

This was Twon first time to the county he had only been to juvenile detention once now that he was seventeen there was no more juvenile for him he had to be with the grown men.

Once he made it to the Cook county jail, division 10 he was screened to see if he was gang affiliated, he was an UnderTaker ViceLord. He got introduced to the other ViceLords, they gave him a little cosmetics, and food. They offered squares, but he didn't smoke. Afterwards they laid out to him the security measurements . . . .

His first day on the deck was average . . . .

Twon immediately noticed that the county was totally different from the juvenile detention center in many different ways . . . .

On his third day of being in jail he awoke from the sounds the doors being unlocked to eat breakfast . . . .

I can't believe I'm stuck in jail for a body, he thought to his self as he walked to go get his tray . . . .

They had scrambled eggs and oatmeal on the trays. This was his first time eating oatmeal, it was a bomb to him . . . .

In juvenile they'd go to the lunchroom to eat as school kids did, in the Cook county jail there was no lunchroom in his division, the officers brought the trays to the deck, and two or three assigned inmates passed the trays out to the rest of the people on the deck.

Certain inmates would get special trays that revolved around health issues; like hypro trays, and low fat trays . . . .

Twon ate his tray went in cell in attempts to go back to sleep . . . .

Approximately three minutes after Twon laid off in the bunk he heard one nigga say the next time you bitches don't give me my hypro tray we gonna tear this bitch up.

Then one of the niggas that was working the trays yelled out it aint gonna be no next time and hit him in his mouth for calling him a bitch.

In 0.3 seconds the deck went up, he kicked off a riot between the fin ball, and niggas under the six. The fin ball consists of mainly ViceLords, Latin Kings, and Black P-Stones, amongst others. The six mainly consist of G.D's, B.D's, and Latin Folks amongst others.

Twon begin to hear people yelling, the bottom of gym shoes squeaking against the floor.

He jumped out his top bunk to see what was going on, and seen food trays flying back and forth, knives penetrated flesh, as others were getting stumped, and beat . . . .

Twon was on his way out of the cell, but in 0.3 seconds they niggas under the six, and the niggas under the fin separated, both to each side of the deck, as a standoff.

Twon then seen more knives than he'd seen in kitchen sets . . . .

Twon cell was in the back where the niggas under six was so he didn't know what to do, he hoped they didn't run in there on him . . . .

Within no time a gang of C/O's ran on the deck to disperse the violence . . . .

Everybody that had knives tossed them to the ground and ran to their cells as the C/O's came in whupping nigga's and locking them in their cells.

All those that were injured remained out there cells until the paramedics came from the med unit of the county . . . .

Nigga's from both sides got fucked up real bad, from puncher lungs, to broken jaws, to staples in heads, to stitches in faces . . . .

The C/O's found twelve knives . . . .

Twon had heard many bad things about the county before he even made it there, but he never knew that a deck would go up, and niggas get fucked up real bad over a petty hypro tray . . . .

What Twon didn't know was that the individual working the trays gave the man three regular trays and apologized for not giving him a hypro tray, they gave his tray away to someone else by mistake. The man accepted there apology ate the three regular trays and started talking shit.

This was like a welcoming party to the county jail for Twon . . . .

They officer in division 10 decided to split up the deck before they let them off lock down.

When they moved him to another deck he was placed in a cell with a Latin King; which was good for him because Latin Kings and ViceLords were under the fin, allies.

His new celly was nicknamed Loco and he lived up to his name. Twon and Loco hit it off immediately.

The division 10 was still on lock down. Each time someone on any deck got stabbed the entire division would go on lockdown.

Twon hadn't got in touch with his family yet because each time he'd call he'd get no answer. Now that he was on lock down he couldn't call at all.

Loco had been locked up for two years fighting a murder. During those two years Loco had caught all type of assaults on inmates, aggravated batteries for stabbing inmates, and UUW for getting caught with a knife.

Loco was the true essence of a gang banger.

As days past Town begin to open up to Loco and tell his story of why he was locked up. Loco took a liking for him knowing that he wasn't a stool penguin to work with the police and sign a statement on John-John, and Q. Loco knew he could've made all three of them rapy's on Abdula's murder, but he kept his mouth shut.

Loco had a personal vendetta for stool penguins, because his rapy was turning states on him . . . .

"Don't worry about your case, just pray to the creator and leave it in his hands. One of the best things to do while you're in her is read. Reading can take your mind into different areas. It's been times where I been reading a book, and forgot I was even in jail, it was like I was one of the characters in the book, real talk," Loco said. "What kind of books should I read," Town asked? "I read almost anything I can get my hands on, me and you two different people, maybe you should read whatever books that's exciting to

9

you, the ones that keep your mind away from the free world. I got a book for you to read, read this," Loco said as he reached under his mattress grabbed a book and handt it to him.

Twon read the title to himself, The Greatest Sex Stories Ever, Volume 1.

"I don't want to read no sex stories," Twon said. "Go ahead this shit a bomb," Loco said . . . .

Twon got on the top bunk opened up the book and started reading it: Chapter 1, Several People . . . .

Chad and Felicia was a married couple that had been happily married for twenty years. Chad was 43, and Felicia was 50 years of age. Throughout their twenty years of marriage they didn't have too many problems; not once did Chad or Felicia unfaithfully cheat on one another.

Chad and Felicia sex life was average, but they both wanted more excitement . . . .

Chad worked in an office building around many women, but he'd grew a liking for this eighteen year old young lady that had been working there for only a few months. Her name was Rita. Rita had one of the nicest ass any man would love. Each day at work she'd either wear tight jeans, or a full length tight skirt. On top of her nice ass she had a cute baby doll face.

Each day Chad and Rita would conversate, but nothing outta the ordinary, simply casual conversation.

One day Rita and Chad's conversation begin to get a little heated. Rita begin to tell Chad that she'd only been sexually active with one man in her life, her last boyfriend.

By Chad being faithful to his wife he got on to another topic. But in the back of Chad's mind he knew that when a woman told a man such business that was because she was interested in him . . . .

Twon liked the story, and couldn't put the book down, wanted to see what would happen next, so he continued to read . . . .

Felicia would go grocery shopping most of the time by herself. She became acquainted with a young man named Micheal that worked at the grocery store.

Micheal was 22 years old and one of the most hansom man Felicia had ever laid eyes upon.

Felicia and Micheal would have casual conversation when she came to the grocery store, but nothing outta the ordinary.

One day when Felicia was leaving the grocery store Micheal told her that she had a nice ass. Felicia couldn't believe what he'd said. She turned around and asked him "what did you just say." "I said you got a nice ass." She begin laughing, and thanked him for the compliment . . . .

Later on that night Felicia and Chad was watching some stand-up comedy on TV. One of the comedians begin talking about how this younger lady was attracted to him, and of course he made a joke out of it. Chad begin to tell Felicia about that young lady from work that liked him. Felicia begin to tell Chad about the young man from the grocery store that liked her. It was no big deal to either one of them because they had a marriage built of trust.

Before the night end they watched a XXX rated movie. The movie consist of all threesomes. Chad told Felicia he'd like to be involved in a threesome. Felicia told Chad she might if she wasn't married. She didn't want to see her husband having sex with another woman . . . .

After the movie they sexed throughout the night . . . .

The next day at work Rita was all over Chad. Chad was intelligent enough to know she wanted sex . . . . Coincidently on the same exact day Micheal gave Felicia a hug at the grocery store. This wasn't a average hug, this hug was a hug as it was from one lover to another . . . .

Later that day both Felicia and Chad told each other of their experience with the youngsters. Chad admitted to Felicia that he liked Rita, but could never get involved while he was married to her. Felicia said she felt the same way about Micheal.

Out of nowhere Chad said let's invite them to our bedroom one by one. Felicia begin to blush, while giggling and said no in a phony way. Chad had been with her all these years and knew her no wasn't sincere.

Chad didn't say anything else about a threesome for several days . . . .

Within the next several days at work Chad begin to get physical with Rita. He even palmed her ass and titties she enjoyed it.

What Rita didn't understand was why he didn't want to creep off and have sex; Chad didn't want to cheat on his wife, the times he palmed her ass and titties was when his dick got hard and he got out of control . . . .

A day later after he palmed her merchandise they was at work talking about various things. Out of nowhere Chad kissed Rita. After kissing her he told her that he wanted her but didn't want to cheat on his wife. She told him what she don't know won't hurt her . . . .

Twon begin to really get excited, thinking to himself that they should make a movie out of this shit . . . .

"I just can't cheat on my wife. I even told her about you and she'd enjoy meeting you. The only way you and I could get together was in a threesome," Chad said.

Chad paused hoping she'd say she wanted to have a threesome that would've been like a dream come true for Chad. As he paused she paused, confused not knowing how to reply . . . .

"Well in order for me to have a threesome I'd really have to like the man a whole lot to involve myself in that," Rita said. "Do you really like me," Chad asked? Rita begin to smirk. "You got a valid point because I really do like you a lot. I like that you don't want to cheat on your wife, most men wouldn't turn down pussy married or not. First let me meet your wife and we will see how it goes," Rita said . . . .

Chad went straight home from work. When he got there Felicia was naked ready for sex, and he gave her sex, great sex . . . .

After sexing Chad told Felicia all that happen between Rita and himself he left out the part when he palmed her ass and titties. Felicia told him she didn't know about a threesome . . . .

As days passed along Chad continued to ask Felicia of a threesome. She told him that if we have a threesome it would have to be with another man. Chad told her to let's try it with Rita first . . . .

"You'd let your wife have sex with another woman," Felicia asked? "Yes if I'm involved," Chad said . . . .

Felicia remained silent for a little while . . . .

"Forget it let's give it a try with Rita, but if I don't like it I'm not doing it anymore," Felicia said . . . .

The next day at work Chad told Rita, "My wife wants to have a threesome with you." "How do you know that she don't even know me," Rita said. "Although she don't know you I've been telling her good things about you. We've been together for twenty years and my wife and I are in love, therefore we do what it takes to make each other happy. This threesome will make all three of us happy," Chad said . . . .

Later on that day Chad showed up at his home with Rita. Dinner was already ready. All three sat down and ate dinner. While eating dinner Rita and Felicia begin to conversate about girl things, they seemed to be getting along well.

"You look nice," Felicia said to Rita. "I was thinking the same thing about you," Rita said . . . .

At that very moment Chad knew that they wanted to get it in.

Chad went into the living room and placed on a XXX rated movie; of course the movie was of a sexual threesome. He then called both women in to watch the movie.

To his surprise as they begin watching the movie the girls acted like they couldn't take their eyes off of it . . . .

In the process of Chad and the girls watching the movie Chad spontaneously upped his dick and told Felicia to suck it. Felicia begin sucking it like never before. It was as she'd studied the art of deep throating.

As Rita sat and watched she was amazed of how long his dick was. Rita was afraid to have his big dick in her little pussy.

As Felicia continued sucking on his dick she looked out the corner of her eyes to see Rita's facial expression. Rita's facial expression looked as if in the back of her mind she was saying hurry up bitch I'm next.

In no time flat Chad begin to bust a nut, he released it in Felicia's face; at that very moment it was as Rita felt like she was releasing her orgasm . . . .

"Take them panties off," Chad said in a low firm, sensual tone of voice . . . .

The women didn't say a word as Rita laid on the couch Felicia snatched of Rita's pants, then her panties, then her shirt, and bra. Then Felicia laid on the couch as Rita snatched of all her clothes . . . .

They both were ready to eat away at each other's pussy but Chad told Felicia to get on all fours. Chad banged Felicia pussy as Rita watched Felicia continuously licked her tongue in and out at Rita while hollering unable to take the dick as usual . . . .

Chad stop fucking Felicia and told Rita to get on all fours. As he stuck his dick in her she tried to run from it, Felicia held Rita's hands down, as Chad gripped her waist tightly and started slamming his dick in, and out the pussy. Chad couldn't believe how good, wet, and tight her pussy was.

As Rita was hollering Felicia continued to hold her hands down, and kissed her in the mouth, as their tongue connected Rita could feel herself cumming . . . .

Felicia stop kissing her, but continued to hold her hands down as Rita looked at Felicia with her eyes slightly open breathing heavily, and moaning saying, "oh his dick is too big, his dick is too big, his dick is too big." Felicia kissed her again, and then told her, "Just take it baby."

Chad started banging Rita even harder because he was getting ready to nut, and Rita knew this . . . .

"Please take it out, and nut my mouth," Rita said . . . .

Chad took it out, but before he could put his dick in her mouth his nut splashed all across her lips. She liked the nut off her lips, and then licked the nut off his dick, and set on the couch as he stood straight up she begin sucking his dick.

Her mouth is fantastic, Chad thought to himself.

As Rita continued sucking on his dick she could feel Felicia sucking on her titties, and trying stick her hand up her pussy, as Rita tried to control Felicia's hand, as Chad was force feeding her his dick she felt overpowered and bullied, and she loved it . . . .

Then Chad started eating Rita's pussy while Felicia sucked on his dick, as Felicia fingered her own self all at the same time.

We should've been done a threesome, Felicia thought to herself . . . .

Then Chad begin eating Felicia's pussy while she ate Rita's pussy, all at the same time . . . .

Before they even begun sexing Chad just knew that at least one of the girls wouldn't cooperate with some of the sexual acts, oh how he was wrong.

Then Rita got on her knees to suck Chad's dick again while Felicia finger fucked Rita's pussy, and ass at the same time . . . .

Chad was really enjoying himself, but the girls were enjoying themselves even more . . . .

All night Felicia, Chad, and Rita sexed thoroughly . . . .

The next morning all three got into the shower together. Afterwards Felicia went to work. Chad took Rita to her house to change clothes, and then Chad and Rita went to work . . . .

All day at work they gazed into each other's eyes with lust built within . . . .

After work he hugged her and told her he'd sat up a date when Felicia, her, and him could hang out, even if she didn't want to sex again. He told her the date would probably be tomorrow.

Both Rita and Chad was in a hurry so they immediately went their separate ways . . . .

He rushed home from work hoping Felicia was there. He wanted to privately ask her how much she enjoyed intercourse last night . . . .

Once he made it from work she was there. Soon as he walked through the door she begin tongue kissing him like never before.

Afterwards they sat down, and talked . . . .

"How did you enjoy the experience last night," he asked? "Last night was wonderful let's do it again tonight," she said . . . .

He begin to smile knowing that he'd open up this wonderful door of group sex at its best . . . .

"No we aint going to do it tonight, let's wait a few days, we don't want to seem too eager," he said . . . .

Right then and there she begin tongue kissing him, and they undressed and fucked for hours . . . .

Later on that night Felicia begin to tell him about her secret freaky desires. The one freaky desire that fascinated him the most was when she told him she wanted to have sex with a group of only men as they treated her like a cheap hooker. He begin thinking to himself like damn I'm married to a closet freak. He felt good that he'd brought the freaky side outta her . . . .

The next day at work he walked up to Rita and hugged her liked he hadn't seen her in years, and was happy to see her . . . .

"Did you enjoy yourself the other night," Chad asked Rita? "Yes I did I aint never felt that good before," Rita said. "Which part did you like the best," Chad asked? "I liked it the best when you, and your wife was taking turns performing oral sex on me, but actually I liked all of it, but when you and her took turns performing oral sex it was a little better than all the rest. I wanted to tell you yesterday, but we didn't do too much talking yesterday," Rita said. "Yeah I felt the same way but I believe that when you and my wife took turns sucking my dick that was the best part for me," Chad said. "Sshhhh, you don't have talk all loud we don't want anybody in our business," Rita said. "Sorry about that," Chad said . . . .

She then kissed him on the cheek and said, "Thanks for bringing me to life the other night. When are we going to do it again," she asked? "Honestly me and my wife enjoy having you around without sex, but we'd love to have sex with you more often, but it's only one problem," he said as he looked out the window in order for her not to be looking at him face to face. "What's the problem," she asked? "Me and my wife wants you to do everything sexually," he said. "Sure it's not a problem," she said . . . .

Chad came at her like that to insure that he could have his way with her this time and every other time . . . .

15

"Once our day at work is over I'll take you home with me," Chad told her. "Okay that's cool," Rita said . . . .

Chad and Rita showed up at Chad's home unexpectedly. As they entered the door Felicia couldn't believe it she became overjoyed, instantly smiling and undressing. In 0.7 seconds Felicia was totally naked tongue kissing Rita.

Chad and Rita then undressed. Chad ordered Felicia to suck his dick. Rita just stood there naked watching.

Within minutes Chad bust a nut in Felicia face. He then ordered Rita to suck his dick; she acted like she didn't want to do it, but she got on her knees and did it anyway . . . .

Chad grabbed the back of her head and begin fucking her face, once he got ready to nut he released it in her mouth.

Chad stood Rita up bent her over and begin fucking her from the back. Chad liked Rita's pussy, it was much tighter than Felicia pussy.

While Chad fucked Rita from the back giving her the dick in the hardest rawest format Felicia stood up watching while fingering her own pussy with her index, and middle finger while sucking on two of her fingers from the other hand.

When it was time for Chad to release his enormous load of nut he let it loose on Rita's ass cheeks as he jagged all of the nut of his dick . . . .

As Twon continued to read the book he begin to think to himself like damn this shit better than a porn movie. Loco was right reading a good book takes your mind away from being in jail.

The book was so good that Twon actually felt like he was living it himself. He felt like he was married to Felicia, and at that very moment he was the one busting nuts on Rita's ass cheeks.

Twon dick was harder than it ever been reading that sex story . . . .

Loco laid on the bottom bunk remaining silent knowing what Twon was experiencing off reading the book. Loco knew that this book captivated readers, because the sex scenes were incredible . . . .

Twon continued to read . . . .

"Felicia lay on the couch, now Rita stick your tongue as deep in her pussy as you can," Chad said . . . .

She stuck her tongue in Felicia's pussy, and started eating . . . .

While she was eating it Chad whispers in Rita's ear . . . .

"Rita you're doing a great job I'm proud of you. Me and my wife loves you," Chad said . . . .

Of course Rita knew they didn't really love her but she still liked hearing it . . . .

"Yes, yes keep eating that pussy just like that," Chad said while fingering Rita's pussy . . . .

Chad stops fingering Rita and started eating her pussy.

After Rita came twice Chad stuck his dick off in her which made her eat Felicia's pussy even better . . . .

After Rita was done eating Felicia's pussy, and Chad was done fucking Rita, Chad sat on the couch to relax and take a break. The girls didn't want a break. Rita begin sucking on Chad's dick while Felicia was licking on the crack of Rita's ass . . . .

After sexing for hours all three showered together and then Felicia and Chad dropped Rita off at home . . . .

A few days later Felicia begin to ask about Rita because it had been a few days since the last time she'd seen her, and she'd wanted to fuck her again.

Chad would see Rita at work every day, but figured he'd wait a week or two before he brought her home again Chad and Rita had got real close, they'd even start going on lunch breaks together . . . .

One day while at the grocery store Felicia wasn't even thinking about Micheal, and outta nowhere he approached her looking good as ever. He had a smile on face that would light up the world, and that particular day he'd been to the barber shop . . . .

"You look good with your new haircut," Felicia said. "Thought I'd try a new look. I haven't seen you shopping in a few days," Micheal said. "That's because I didn't need any groceries until today. How are you doing," she asked? "Well I'm doing alright, tired of this job at the grocery store," he said. "You know you gotta do what you gotta do to pay the bills," she said. "Yeah you right about that," Micheal said . . . .

"You starting to get thick," Micheal said. "That's your second time making a comment about my ass, keep your eyes off my body parts, I'm married," she said. "But you do have a nice body," he said. "Thanks," she said.

"I can't lie I cherish the moments we share together when you come to the grocery store. Each day I watch the front doors in hopes of you entering one of them. My day isn't complete unless I see you," Micheal said. "Is that right," she said. "To keep it real I wish we could be together all day every day. They stood in the aisle of the grocery store and talked for almost an hour non-stop.

After an hour she purchased her grocerys, as Micheal escorted her to her car . . . .

Before she knew it she was in Micheal's apartment getting fucked . . . .

After having sex with Micheal she felt bad that she cheated on her husband. She started to tell Mike how she was feeling inside . . . .

"Mike I'd been with this man for twenty years and not once did I cheat on him until you came along," she said. "But at least it was with someone who cares about you. He'll never find out about us if things get deeper," Mike said. "It's not the point of him finding out it's the fact that I did cheat on him," she said . . . .

Felicia laid on Mike's bed with her hand over her face. Mike assumed she was crying, but she wasn't. She was hiding her shame, while mentally going through a thing.

Mike started to eat her pussy to make her feel better, and it worked . . . .

Later that day Felicia moped around the house . . . .

"What's wrong you aint been your normal self, all day," Chad said. "It's nothing wrong, I feel good actually," Felicia said. "Stop it, I been knowing you all these years, and I know when something is wrong with you," Chad said. "There's nothing wrong," Felicia said with confidence . . . . Chad knew she was lying . . . .

For days Felicia walked around feeling sad . . . .

Chad knew something was wrong, he decided to take her out to eat, and to a dance club, Felicia loved to dance . . . .

Once they made it back home Chad hugged Felicia, and held her in his arms, and told her that he loved her, which made Felicia feel even worser . . . .

Felicia went into the back room and came right back out . . . .

"I love you, and wouldn't ever want to lose you," Felicia said. "Don't won't too lose me," Chad said. "I got a secret to tell you," Felicia said. "Aw that's why you been all sad for the last few days," Chad said. "It's a problem with me telling you my secret, I don't want to be handt no divorce papers," Felicia said. "I'm your husband you can talk to me about anything," Chad said. "I didn't play fair ball I cheated," Felicia said. "With who," Chad said. "The young guy at the grocery store," She said. "I knew that, that's why you been all sad, and that's why you ask me earlier, what would I do if I was married to a woman and caught her cheating. Well I gotta secret to I been cheating on you with Rita," Chad said . . . .

Chad began hugging her tightly . . . .

"I can't believe you're not mad," Felicia said. "Actually I'm glad I married someone like you, how many women you know that would cheat, and then come tell their husband about it, how many women you know that would have a threesome with their husband," Chad said. "Where's Rita," Felicia asked?

Chad began laughing knowing Felicia wanted action . . . .

"I'll bring her over tomorrow," Chad said. "Thank you, I really need, and want her," Felicia said. "Do you want to have sex with the guy from the grocery store again," Chad asked . . . Felicia paused before answering the question . . . . She looked Chad in his eyes, and said yep. Chad gave no remarked, instead he just smiled.

The next day he brought Rita home both Rita and Felicia was so happy to see one another that most of the night they had sex with only one another like he wasn't even there . . . .

The next day freaky thoughts begin racing through his head . . . .

"What's the guy named that work at the grocery store," Chad asked? "His name Micheal, I just call him Mike," she said. "Why don't we invite him, and Rita over for dinner, then we can have a foursome," Chad said . . . .

Felicia begin smiling, and laughing . . . .

"A foursome I never heard of that before, I can invite him, but I don't know if he'll be interested in coming," she said. "He will be interested in having sex with two women at the same time, trust me," Chad said. "So you going to have sex with another man," Felicia asked? "Hell naw, me and him gone have sex with you, and Rita," Chad said. "Okay I'll go to the grocery store tomorrow to ask him," she said. "Don't you have his phone number," Chad asked? "No," she said. "You rotate with a guy, having sexual intercourse with him, and you don't have his number," Chad said. "No, I only sex with him once when we rotate with each other it's always when I come to the grocery store, I'll see him at the grocery store tomorrow, and I'll ask him," Rita said . . . .

The next day Chad, and Rita was in Chad's kitchen preparing dinner. All the while, while they were cooking they hoped that Felicia would bring Mike home for the foursome. As the food was done cooking, still nice, and hot they laid it out on the table like a Thanksgiving dinner.

Chad and Felicia didn't eat they waited for Mike and Rita. They just sat at the table reminiscing . . . .

About forty five minutes after the food was done, to Chad, and Rita's surprise in comes Felicia, and Mike. Chad, and Rita was so happy that they jumped straight up out their chairs hugging Mike one by one as if they'd known him all their lives . . . .

They sat down, and began to eat dinner, as the four of them continued to smile with nasty sexual thoughts running through their heads . . . .

Felicia got up went to the bathroom, and came back naked as the day she was born. Mike mouth drop knowing it was time for action . . . .

Chad stood up upped his dick, Felicia got on her knees and began sucking his dick. Mike stood up and watched in amazement . . . .

Rita got on her knees unzipped Mikes pants, he stuffed his dick in her mouth as she begin sucking on it as if it was a lolly pop . . . .

Mike watched his own dick go in and out of Rita's mouth feeling the joyous pleasure of what sex brings within this life . . . .

Her mouth is fantastic, Mike thought to himself.

Mike continued to glance over at Felicia's performance and couldn't wait to get a piece of her.

Outta nowhere Mike felt his dick get harder as the nut exploded in Rita's mouth as Rita swallowed all of it like a champ.

Mike couldn't believe Rita made him nut it was hard for a woman to suck his dick and make him nut . . . .

Mike walked over to Felicia and stood her up, as she was now on her feet bent over still sucking Chad's dick Mike stuffed his dick in her pussy, and begin fucking the shit out of her . . . .

As they could hear Felicia slightly moaning although Chad dick was on her mouth, Rita begin playing with her own pearl tongue, and started sucking Felicia titties nipples one by one . . . .

I can't believe I got a dick in my pussy, a dick in my mouth, and another woman sucking my titties all at the same time, Felicia thought to herself.

Felicia kept cumming back to back hoping that all three wouldn't ever stop . . . .

Felicia opened her eyes looking up at Chad, as she felt Chads dick getting harder she knew he was getting ready to nut so she took his dick out of her mouth and begged him to nut in her face, and he nutted in her mouth and face . . . .

Mike laid Felicia on the couch on her back wanting more of that pussy he held her legs in the air and started stuffing his dick in and out of it . . . .

"Get on all fours on the floor," Chad told Rita . . . .

Chad stuffed his dick in Rita hard and fast as if he was made at the world, and she loved it. Chad worked the pussy, while she played with her own pearl tongue desiring to cum quicker and more pleasurable, and she did a great job of it . . . .

Chad told Rita to lie on her back on the floor, as his commence to tonguing and sucking her pussy. Mike stop fucking Felicia to eat Rita's pussy after Chad. Then Felicia ate Rita's pussy after Mike . . . .

Mike laid on the floor and both girls started sucking his dick at the same time, as Chad started taking turns fucking both girls from the back . . . .

As Mike nut came out he let it go in Felicia face and mouth. Then the girls started kissing each other as Chad continued stuffing his dick in and out of Felicia's pussy . . . .

After sex that night they showered and Mike drove Rita home . . . .

After that night Chad and Felicia did foursomes with Mike and Rita, and sometimes threesomes with Rita, and sometimes threesomes with just Mike . . . .

About nine months after that night Felicia, and Mike got married, and their marriage turned out to be a happy one . . . .

"Loco this book is a bomb fam," Twon said. "I knew you'd like it that's why I gave it to you, reading a good book takes your mind off bullshit," Loco said. "I only read chapter one, but it was hot, I couldn't stop reading it," Twon said. "I know that's why I gave it to you. I got a gang of books for you to read. I only read erotica when I'm alone. I mainly read nonfiction, and spiritual guidance books. I'm finna go to sleep so I want to cut the light off man, so can you wait to tomorrow to do some more reading," Loco said. "Yeah I'm cool on the light, you can cut it off," Twon said.

Twon laid back on the top bunk with constant visions of Rita, and Felicia having threesome with him. Twon dick stayed hard for hours, it was like he had popped some Viagra or something . . . .

Chapter 2

A few days later they were let off lock down Twon was able to get through to his family; they were happy to hear from him and disappointed that he was locked up for a murder. They immediately start sending money orders and religious pamphlets amongst other things. They were anxious for visiting day to come so they could come see him . . . .

Once visiting day came Twon, and everybody on the deck was preparing for visiting day.

Twon got quite a few visits from family members and friends showing love and support. They all promised that they'll always be there through the trials and tribulations of his case.

At the end of the day Twon last visitor showed up; it was his four month old pregnant girlfriend . . . .

Tears ran down her face in the visiting room as she cried out to Twon because she needed him there for support, and she knew that Twon wouldn't be there when the baby was born.

Twon left the visit early sad and confused knowing he wouldn't be there when the baby was born . . . .

Once he made it on the deck Loco could look at him and see and feel the sadness . . . .

Shortly after Twon's last visit they C/O's yelled out, "lock up time."

Once Twon and Loco made it within their cells Loco begin fixing burritos . . . .

"You think we should hook up all meat burritos, or this pasta I saved from dinner," Loco asked? "It don't matter," Twon said. "What's wrong, why you looking all sad for," Loco asked? "My girl on visits crying, talking about she can't do it without me, and that my baby gone be born without his daddy there, everything she said was the truth, sometimes the truth hurt, and it really hurted," Twon said. "Man, you got a body you might be fighting for two or three years, and then get found guilty, and gotta work on appeals. I understand how you feel because I got kids to, but you got a body man you gotta get with the program. I know I aint gone never see the streets again I got to many cases, my rapy turned states, and I done caught gang of cases since I been in here and I might catch some more. But I don't let shit get me down I keep my head up to the sky, and just keep, keeping on. I must admit I aint been to church in a long time but I do pray to God; what you need to do is pray, theirs power in prayer," Loco said. "I got to do some reading tonight. How long you gone be with them burritos," Twon asked? "Be patient they'll be ready in no time, let the young chef work his magic," Loco said, as they both begin laughing . . . .

"Damn these burritos is a bomb, what you put on them some Mexican dip or some shit," Twon said as they begin laughing. "Naw that some homemade bar-b-que sauce," Loco said. "Whatever it is it's a bomb," Twon said . . . .

I wonder what I'm going to read tonight. I can't read no sex stories while Loco in the cell with me them sex stories to hot, Twon thought to his self as he continued eating his burrito . . . .

Loco reached under his bunk and went in his brown paper bag filled with books, and pulled out a book that was average size in length but small in width. The book was only a hundred pages. He handt the book to Twon . . . .

"What kind of book is this," Twon asked as he reached for the book. "This a book poetry, it aint regular poetry it's called ghetto poetry it's kind of like handwritten rap mixed with hardcore open mic poetry, you'll like it trust me," Loco said.

Twon looked at the cover of the book, it looked like the cover of a rap C.D. He seen this little short big head bald head dude, with a black, and gray fur vest on the cover, which was the author. He read the title ghetto poetry by Flame.

"What kind of name is Flame," Twon asked? "It's not his real name, some authors use a pen name just like how rappers use different names, some authors do the same," Loco said. "I don't want to read no poetry," Twon said as he tried to hand him the book back. "Read it you'll like, remember when I gave you the sex stories you was acting the same way, then when you start reading it you feel in love," Loco said . . . .

Twon didn't respond but instantly got on the top bunk, and began reading the book. He skipped through the acknowledgements and went straight to the first page and began reading:

1
New

On the new investigated to see if black and gold, red and black or
black and blue. Visions never knew the goodness of the truth.
We were self-made kings, and queens, and humanized gurus.
Never knew it was designed for the black beauties to improve.
Lost and confused a minute issue was overdue.
Stabbed up a hundred something times, by his own multitude.
A fool sacrifice his own life, tossed away like rotten fruit . . . .
He never knew, never growed, never grew.

That poem was decent, Twon thought to
himself, as he decided to read more:

2
Friends

Friends that was once friends changed on me in the
end. Literally murdered my uncle, my next of kin,
while I resided in the belly of the beast within.
To his killer they be-friend.
In God we trust, not men.
Fake tears at funeral, basement tattoos on skin.
Open up on his joint claimed it as their own land.
Sexed his girlfriend.
Once I was released they walked up to me to
shake my hand as nothing never happen.
In the beginning and the end problems
occurred through my so called friends.

3
A Way To Live A Way To Die

Pitiful Cries.
Whip away tears from eyes.
Knowing that it's heaven above the skies when we die.
First you must be baptized, free from all sinful ties,
be a product of Godly things in others eyes.
Speak the truth not a lie.
Use scriptures to abide by the Lords
guide, and as a way to survive.
Worship God until you die.

4
Love and Hate

It's a thin line between love and hate.
Be careful, watch for chameleon of snakes,
even your homies, and ones you date.
Demons that made the creator close heavens
gates, enemy of the states.
Control fate.
Be careful not to cross that thin line between love and hate
where firely sparks have already set a date, sealed fate.
Kill and take.
Love and hate.

5
She Wanted To Fly

She said she wanted to soar like a bald eagle, so high.
I asked her how high.
She said she wanted to reach the sky.
She really believe she could fly, she literally wanted
to touch the sky one day before she die.
She sat by looking out her project window smoking a dip
cigarette to get high with no hesitation jumped out of the

window saying, "I can fly, I can fly, I can fly," right before
her skull hit the ground cracking open a thousand times.
She wanted to fly a suicidal way to die.
Could never be forgiving for that suicidal sin
she had to try, no heaven in the sky.
Her soul shall forever burn in eternal fire.
Right before she die, she wanted to fly.

"Loco, these ghetto poems cool, who put you up on these," Twon asked? "A lot of people know about Flame he from the streets, I heard the nigga did fifteen straight for attempt murders. The niggas that use to work for him fucked up some money, and he fucked them up, and they got down on him in court. While he was in jail he wrote a gang of books then he got out, he got them published and got rich," Loco said. "Straight up?" "Yep. I heard he was one of them Travelers from off California, and Flournoy," Loco said. "Aw yeah," Twon said. "How long you gone be with the light man, I'm about ready to go to sleep," Loco said. "I wanna finish reading this book it won't take long. Soon as I get finished I'll cut the light off," Twon said. "Hurry up, nigga," Loco said, as he laid on the bottom bunk putting the blanket over his head . . . .

Twon continued to read the book, it seemed as each individual poem got even better each time he flipped to another page . . . .

In no time Twon finished the book hit the light, and laid on his bunk. It was hard for Twon to go straight to sleep because they were hollering out the doors for hours. He couldn't wait until they shut the fuck up . . . .

The next day the deck went up Loco stabbed a nigga in his eye for making that noise while he was trying to sleep the night before in return Loco was stabbed five times in the back, Twon got stabbed once in the hand, and others from both side the fin and the six got fucked up real bad . . . .

Loco was sent to the outside hospital. Once released from the hospital he was sent to seg with Twon amongst a bunch of others, some had went to the health care part of the county jail. Loco caught a new case which was nothing to him.

Twon and Loco stayed in seg. For thirty days. When they got out they were placed on the same deck, but not the same cell . . . .

This time Twon was smart he found a way to get a hold to some knives for security purposes. The ViceLords on that deck had plenty knives but he wanted his own for protection . . . .

The next day after Twon was released from seg. it was Twon's first court date. He went and met his public defender for the first time.

His public defender was an African he hadn't look over any of Twons evidence yet, but scheduled the next court date to the next month . . . .

Twon made it to the deck, and his celly was on a special out of town visit, so Twon decided to ease his mind by reading a sex story . . . .

Twon begin reading this erotica book called Sexy Love, it was a book he got from Loco the day before . . . . Chapter 1

Starving Artist

Here I was a twenty seven year old starving artist . . . .

All through high school I tried to figure out what I'd major in once I started college. Well it wasn't anything that I'd like to build a career in; until my senior year in high school.

In my senior year of high school I begin to visit art galleries with one of my friends and I really begin to take a liking in art . . . .

I started to read stories about ancient artist. One of the main things I liked about some of the artist, that they would paint portraits that wouldn't look like anything in particular, and they wouldn't make any sense to the eyes of the beholder, but the public still loved them.

After I graduated high school I decided to take art classes that taught students the very essence of painting artwork. I had already been doing drawings since I was a kid, therefore the classes were easy for me.

After I completed the art classes I decided to move out of my moms and dads home to a apartment on the other side of town.

I first started doing paintings of average things like cartoon characters, the president, and celebrities which sold a little through my Facebook page, and some viewers would come to my apartment to buy paintings.

My family and friends started asking me to do personal paintings of them and their family. Other people would see those paintings, and come through for personal paintings as well. But the money I was making still wasn't sufficient to sustain all my bills by myself . . . .

One late night I was searching through my e-mails, one lady had e-mailed me asking if I could paint nude photos of her. Hell yeah, I thought to myself.

I e-mailed her saying yes, she e-mailed me right back asking the time, and place. I mentioned to her that it would be best if she could come over to my apartment the next night.

The next night came, and I awaited for her to come, she was a little late beyond our regularly scheduled time . . . .

I heard a knock at my door, I knew it was her because I wasn't expecting any other visitors. I looked through my peep hole, and seen this old lady standing there. Who is this old lady, this can't be the one requesting artwork of nudity, I thought to myself.

I opened the door she stuck her hand out to shake my hand, and said, "Hi, I'm Mary Ann I'm here to have the portrait painted of me." "My name is Steven, but you can just call me Steve, come on in," I said.

As she stepped in the door I begin checking this old lady out she was strap, she had a body better than most young women. She wore this beautiful full length black skirt with her cleavage showing with high heels on . . . .

She stepped in looking around admiring the artwork . . . .

"So where is the painting of the portrait going to take place," she asked when I became aware of her country accent. "Right here in the living room," I said. "Are we alone," she asked? "Of course," I said while looking directly in her beautiful blue eyes . . . .

She slowly undressed as if it was a strip tease, or as if we were getting ready to partake in the art of love making . . . .

I was stuck in a state of shock staring at this older lady beautiful body, as my cock got hard as concrete, I just wanted to give her vagina my cock in its entirety . . . .

"You must like what you see," she said. "I love what I see," I said . . . .

She laid down flat on her stomach with one of her finger slightly in her mouth, and told me this how she wanted me to paint the portrait . . . .

This old lady looked as if she was in her early forties, but looked wonderful, she was definitely someone I'd be interested in getting with . . . .

I started painting my first nude portrait as her, and I remained silent, it was as my cock refuse to get off hard, as I was on the verge of painting a masterpiece . . . .

Usually when I painted people it would be a problem, because people tend to move, she didn't move not one bit; which was strange that she could just lay there naked for hours . . . .

After the portrait was done I looked at it amazed and proud of myself . . . .

I told her it was finish she got up, and looked at it, and begin jumping up and down in joy. As her titties and butt cheeks jiggled as she jumped up, and down made my cock get even harder.

She paid me my money gave me a hug, and told me she will be back tomorrow to get her painting once it's totally dry . . . .

All night long I dreamed of that lady's naked body . . . .

The next day she came and got her portrait, and told me she'd come back soon for me to paint more portraits', I gave her my cell number so she wouldn't have to go through my e-mail or Facebook to get in touch with me . . . .

A week had went pass she called but I didn't recognize the number so I answered it, it was Mary Ann. She asked when could she come through to get more nude portraits done, I told her right now.

She came through, and I painted a portrait of her standing up naked . . . .

After that day she'd come every three days to get a nude portrait painting . . . .

I'm a human being, and heterosexual therefore I wanted to bang her more than you can imagine; but I didn't want to interrupt our business venture so I kept it professional . . . .

The fifth time she wanted me to paint a close up picture of just her vagina, I thought I was in heaven . . . .

After I finished painting her vagina she asked me to rub some baby oil on her. She laid flat on her stomach and told me to rub some baby oil on her back. As I begin rubbing it on her back she kept telling me to go down further once I got to the end of her back I told her I couldn't go down any further. She asked me why not I told her that I was at the end of her back. She asked me to rub some on her butt cheeks, I couldn't believe it. I started gently rubbing baby oil on her butt cheeks, my gently rubbing then turned to firm grips as she slightly moaned as if my cock was in her. I started to rub baby oil on her vagina as I gently slipped one, two, three, and then four fingers in and out of her, as she looked at me with the cutest sex face . . . .

29

I eagerly pulled my pants down hungry to give her my cock. Before I could stick it in she pleaded with me to give her my cock, and I did just that . . . .

When I first stuck my cock in her it felt wonderful it was tight, and moist it gripped my cock to perfection . . . .

I eagerly fed her vagina all of my cock as hard and fast as I could as she begged me to stop because it was too much pain for her to handle . . . .

Once I was done she begin sucking my cock without me even asking, and of course once she was done I returned the favor by eating her vagina . . . .

She spent a night over my house and we created pornography throughout the night on and off . . . .

Come to find out Mary Ann was fifty years old, and always wanted to show her body off to the the public, but never had the courage until I started painting those portraits of her.

After that night she placed my paintings of her in the nude on Facebook. Thanks to her my paintings sells were boosted. People from all over wanted me to do all sorts of paintings even those in the nude.

I never got the fame I wanted as an artist, as far as my paintings being in art galleries and shows. But I did get recognition from people that wanted personal paintings, and I made a lot of money off paintings . . . .

Maybe one day, possibly after I'm dead art galleries will exhibit my artwork.

As for me and Mary Ann she still comes over from time to time for me to do paintings of her in the nude, and for me to please her sexual lustful ways . . . .

Damn that was a bomb, Twon thought to his self as he begin looking for his bottle of lotion . . . .

Chapter 3

A s time progressed along Twon became half use to and half tired of jail. The family and friends showed love, commissary, and visits every week . . . .

"What you doing man," Loco asked? "I'm getting ready for visits tomorrow," Twon said. "Aw yeah that's right visiting day is tomorrow," Loco said. "How in the hell did you get out your cell," Twon asked? "The police let me out to be the porter for tonight. I didn't wont shit I just stop by your cell to see what you was on, I'll let you finish shaving I'll see you tomorrow when the doors roll," Loco said. "A'ight," Twon said . . . .

Twon finished shaving, did a few push-ups, washed up in the sink, and went to sleep dreaming of the women he'd possibly see in the visiting room the next day . . . .

"Antwon Starks on that visit," the C/O said . . . .

Twon went to the visiting room, and to his surprise it was his pregnant ass girlfriend, she usually didn't come early in the morning . . . .

"What your pregnant ass doing coming up here to see me this early," Twon said. "I miss you," she said. "You just miss this big ass dick," Twon said. "Yeah I miss that to," she said. "I can't wait until you get out, it's just gone be me, you, and the baby," she said. "I aint even gone have time for you, I'm gone be with so many other ho's," Twon said. "Boy I wish you would. Why do you keep writing me them corny ass letters. How you gone be somebody daddy and you can't even spell grammar school words," she said as they both begin laughing . . . .

31

They stayed on visit for a while, both enjoyed seeing each other . . . .
After the visit Twon went back to the deck and couldn't stop smiling . . . .

"Damn nigga you smiling hard, tell me what you so happy for, so I can be happy like you," Loco said. "Nothing much, when the C/O's wasn't looking my girl showed me some things. I miss her," Twon said. "I know you do, don't worry big dick Bob will take care the pussy for you," Loco said, as they begin laughing. "She talking about my letters is corny as hell," Twon said. "Yeah, you gotta learn to be raw with the pen that's how you survive in jail, I'll read one of your letters later or the next time you write," Loco said. "Imma write her tonight when we lock up, if you be the porter tonight I want you to come through and read it," Twon said. "Okay I got you, I gotta go make some calls," Loco said. "Yeah gotta try to get one of these phones myself to make sure my visits get to rolling through today," Twon said . . . .

All the rest of the day Twon got a lot of visits. Loco got a couple visits as well . . . .

"Play time is over you cowards lock it up," the C/O said . . . .

"Fam you finished writing the letter yet," Loco said. "Naw not yet we only been locked up for about ten or fifteen minutes, come back later right before the police lock you up in the cell," Twon said. "Okay, ten, four," Loco said . . . .

"It's been almost two hours, you told me to come back before lock up time, we getting ready to lock up in a lil while, where the letter at," Loco asked? "Here it go," Twon said, as he handt him the letter . . . .

Loco begin reading the letter . . . .

In no time flat Loco begin to laugh out loud, and then handt him the letter back . . . .

"Man is you serious, you can't write no letters like this to no ho's, you can't write no letter like this to nobody. You gotta learn to write letters that's how niggas survive in jail. A gotta go the police calling me to lock up. I'll holla at you in the morning," Loco said. "A'ight love my nigga," Twon said. "Love nigga," Loco replied . . . .

The next morning and days to follow Loco tried teaching Twon how to properly write letters. Twon just didn't get it. Twon barely made it through grammar school, and only went to high school for three weeks before dropping out . . . .

Chapter 4

It was time for court again, and Twon's public defender still hadn't looked over any of the evidence all he did was got him another continuous . . . .

After that day each time Twon went to court it was the same thing, continuous after continuous . . . .

On Twon's fourth courtdate to his surprise his P.D. had brought forth all the evidence the state had against him, which was one surveillance videos, and one eye witness. The eyewitness said she seen him walk Abdula in the store at gun point but couldn't totally make out his face because it was partially covered. The surveillance video showed everything that happen within the store, but didn't fully show Twon's face because it was partially covered . . . .

In reality the only reason he got booked is because the niggas that was with him went to the hood running off at the mouth . . . .

"So if the eyewitness, and the video didn't positively I.D. me, what am I doing in jail for than," Twon asked? "Because the eyewitness picked you out of a line up, which is not proper lawful procedure, because at first she said she couldn't positively I.D. you, then she said in the lineup she was positive it was you. All my years as a public defender I done seen all type of court cases similar to this one, and the defendant still got found guilty, and got a lot of time," the P.D. said. "So do you think you can beat it," Twon asked? "Of course I do, but like I just mentioned I done seen people get found guilty on all sorts of cases where the evidence was faulty. I got to go to another courtroom so I'll see you on the next court date," the P.D. said "Okay thanks man," Twon said . . . .

Twon went back to the deck smiling . . . .

"Fam what you smiling for you must got some good news, Loco said." Not really my P.D. told me that the eyewitness fucked up, at first she couldn't positively I.D. me, then when I went through the lineup she did positively I.D. me. And the P.D. said the surveillance video they got showed my face partially covered," Twon said. "Don't get me wrong I do hope, and pray you beat your case, but I done seen niggas get pinched for bogus murders a gang of times. But that's good you got some good news," Loco said. "I'm sleepy as hell Imma gone to my cell, and lay it down," Twon said . . . .

"Antwon Starks," the C/O said. "Celly wake up you got mail," Twon celly said. "Antwon Starks," the C/O said again. "Celly, celly wake up you got mail," Twon celly said again . . . .

Twon woke up out of his sleep got his mail, sat on his bunk reading the letter, and looking at the pictures that was in the envelope with the mail . . . .

When the doors rolled Twon ran straight to Loco's cell to show him the new pictures . . . .

"Damn fam these pictures hot, I can't even see the thong it look like she showing straight ass shots. She sent a lot of them she must like showing her body off," Loco said. "She is a freak she like doing all type off shit, she take it up the ass and everything. The bitch say the only time she can cum is when see sucking a nigga dick," Twon said. "For real," Loco said. "Yep, so you know her head game is awesome," Twon said.

"She talking about my letters is a joke to her," Twon said. "I been told you, you gone have to step your game up on writing letters, you been locked up to many months not to be raw on writing letters," Loco said . . . .

Later that day Loco tried to give Twon some more game on writing letters . . . .

Chapter 5

"Mom how are you doing," Twon said over the phone. "I'm good, son your daughter looks just like you," Twon's momma said. "Daughter I don't got no kids," Twon said. "Your girlfriend had the baby," his momma said. "She did, when," Twon asked? "A few days ago," his mom said. "Make sure to bring the baby on visiting day," Twon said. "We might can't bring her the first visiting day, depending on the weather. We took a lot of pictures of her I sent them off yesterday," his momma said. "Mom, what's her name," Twon asked? "She came out looking like one of God's Angel so we named her Angel," his mom said. "Angel . . . . Angel that's a nice name," Twon said . . . .

For a little while they talked over the phone mainly about the baby, and up coming family social events . . . .

Twon ran to tell Loco about Angel, Loco was happy as if it was actually his very own child being born . . . .

They celebrated by drinking homemade liquor, smoked a little weed, and cooked all meat burritos . . . .

Twon received the pictures of Angel a couple days later, he couldn't believe how much she looked like him . . . .

Visiting day came and went, he got a lot of visits but not one of his baby momma, nor his new born Angel . . . .

The next visiting day came and his baby momma, and his daughter Angel showed up. Seeing his new baby brought an overwhelming joy that he had never received in life. Once the visit was over he didn't even wanna leave the visitors room, but had no other choice . . . .

He promised his self that upon his release from prison he'd definitely be a good father to his daughter, unlike his father had been to him . . . .

Throughout a year in the county Twon continue to get love, and support through family members, friends, his baby momma, and from other ho's . . . .

"Your last day of trial is today, blessings," Twon said to Loco. "I already know what it is I aint getting out of jail, but it is what it is," Loco said. "You gotta think positive," Twon said. "True that, but I'm a realist I'm not gone beat this body, and if I do I got to many cases I caught in jail, and I'll catch some more if a nigga want some trouble," Loco said. "I got faith that you gone beat your case tomorrow," Twon said. "I already know what it is," Loco said . . . .

The next time Loco came in from court what a grin on his face . . . .

"I see you smiling so that's how I know you beat the case," Twon said . . . .

Loco begin laughing devilishly . . . .

"Naw I aint beat it all twelve people outta the jury found me guilty," Loco said. "So, why you smiling," Twon asked? "I just seen this thick ass new C/O down stairs," Loco said. "Man that's fucked up they found you guilty," Twon said. "I already knew they were, I just hope they don't give me the death penalty," Loco said . . . .

Twon got quiet started to think about his case, and how he'd feel if he got found guilty . . . .

"Don't tell nobody, nobody that I got found guilty," Loco said. "You know I aint gone say nothing. When you go back to get your time," Twon asked? "Next week, I'm finna lock up in the cell fall back, and do some reading, I'll holla at you later," Loco said . . . .

All day and the rest of the night Twon started to worry about his case more and more . . . .

The week to follow Loco came back from court and told Twon they gave him sixty years. Twon felt sorry for him. But Loco was happy that he didn't get a natural ball, or the death penalty, and his lawyer had filed his appeal . . . .

The week after that Loco was shipped off to the joint to start his bide. When Loco left a piece of Twon left with him. Loco was Twon right hand man, a true friend. Twon had other niggas he fucked with on the deck, and in the building, but he didn't fuck with them to the fullest degree like he had did Loco . . . .

Shortly after Loco left Twon's world seem to be falling apart: money orders and visits started to get slow. And even his baby momma started playing games; she even slowed down on bringing the baby to see him . . . .

Chapter 6

After Twon's second year in the county his P.D. was preparing him for trial . . . .

"As you know your case carries twenty to sixty years, therefore if found guilty you can get up to sixty years. By this being you first adult offense I can go into a 402 conference with the state and judge, and try to get you approximately twenty five through thirty years. With this state it'll be rough to get twenty five through thirty years, but I can try," the P.D. said. "Man is you done lost your damn mind, twenty five or thirty years," Twon said. "That's better than getting found guilty, and getting the whole sixty. You're a young guy you can get thirty years, and be out of jail while you're still young, you'll be in your early thirties," the P.D. said. "I aint doing no copping out. I thought you said the evidence against me was good in my favor," Twon said. "Yes, that's true, but daily defendants are wrongfully convicted," The P.D. said. "Naw I aint doing no copping out," Twon said. "Well I'm going to be setting your trial date to the end of next month. Will you be taking a bench trial or a jury," the P.D. said. "Which one do you think is best," Twon asked? "I don't know you got to figure out which one is best for you," the P.D said . . . . "I'll go with the bench," Twon said. "Well its official trial will be set for the end of next month," the P.D. said . . . .

The end of the next month came in no time . . . .

As Twon entered the court room he seen his family, and friends sitting in the back all anxious to hear a not guilty verdict. Twon looked and seen his baby momma looking like a drug addict . . . .

Trial begin first with them showing the surveillance, which didn't clearly show Twons face. Then the witness got on the stand first she said she was unsure if it was Twon or not. Then she said she was positive it was him; right then and there Twon knew that he'd be going home at the end of the day . . . .

After the state's attorney and his P.D. went through long rebuttals of explaining view points of the evidence, it was time for the judge to give the verdict . . . .

"Mr. Antwon Starks I find you guilty of first degree murder," the judge said . . . .

The court room was in shock, even the state's attorney couldn't believe he had got found guilty . . . .

Tears begin to roll down his mom, and his baby moms face . . . .

Twon took off running to the door trying to get away but never made it as he was tackled, and shackled by the C/O's . . . .

The P.D. then filed his appeal, and his next court date was next week to come back and get his time . . . .

Twon figured by this being his first adult case that they would give him the minimum of twenty years . . . .

He came back to court the next week, and the judge gave him thirty years . . . . Twon couldn't believe it, his inner soul cried out to be free . . . .

Right before he left, and went to the joint everyone came to see him, they all told him don't worry they'll always be there, and to rely on his appeal which could set him free in a couple years . . . .

The state sent Twon to this medium security joint. Once Twon made it to the unit he noticed half of the deck was in street clothes instead of jail uniforms. He immediately sensed a sense of peace.

The officer gave him his key, and he walked to his cell. As he walked to his cell everyone stared wondering who Twon was, and what he was . . . .

Twon had heard all about the joint, but he still couldn't believe the difference of the county jail. Just off one look the joint was like paradise compared to the county jail . . . .

After he unpacked his things within his cell he went out in the dayroom to try and meet a few people. Many people didn't want to meet him scared that he was going to start asking for shit . . . .

It was two of the ViceLords that introduced themselves to him; one was a Cicero, Insane, the other was a Mafia. Mafia was old school damn near fifty years old still gang banging . . . . Mafia gave him toothpaste, and a soap, genuinely . . . .

During the next few days as Twon awaited on I.A. to approve his telephone list of numbers, and his visiting list he seen how phony the ViceLords, and everybody else on his unit was . . . .

Twon's numbers finally got approved, and he noticed that almost everybody had blocks on their phone. He assumed that the blocks were on the phones because people didn't pay their bills; his assumptions were wrong, it was blocks on phones because a lot people had turned their back on him after he got that time . . . .

Twon was able to get through to his mom, his mom told him that she was low on cash, therefore she couldn't send a money order just yet, and that his baby momma had left Angel with her for a week, and she didn't know where she was . . . .

During next few weeks Twon still wasn't getting through to his family . . . .

"Lord, you want some of this food I cooked," Mafia asked Twon. "Naw I'm cool," Twon said. "Why not, I cooked enough for me and you," Mafia said. "Naw I'm cool," Twon said not being full hearted. "Why not," Mafia asked again? "Cuz man you been looking out for me since I been here," Twon said. "I suppose to look out for you, you one of the brothers. Let me go get this food for you," Mafia said . . . .

Mafia went next door to his cell and came back with Twon a big bowl of food, some cakes, and a pop . . . .

"This shit a bomb," Twon said. "Yeah I do my chef thing when I can. When you get out," Mafia asked? "I got a while to do," Twon said. "How long is a while one year, two years, or three years," Mafia asked? "Thirty years," Twon said. "Thirty years, damn that's fucked up you still a baby. What you got a body," Mafia asked? "Yep," Twon said.

Mafia got quiet and left the room feeling Twon's pain . . . .

The next day Mafia went and talked to Twon to uplift him and give him a revelation about the things that was to come within bidding . . . .

"Since you gone be here for a while you need to get with the program," Mafia said. "I probably won't be locked up for no long time I'm waiting on my appeal to come through," Twon said. "I hope your appeal do go through, but appeals aint guaranteed to get granted no matter how bogus the case is. You need to start working out get you a job, and start taking college courses," Mafia said. "I aint even on none of that right now," Twon said. "You need to be on that, that's how you make you time go by. It's a part of ViceLord lit, that goes as follows, while in prison you should serve your time more constructively so that upon your release you can be more useful to your community, your family, and yourself as a whole," Mafia said . . . .

I don't know what Mafia talking about I'm going home on appeal, Twon thought to himself . . . .

Twon finally got a money order for two hundred from his momma; he only needed approximately thirty more dollars to get his TV. Twon decided to wait to get the TV. because he didn't know when or where his next money order was coming from.

Twon went to commissary and bought a pair of gym shoes for twenty five dollars, a radio for twenty five dollars, and spent a hundred and fifty on food.

Twon had so much food that two of the commissary workers had to help him back to his unit with the food . . . .

As Twon walked through the doors with all his commissary everyone stopped and stared.

Later on that night niggas off the deck tried to befriend Twon . . . .

"Mafia, it seems like every nigga on the deck trying to start fucking with me," Twon said. "That's because they seen you come from commissary with all them bags, other than that they wouldn't even fuck with you," Mafia said. "Aw, that's why everybody been trying to kick it with me," Twon said.

"These niggas phony ass hell, they didn't wanna help you when you was on the new now all of a sudden everybody wanna act like they your homie," Mafia said. "Aw you peep that to," Twon said. "I pay attention to every little thing a nigga say and do, that's how I been surviving all these years. These nigga call themselves ViceLords and aint nam nigga offer you shit when you came on new, not a bar of soap or a pack of squares or shit. Now they see you might be having shit, they wanna kick it with you so they can start asking for shit. If I was you I wouldn't even start fucking with these niggas, fall back and do your own time. The joint aint like it use to be, like it is in the county where niggas still standing on nation business, it's every man for themselves," Mafia said . . . .

"It's almost lock up time, what books you got I can read," Twon asked? "I got three different Donald Goines books, I got Dopefiend, and Kenyatta's Last Escape, I forget the name of the other one. Have you ever read Dopefiend before," Mafia asked? "Naw I aint read none of Donald Goines books, but I read alot other urban novels, by other authors," Twon said. "Donald Goines, and Iceburg Slim the ones that invented the shit. They were the first ones writing urban novels before they were even called urban novels. Here take the book before they call lock up, you gone like it trust me," Mafia said. "We still got another minute or two before lock up. Have you ever read some of Flames urban novels," Twon asked? "Yeah, I done read some of his shit before it even got published, I was locked up with Flame in three different joints. I was in and out of jail, he was stuck in the motherfucker waiting on appeals, steady getting kicked out of joints for being a bad boy.

"Flame write books of poetry, urban novels, nonfiction, music, screenplays, and all type of shit. The man use to always tell me when I get out I'm gone get on. And he did it, and never looked back. I heard he finna start his own publishing company, and a record label. Donald Goines, and Flame are my two favorite authors of all time," Mafia said . . . .

"Here come the police finna lock us up, I'll rotate with you tomorrow," Twon said . . . .

Twon went into his dark cell, his celly was asleep, and had the light off. Twon quietly got on his top bunk cut on his night light and started reading Dopefiend. The book was so good to Twon that once he started reading it he couldn't put it down . . . .

After thirty minutes of reading it he couldn't believe how realistic the events in the book seemed.

This nigga Donald Goines must've been a dope fiend to write a book like this, Twon thought to himself . . . .

The next morning when they unlocked the cell doors for breakfast Twon ran straight to Mafia's cell . . . .

"Man, that book was off the chain," Twon said, as he handt Mafia the book back. "I told you it was gone be a bomb. I'll give you the other two later. Let's ride they calling us out for breakfast," Mafia said . . . .

Later that day Twon awoke from his sleep by a knock from his cell door. He looked up and seen Mafia standing there . . . .

He jumped out of his bunk and unlocked, and opened his cell door . . . .

"What's going on fam," Twon said. "Here go these other two books. Why you didn't go to chow," Mafia asked? "Damn I missed chow, what time is it," Twon asked? "It's twelve o'clock," Mafia said. "Fuck it, it's cool I gotta little food in my box," Twon said . . . .

Twon read the books title to himself, Kenyatta's Last escape, and Crime Partners . . . .

"I'm getting ready to read these now so I'll holla at you later," Twon said. "Okay," Mafia said . . . .

Twon brushed his teeth washed his face sat on the top bunk and looked at both books wondering which one he should read first . . . .

He decided to read Crime Partners first . . . .

Half way through the book he fell in love with it . . . .

He ended up missing dinner, and staying in his cell the rest of the day reading the books . . . .

The next day at breakfast he went to Mafia, and gave him both books back . . . .

"Man these two was better than the first one. Jeff and Mutt was ignorant," Twon said. "I told you Donald Goines the shit. I think one of my guys on another dec got some more of Donald Goines, and Flames new book, I'll check for you later when they call yard," Mafia said . . . .

Later that day Twon woke up anxious to read some more of Donald Goines other material . . . .

"Did you go to yard," Twon asked Mafia? "Yeah I got the book calm down nigga," Mafia said. "Which one you get," Twon asked? "I got Flames new joint, The Evil That Men do," Mafia said as he reached in his jacket pocket pulled out the book and handt it to Twon. "The Evil That Man Do sound like a bomb," Twon said. "Anything Flame write is a bomb," Mafia said. "True dat," Twon said . . . .

Twon spent right off, and went to his cell and started reading it:

Chapter 1

Momma, I don't feel like going to church today, Oliver said. "Hush up now boy, you going to church every time services being held," his momma said. "But why mom," Oliver asked? "Why, because God so loved the world that he sacrificed the life of his only begotten son for our sins, God gave you life to live, he let you live, the air you breathe, the food you eat, everything you're able to do comes from your father whom are in heaven. God loves you, and you should always love him and praise his name," his momma said . . . .

How do God love us so much that we barely making it to pay the bills, a few times our lights even got cut off you had to read the bible under candle light, Oliver thought to himself . . . .

———

"We need to go to church today," Ralph said. "Naw man fuck going to church," Ronnie said. "Man, we need to go to church," Ralph said. "All this dirt we been doing we done robbed everybody, and they momma, we don't need to go church," Ronnie said. "I'm going, I talked to James last night he said he was going, that's on you if you wanna miss out on your blessings, I'm about to get ready right now, and go pick up James," Ralph said . . . .

Yeah I don't want to miss out on my blessings, Ronnie thought to himself . . . .

"Fuck it I'm going," Ronnie said. "You betta hurry up soon as I get dressed I'm up," Ralph said. "I'll be ready in no time Imma wear the suit I wore to my cousin's funeral," Ronnie said . . . .

James got in the car and slammed the door hard . . . .

"What took you so long to come out," Ralph asked James. "I was taking a shit. What church we going to," James asked? "It's called Divine Christ," Ralph said. "Where that's at, James asked? "You'll see when we get there," Ralph said . . . .

Ralph stopped at a red light and looked in the back seat at James . . . .

"Damn nigga you fresh to death, that suit brand new," Ralph asked? "Not all the way brand new I wore it twice before," Ronnie said . . . .

They pulled up to the church in which seemed as if it was in the country on the back of one of those dirt roads . . . .

"This way in the boondocks, look like some shit off a Steven King movie," Ronnie said. "That's why I picked it because it's way out, and a big congregation so I know it's going to be a lot of love," Ralph said . . . .

As they entered the church they walked up this long hallway filled with small statues, and portraits of a black Jesus. Once they made it to the front of the church one the deacons that was preaching the word of God to the kids paused . . . .

"Hi, God bless you brothers, how are you doing," the deacon asked? "We're doing good," Ralph and Ronnie said simultaneously. "God bless you to brother, and I feel wonderful blessed to be able to attend church this morning," James said. "This must be you brothers first time coming to this church, because I never seen neither one of you before," the deacon said. "This is our first time here," Ralph said. "Well I'm glad God put it on your heart and mind to come, you're always welcomed here in the house of the Lord. Hopefully you'll decide to become members of this church," deacon said. "Well I'm teaching Sunday school to the kids, but I'd love to talk to you more after church. Well the way we do Sunday school is off the age brackets. Follow me, and let me escort you to the Sunday school class that fits your age brackets," the deacon said . . . .

Once Ralph, Ronnie, and James walked passed Oliver he looked at them in disgust . . . .

These studs don't look right, Oliver thought to himself.

During Sunday school, and throughout the rest of the day in regular service Ralph, Ronnie, and James listen to the deacons, and pastor preach the word of God . . . .

Ronnie looked at the clock on the wall and seen that it was three thirty p.m . . . .

"It's three thirty the pastor said church over at four, so I guess it's time to receive our blessings," Ronnie said . . . . Ralph begin to smile. "Yep showl is," Ralph said then begin laughing . . . .

Three gun shots rang out back to back, as Ralph's .44 shattered the roof of the church. People in church immediately duck down, surprised, and afraid not knowing what to do . . . .

The pastor ducked down after the first shot; after the third shot he didn't hear no more shots he stood up, and seen Ralph, Ronnie, and James with two guns a piece in their hands . . . .

"Satan I rebuke you," the pastor yelled out. "Naw bitch I rebuke you," Ralph said . . . .

It was only one way out, one way in . . . .

A few members outta the congregation tried running out the door, but couldn't because Ronnie stood there with two guns in hand.

Ralph ran over to the pastor and brought him down off the pulpit; James and Ralph made the entire congregation line up, side by side. Then they made all the men lay face down on the floor. Ronnie told all the women to get naked. The women didn't obey him until the pastor told them to cooperate.

Ronnie, Ralph, and James felt blessed by being able to see all these naked women all at the same time.

After the women all got naked Ronnie, and Ralph made them lay on the floor . . . .

Ronnie, and Ralph confiscated all of the money from the offerings, and went through everyone's, pockets, purses, and wallets taking any, and everything that was valuable . . . .

After they finished robbing the church, Ralph, Ronnie, and James begin walking swiftly up the hallway. As they were almost at the door they looked back and seen the pastor running towards them at full force . . . .

"What the fuck is he doing, I should hand him one," James said. "Naw, don't get him, let's hurry up, and get up outta here," Ralph said . . . .

As Ralph exited the church door right before Ronnie, and James exited they heard multiple gun shots, before they could even look back Ronnie felt something hit him hard in the back of his head. Ronnie looked back and seen James laid out on the floor with his brains hanging, as the pastor was steady running his way . . . .

The pastor had shot James in the head, James fell and his head hit Ronnie's head . . . .

The pastor stepped over James, and ran behind Ralph's car busting his last two shots but didn't hit shit . . . .

The pastor went back to James examined him seen his brains hanging, spit in his face, and then splashed blessing oil in his face, took off his own suit jacket, and put it over James face, and looked up . . . .

"Heavenly Father I come to you once again begging you to have mercy, and forgive the young man whom is laying here dead. As well father I begging you to forgive me for I have committed a deadly sin by violating one of the Ten Commandments, thou shall not kill," the pastor said, as other male members came up examining the body . . . .

"The pastor wacked James the man brains was hanging out," Ronnie said. "Fuck that nigga I didn't want to split the money three ways no way, I'm glad he aint get me you see how he was yaking at us chasing the car down," Ralph said as Ronnie begin laughing. "You are a mess," Ronnie said . . . .

In due time the police had found out about Ronnie and Ralph robbing the church; they eventually got convicted of arm robbery and sentenced to excessive time in prison. The pastor was eventually convicted of James body, and received twenty five years in prison . . . .

All that night Oliver wondered to himself, how could all that violence occur in the house of the lord . . . .

"Mom buy me a ice cream," Oliver said. "Boy we almost home, we got ice cream at home," his mom said. "But we don't have any strawberry short cakes at home," Oliver said. "Alright I'll buy you one ice cream bar, that's it," his mom said . . . .

As they were second in line at the ice cream truck a guy ran out of an alley at top speed. Within seconds another man ran out of the alley chasing the first man while busting shots.

One of the stray bullets hit Olivers mom in the back as she instantly begin throwing up blood on Olivers face, and then she fell to the concrete . . . .

Oliver got on his knees holding his mom and crying out . . . .

"Mom, mom, mom, please don't die, please," Oliver said . . . .

The police and paramedics arrived in no time snatching Oliver away from his mom vacating the area of all the other people that wasn't law officials or medical assistance . . . .

Little Oliver cried out that his mom would continue to live. But it was too late they had pronounced her dead . . . .

A week later the funeral was held Oliver cried and screamed his screams was that of a horrifying nightmare that came to reality. Later within life his screams would haunt people's dreams turning them into nightmares . . . .

Oliver never knew his real dad, his dad took flight once he found out his mom was pregnant. Olivers grandparents was dead before he was even born. Majority of Oliver's mom family lived in other states, so his mom was all he ever really had . . . .

Every day after his mom was killed he'd blasphemy the Lords name . . . .

Why, why did she out of all people have to be killed, she worshipped God, and his son Jesus Christ faithfully, if God so call loved his children why would he let her get killed, Oliver thought to himself . . . .

Oliver's mom had one sister that lived in the same city, she ended up getting custody of Oliver not out of love, only because she felt sorry . . . .

From the very first day that Oliver moved in with his auntie, her husband, and their three kids he could see how phony they was. Although he was still a kid, and had lost his mom he continued on with his life promised his self that he do the things to make her proud as if she was still living . . . .

By the time Oliver was eighteen he went off to college to study psychology; he was fascinated by the power in which minds behold, and he wanted to be a psychiatrist . . . .

After a short period of time in college he seen how most college students would party hard, he wasn't interested wanted to spend time studying for a higher learning . . . .

One thing stayed with Oliver since he was a kid was that he'd always harshly blasphemy the Lord's name; he felt that if the Lord really loved his children why was it so much pain, and suffering in the world, and how, and why did the Lord allow his mom to be slayed . . . .

Oliver spent a lot of time at the library studying, and reading differnt nonfiction books. One day he decided to order the satanic bible off line to study the way the devil thinks, and how the devil's mind coincides with humans minds . . . .

Chapter after chapter Oliver begin to understand devilish things of the past that is currently going on today. How the devil works into peoples mind for them to think, say, and even act out devilish deeds . . . .

The city that Oliver went to college in was filled with devilish crimes. Quite often Oliver would see on the news or hear about crimes in his city . . . .

One night Oliver had borrowed a friend's car and was driving back to campus, and seen this man up a knife on this old lady, and took her purse. Oliver wanted to get out, and help the lady but was afraid the guy would possibly stab him; so Oliver just followed the guy to his destination which was his home . . . .

All night Oliver stayed up wondering what could he have done to stop that man from robbing that lady . . . .

Although Oliver would always use the Lord's name in vain Oliver still wasn't a bad sinful guy . . . .

More and more Oliver wondered to himself what could he do to stop violence . . . .

On the weekend, at night while party's was jumping off everywhere Oliver would roam the streets of the ghetto, and observe the evil that men do . . . .

One day on the CNN news they talked about how a mother was killed in broad daylight in front of her own kids. Oliver went into a mental rage thinking of how his very own mother that was killed right in front of his eyes . . . .

Oliver begin snapping out, threw the T.V. in a tub of water, and begin breaking lamps, amongst other things he could get his hands on . . . .

Oliver decided to take target practice whenever he had the time. First he starting going to the shooting range, then he started going dear hunting with one of his teachers . . . .

Oliver decided to get some guns, and bow, and arrows for personal use. He was too young to buy guns, and bowing arrows from stores so he went through one of his classmates that had family in the streets. Once Oliver came up with the money, getting the guns and bow, and arrows wasn't a problem. They gave him the guns, brand new still in the box with a gang of bullets. He only paid for one bow, and arrows, but they were players so they gave him two bows, and arrows. Oliver's classmate knew about the streets so he kept everything silent . . . .

One night after Oliver finished his homework flashes of his momma being killed and throwing up blood raced through his head. He started to think about what he'd seen on CNN, how a mother was killed in front of her kids . . . .

He grabbed the bow, and arrows put it in a black laundry bag and took it to the streets . . . .

He drove through the ghettos seeing massive amounts of drug addicts in lines, rocks and blows they was buying as Lucifer's madness was steadily inclined . . . .

He begin to remember when the guy robbed that old lady, and he followed him home. He went over to that guys house and parked waiting on him . . . .

Oliver winded up dosing off going asleep . . . .

Oliver was woken up by a knock on the window . . . .

The knock on the window scared him . . . .

Oliver slowly let the window down . . . .

Before Oliver could say a word the guy that was knocking on the window spoke first . . . .

"Hey, guy do you got a square I can buy from you," the man asked Oliver. "No I don't even smoke, you should stop smoking it's bad for your health," Oliver said. "It's a lot of shit that's bad for our health, and we still do it, but uhhhh sorry for waking you up, you can gone back to sleep," the man said as he turned his back to walk away . . . .

After the man took a few steps away from Oliver's car an arrow went through his head, before his body fell to the ground another arrow hit him in the back, leaving him for dead . . . .

Oliver pulled off as his tires burned rubber he left the scene scared to death . . . .

Once Oliver made it back to campus he went to his room locking the door frightful as if someone was after him . . . .

He laid on his bed reenacting the crime within his mind . . . .

I can't believe I was looking for this guy, and he walked up to my car asking for a cigarette, Oliver thought to himself.

The next day at school Oliver went in did his work, and past his tests all with A pluses, like nothing never happen the night before . . . .

One day Oliver was riding to do some shopping for clothes and rode pass the ho stroll . . . .

How could these women deprive themselves of selling their bodies for money, and for short sums of money at that, Oliver thought to himself . . . .

Oliver decided to go back around and see if he could talk to them, and maybe find a way to help them get a job . . . .

As soon as Oliver pulled up before he got a chance to park, one white chick ran up to his car pulling down her pants . . . .

"You want some of this pussy, don't you," the white chick asked?

Then four more other women, ran up to the car showing him there body, begging him to let them suck his dick, and to do other extreme sexual acts.

Oliver didn't waste his time trying to convince the ladies to stop hoing, he knew it was too late for that . . . .

So Oliver decided to get his dick suck by the first white chick that ran to his car . . . .

Once he got her in the car he tried to pick her brain to see where she was at, and how did she start selling pussy.

Come to find out she came from a middle class home, and started selling pussy to maintain her drug habit. Just like most of the woman that was hoing was drug addicts, although some didn't look like drug addicts they were . . . .

Oliver drove far away from the ho stroll pulled up in an alley, parked an unzipped his pants, as she snatched his dick out his boxers, and started eating his dick . . . .

Awww awww this feels so good, Oliver thought to his self, as she continued eating his dick.

As Oliver could feel his dick getting harder as his nut start coming, then unloading it in her mouth as she drank all of it thirsty for more . . . .

After swallowing the nut she jumped up . . . .

"A'ight give me my twenty dollars," she said . . . .

He reached in his pocket, and gave her the twenty dollars . . . .

"Step out the car and look at the back tire, it fills like the tires are low," Oliver said . . . .

She stepped out of the car looking at the back tire, before she could look up a arrow went through her skull instantly killing her. Oliver get in his car pulled off leaving her for dead . . . .

Oliver decided to kill the ho because she was part of the reason people catch diseases that it's no cure for, like H.I.V. that's fatal . . . .

In time Oliver begin to read more of the satanic bible, and he'd compare it to the lives of human beings. Oliver became aware of how the devil works in the minds of almost, if not all human beings. The devil would even work in the mind of those that's righteous even if only for short period of time . . . .

Oliver watched a lot of news on TV. And the Bloods and Crips were warring against each other, killing one another . . . .

Late nights Oliver would go kill a blood, then the next night kill a Crip . . . .

On many occasions Oliver would see on the news the police committing criminal activities themselves and getting away with it. Oliver hated the police just seeing them made him sick to his stomach . . . .

One cold, cold winters night Oliver road to the police station, listening to Adele's song Chasing Payments . . . . Once he made it to the police station he parked, and went inside the police station, and seen that it was no one in the inside, but police officers he went to the front desk, and was greeted by this openly genuinely nice female officer . . . .

"Hi what can I do for you today," the officer said . . . .

Oliver didn't reply immediately he just looked around the inside of the police station. He noticed that it was two more other officer's sitting at the long desk . . . .

He looked back at the officer looking her in her pretty baby blue eyes . . . .

"Yes, it's a place called hell were solders of war felled were sinners dwell in a pool of burning fire where demonic spirits couldn't go higher where gang members never retire. Some say that a particular race got they heaven on earth, that's a lie it's hell on earth, and it's no heaven in the sky after we die," Oliver said . . . .

The officer stared at Oliver confused not knowing what to say or do . . . .

Oliver upped a long ass chrome gun the officer was scared to death not thinking in her right state of mind she reached for Oliver's gun as she caught two bullets in the face one in the eye, and one in the forehead, in which killed her. Oliver then shot the other cop that was close by him whom was reaching for his gun. The other officer that was at the large front desk begin shooting at Oliver hitting Oliver once in the chest once in the arm, as Oliver was shooting back he shoot him once in the leg as every police in the back of the station came and shot Oliver up fifty something times, taking his life away . . . .

Oliver really believed it was hell on earth, but just to make sure he was going to hell he went into the police station shooting knowing that they would kill him, that was Oliver's version of suicide. Oliver knew that God didn't forgive those for committing suicide, so if there was a hell his soul would forever burn in eternal fire . . . .

Later down the road once the police did a background check they came to see that Oliver had no history of criminal record not even a misdemeanor, or a traffic violation. Oliver's family was confused, sad, and devastated; they couldn't believe what Oliver had done, and that he was dead. Oliver never was a bad boy, never did anything violent . . . .

No one never knew the pain Oliver felt, because of the evil that men do . . . .

Twon ran out his cell to Mafia . . . .

"This shit was a bomb," Twon told Mafia. "Damn you read that whole book that quick," Mafia asked? "Naw I just read the first part, its four parts to it, its four short stories. The first one was called Oliver, Oliver was a nut," Twon said. "Don't tell me about it I wanna read it myself, you gonna ruin the surprises. Oliver . . . . I think I read that book before," Mafia said. "How did you read it before if it just came out," Oliver asked?

"A lot of material Flame be putting out, he wrote years ago when we was locked up together, he use to let me read it so I could give him my criticism. A lot of nigga's didn't even like talking to Flame, because that's all he use to talk about was book shit, all day every day, but the nigga is smart than motherfucker. He got out put his books out there and they took off. That's what I be trying to get you to be on you can do some positive things right now while you're in prison then once you get out, you aint gotta sell drugs or be in the streets no more. When you get out you can sit back, and cash fat checks," Mafia said. "So, why you didn't do something positive with yourself all those times you been in prison," Twon asked? "Well I did do something positive I made sure all my kids was raised right, all my kids went to college, and got married. Even though I was in and out of jail I still had a influence over my kids life. I know I ain't on shit Imma dopefiend I'm going to be a dopefiend til I die," Mafia said as Twon begin laughing. "You laughing I'm serious soon they let me out the gate I'm going straight to the dope spot. But I'm not a hypocrite by preaching to you about being constructive, I'm trying to get you to not be like me, do something with your life, you can turn out to be a positive remodel," Mafia said . . . .

Mafia, and Twon paused both thinking to themselves about the past, present, and future . . . .

"Why do these same niggas keep trying to fuck with me more, and more," Twon asked Mafia. "Fuck these niggas, keep these phony ass niggas away from you. These niggas just wanna fuck with a nigga just to see what they can get up out you, or to try to get to know a nigga to be all in your business. You see how I don't talk a lot these niggas phony. You see how they didn't even hit you with shit when you first came on the deck definitely stay away from the ViceLords they'll have you in some bullshit. A lot these niggas say they ViceLords but aint real with it. I done been around some of the finest Vicelords, Walter wheet, K.T., King Wallace, and Prince God," Mafia said. "Who the fuck is King Wallace," Twon asked? "That's King Neal, his last name Wallace, a lot of us old school nigga's call him Wallace, or Mr. Wallace," Mafia said. "Didn't the Travelers have two princes, Prince Black, and Prince God," Twon asked? "Naw a lot of people get that mixed up, Black, and God that's the same person. Black got drafted and had to go to Vietnam, while in Vietnam the soldiers named him God, so when he came back from the war, and hit the streets again he kept the name

God. I'f Wallace was still living he would have the king of kings slot, he would've been king of all Vicelords," Mafia said. "Aint the Insanes prince named Black to," Twon asked? "Yep, I met him before in jail he a good nigga to," Mafia said . . . .

For about an hour Mafia kicked it with Twon about ViceLord history . . . .

Chapter 7

"Mafia what you doing with that yellow suit on," Twon asked Mafia. "It's time to go home, time for me to take my show on the road," Mafia said. "Awww man you was finna sneak up outta here you didn't even tell nobody you was short, I thought you still had a couple of years left," Twon said. "Naw I wasn't going to sneak up outta here on you, you my man. Help me take my shit over to property," Mafia said . . . .

As they carried Mafia's belongings to property they reminisced joyfully . . . .

"I hope everything works out for the best on your appeal, just keep praying on it," Mafia said. "Things aint gone be the same without you," Twon said. "Don't worry you'll be a'ight you cool now moms made sure you got your t.v, and all your electronics. But just remember what I told you, don't start fucking around with them niggas, do your own time, and get your job in dietary, start college, and fall back until it's time to start your big debut in the free world again," Mafia said . . . .

Twon gave Mafia a hug. "You be easy out there," Twon said as he left the personal property room without looking back . . . .

After Mafia left and went home it seemed as Twon was all alone, Mafia was the only genuine friend he had since he first stepped in the joint . . . .

Twon heard a knock at his cell door which awoke him outta his sleep. He got up and looked through the glass of his cell door, didn't recognize the face so decided to open the door to see what he wanted . . . .

"What you need homie," Twon asked him? "Your name Taker," dude asked? "Naw my name Twon, but I am a Undertaker," Twon said. "My name Rob I'm a taker to, I just come to meet you." "Where you from Lord," Twon asked? "I aint from Chicago, I'm from Danville," Rob said. "Danville, I didn't even know it was takers in Danville," Twon said. "Yeah it some Takers in Danville," Rob said. "How long Lord, let me put brush my teeth, and put my clothes on I'll be in the dayroom in a minute," Twon said . . . .

Twon brushed his teeth, washed his face, put on his clothes, and went into the dayroom, and kicked it with Rob for a long ass time . . . .

Twon begin to rotate with Rob heavy, but after a few weeks he begin to notice that Rob was a dummy so he started to stray away from him a little bit . . . .

"Let me use your hot pot," Rob said. "Go in my cell, and get it," Twon said . . . .

Later the same day Twon was in his bunk reading, and heard a knock at his cell door. He got up and open his cell door, and there stood one of the ViceLord with his pot in his hand . . . .

"Here go your pot," Lord said. "How the hell you get my pot," Twon asked? "Rob gave it to me," Lord said. "Aw yeah that's right I did give it to Rob, anytime you need to use it feel free to ask me," Twon said. "A'ight," Lord said. "Hold on lord, why the bottom of my hot pot loose," Twon asked? "I don't know," Lord said. "Hold on let me plug it up to see if anything is wrong with it," Twon said . . . .

Twon filled his pot with water plugged it up and seen it started boiling harder than it normally did . . . .

"One of ya'll rig my pot up so it could boil hotter, ya'll know them people be sending nigga's to seg for that," Twon said. "Nigga fuck you, you tripping of a petty ass hot pot, nigga you a bitch," Lord said . . . .

Before Lord knew it Twon had dropped his pot, and swiftly handt him five stiff ones in the face knocking out one of his teeth and breaking his jaw . . . .

Twon got sent out the joint for that ordeal which was an inmate assault. They sent him to a max joint . . . .

56

On the bus ride to the max joint all Twon could think to himself is that I should've listen to Mafia, I should've never even started fucking with them nigga's . . . .

When the bus first made it to max joint Twon noticed that it look like a place that was built in the eighteen hundreds.

Once Twon made it to seg. He noticed that it had bars instead of cell doors like the medium joint he had just left . . . .

As he slowly walked up the gallery escorted by the c/o's as his wrist, and ankles were shackled other inmates begin yelling . . . .

"Hey lil bitch were you from," one guy within a cell asked?

"I'm the grand dragon of KKK I hate niggas," one white guy said as he passed his cell.

"A pussy ass bitch is your momma still sucking dicks for rocks," another guy said as people on the gallery begin laughing . . . .

Twon couldn't believe the disrespectful shit that they was saying. What Twon didn't know was that, that's how they get down behind the wall in seg. because there was no way for you to get to them. Inmates went to the shower once a week one by one shackled up, breakfast, lunch, and dinner was brought to the cell by an officer. Once someone was released from seg. they'd be going straight to another joint or home. And even if they were going to population chances are you'd never see them, because the joint was so big . . . .

Once Twon made it to his one man cell, he entered as the officer slammed the cell door extremely hard, reached through the bars, and uncuffed Twons wrist, and ankles.

Once the police left Twon looked around the cell, and noticed that all of his property that he was allowed to have in seg. was already there: his pictures, his books, his letters, writing supplies, cosmetics, three pairs of boxers, three pairs of t-shirts, three pairs of socks, etc . . . .

"Hey little homie on the new," Twon heard someone say. "Yeah what's up man," Twon replied. "You from the city," the guy asked? "Yeah," Twon said. "Where at," the guy asked? "I'm from out west," Twon said. "What you is," they guy asked? "Imma a undertaker," Twon said. "I'm a ViceLord to I'm a Double I from up north, they call me Double I the guy said . . . .

Twon and Doub kicked it for a little while. Doub explained to Twon that people always yelling, arguing, and saying ignorant shit just to past time, so he betta get use to . . . .

Later on that night Twon seen that Doub wasn't lying. Twon couldn't get no peace, no sleep, all night none stop they yelled out on the gallery. To Twon it seemed as hundreds of maniacs were yelling in his face screaming in his ear, he even prayed that they would shut up, but they never did . . . .

After a couple weeks Twon got use to the yelling, and hollering because they did it all die and night . . . .

Twon finally received his review for his ticket of inmate assault he got six months in seg. and six months loss of good time conduct . . . .

After three months in seg. they moved Twon to a different building were the inmates in seg. had a noise ordinance policy. Twon got over there and couldn't believe how quiet it was. To Twon it was a beautiful thing to finally get some quiet time . . . .

Since Twon stepped in seg. all he did was read constantly . . . .

After six months in seg. they released him to population, put him in west house three gallery . . . .

Once he made it to his cell he noticed how clean it was. Once he made it in the cell the officer slammed the door his celly jumped upped from under the covers . . . .

Twon immediately noticed how tall he was, and all the tattoos he had that looked as if they was done professional . . . .

Twon's new celly took off his doo-rag, he had fresh 360 waves . . . .

"You plugged," he asked Twon? "Yeah I'm a ViceLord," Twon said. "I'm a ViceLord to, four corner hustler, the call me Manny," he said, as he reached out to shake Twon's hand.

Twon begin unpacking his shit, and inquiring about how they rotate knives, and do security, and how ViceLord was being ran . . . . Manny begin laughing . . . .

"They don't get down like that no mo, that was in the 80's, and in the early 90's the joints shut down we barely come out the cell when we do it's for only a hour yard, unless we going to commissary, or on call pass to the library or something. If you get caught with a knife or taking care of to much nation business they sending you to Tamms," Manny said. "I heard that in Tamms they don't even come out the cell for nothing. I heard they bring the shower to their cell doors, and it's made of unbreakable glass, and they connect it to their cell doors, they take a shower and go right back in their cells. I heard they gotta read their mail of a screen. That sound like some shit out the movies," Twon said. "It may sound like some shit out the movies but its real life homie. Don't get me wrong they still take care of nation business, and it's a few knives floating around, but not like that. Your best bet is to chill, keep you a small circle of niggas you fuck with, and do you. How much time you got," Manny asked? "Thirty years," Twon said. "I wish I had thirty years," Manny said. "You saying that like thirty years aint shit, that's a long ass time," Twon said. "It is a long time, but it aint shit to me because I got two natural balls," Manny said. "Damn you got to natural lives," Twon said. "Yep, but I'm trying to get back on appeal," Manny said. "Yeah, me to," Twon said . . . .

After Twon finished straighten up, and putting up his property him, and Manny kicked it for hours . . . .

As days followed Twon went out to yard each morning rotating with the brothers, and kicking it with some of his childhood friends that was in the joint, some was from his hood, some wasn't, some was getting outta jail, and some wasn't. Twon even got a chance to meet some of the original ViceLord chiefs that Mafia had told him about, that had been locked up since the 70's and 80's . . . .

Twon had learned from his mistake of fucking with the brothers, but he still rotated with the brothers a little because it was hard not to in prison . . . .

Twon begin to notice that Manny would get a lot of mail almost every day . . . .

"You get a lot of mail," Twon said. "That be letters from ho's I met off the internet," Manny said. "You talking about one of them prison pen pal sites," Twon said. "Yeah, it's this one called Prison Pen Pals. Com that I was on, and a gang of ho's wrote me off it, ho's all from Russia start writing me," Manny said. "I heard them sites aint guaranteed," Twon said. "Naw they aint, I know alot a niggas that did it, and aint get not one ho to write them. I been on about ten other prison pen pal web sites, and didn't get not one ho to write me. But once I went on Prison Pen Pal I kept getting letters from ho's, so many ho's was writing me I gave they address away. A lot of niggas be coming up on ho's off the internet and be trying get money out of them, me I don't be on none of that, I just been trying to rotate with a ho that's genuine. You gotta think if a ho just out the blue start writing a nigga in jail that she didn't even know she gotta have some type of good morals, and values," Manny said. "Them the only ho's you be having rotating with you," Twon asked? "Yep, the ho's I was fucking with in the world they broke bad on me as soon as the judge gave me my time," Manny said . . . .

Manny tried hooking Twon up with some of his pen pals friends; a couple chicks started writing Twon but it didn't last long because they wasn't sincere . . . .

Twon decided to place his picture, and ad on Prison Pen Pals.com, which cost eighty dollars for a year . . . .

As the first few months passed along Twon didn't get any respond from nobody off Prison Pan Pals.com so he just gave up . . . .

By the time it was eighteen months after Twon appeal was filed he got a letter from the appellate court denying his appeal. Twon couldn't believe it, his inner spirits was crushed, as his inner soul cried out for freedom . . . .

I been going to the library helping my appellate defender researching case laws, and everything, and they still denied my appeal, Twon thought to himself . . . .

Twon start going to the law library working on his post-conviction . . . .

After about nine months of him being behind the wall his transfer was approved he was sent to another medium joint. As soon as he made it within the joint he seen some of his homies, some he knew from the world, some he met jailing.

Majority of his homies were in school so he decided to sign up for school just to kick it with them . . . .

Once he started taking G.E.D. classes he seen how easy it was he liked it . . . .

One day while sitting in his cell waiting on mail he received two letters one was from his mom telling him how his baby momma keep leaving his daughter Angel with her for long periods of time as usual. The second letter was from a Lisa Santana . . . .

I don't know no Lisa Santana, Twon thought to himself.

Twon eagerly read the letter, and came to find out it was a chick that wrote him off Prison Pen Pals. Twon immediately wrote her back . . . .

In time as Twon and Lisa's friendship grew, his baby momma would continue leaving his daughter with his momma.

Twon constantly wondered why his kids momma would run off, and leave the baby with his momma. He couldn't ask nobody from the hood cuz he had no ties to the streets everybody moved on with they life. In the past one of his homies told him his baby momma was getting high smoking cocaine, he didn't believe him, because when he was out she wouldn't even smoke weed or drink liquor . . . .

Over time Twon decided stay focused, and not let his situation bring him down . . . .

After he got his G.E.D. he decided to take some college English courses mainly to be around his homies, and to be able to write more better letters to Lisa . . . .

Twon couldn't believe how easy college was.

After he finished taking one college course he took another English class, then another one, before long he was taking all type of college classes, not just English . . . .

Eventually the courts denied his post-conviction which broke his heart he still didn't give up going to the next stage of appeals . . . .

Chapter 8

"I got your letter last night it was good. I remember years ago you didn't even know how to write letters now you write sex stories, your sex stories you write to me are better than some erotica books I've read. You need to consider writing a book you're real intelligent. I'm working on writing a book myself," Lisa said to Twon over the phone. "You know a lot people told me that when I first got locked up and I never even considered doing it. Do you know that I read almost any and everything, and write short erotica stories for everybody on the dec. You know how I learned how to write, writing back and forth to you all these years, and from taking all those English courses helped me to write," Twon said. "How long have we been together," Lisa asked? "About seven or eight years," Twon said. "Wow, it's been that long," Lisa said. "Yep, funny how time flies," Twon said. "What's up with your appeal," Lisa asked? "Well they denied another one, as usual so I gotta appeal the appeal they denied. I'm getting tired of appeals, I'm about to give up on appeals, I'm short now I don't got nothing but five years left, since I done got back all the good time I done lost," Twon said. "You should never give up, you should keep fighting to the bitter end," Lisa said. "Yeah, you right about that but fighting them appeals is a headache," Twon said. "Well take you some aspirins for that headache, and keep going round for round with appellate court until they release you," Lisa said. "So since you got your new boyfriend you act like you don't know me no more," Twon said. "No it's not like that I got a life to, besides I really care about him, and he cares about me. You should want to see me happy even if it's not with you," Lisa said. "I do want to see you happy," Twon said. "Well alright than if you don't hear from me a lot be more understanding," Lisa said. "Unfortunately Ms. Santana I gotta go its lock up time," Twon said. "Okay, I love you," Lisa said. "I love you to," Twon said . . . .

After that phone call Twon would only hear from Lisa like once every two months, she got caught in a genuine love affair with her new boyfriend . . . .

"Starks you gotta a package at personal property," the c/o said . . . .

As Twon walked to property he wondered what it could be, because he didn't order anything . . . .

Once he made it over to personal property a c/o opened up a brown envelope from Lisa Santana, and handt him a book . . . .

I wonder why she decided to send me a book, Twon thought to himself . . . .

Twon left property than read the title, Deniros. Twon decided to read the back of the book, and seen Lisa picture. After seeing her picture on the back he then he turned back to the front of the book and seen her name at the bottom as the author.

Damn she wrote a book, aw yeah that's right she did tell me a while back that she was writing a book, Twon thought to himself.

Twon went back ran straight to his cell and read the back of it.

Aw she wrote a urban novel, Twon thought to himself.

Twon immediately opened it up, and started reading it, and finished it in no time he liked it.

He went on the deck, and shared it with others.

Twon remembered what Mafia told him years ago, that he should write a book. Then Twon remembered what Lisa told him, that he was intelligent enough to write a book . . . .

Twon started writing short stories of erotica in which he had been doing for years, but not trying to make a book outta them . . . .

Twon would let people on the deck read his erotica stories he wrote, and they loved them. He knew they would like them, because they liked the erotica he wrote free styling when he wasn't writing a book . . . .

"Here come this nigga Twon always talking about this book shit," one guy told the next guy standing on the side of him. "Hey man what's the best erotica book you ever read," Twon asked? I knew he was getting start talking about some book shit, one guy thought to himself, as both guys spent off faking like they had something to do.

Every time you'll see Twon he was always talking about writing books. He came to find out a lot other niggas in the joint was writing books to of all sorts of genre, majority was urban novels . . . .

Right before, and after Twon got the book Deniros from Lisa he wasn't hearing from Lisa, but eventually she wrote, and told him she get paid two dollars per book . . . .

Two dollars per book aint shit what Imma do with two dollars per book, Twon thought to himself . . . .

Twon went to the library to meet up with one of his book writing homies, Busta . . . .

"Busta Lisa talking about she get two dollars a book, that aint shit," Twon said. "Is you crazy two dollars a book is a lot of money, some bestselling authors don't even get that, some publishing houses only give fifty cent, or a dollar per book. Most publishing houses give checks called quarter royalties," Busta said. "Why they call it quarter royalties," Twon asked? "Cuz they give you the check each quarter, every three months. So just imagine if you sell ten thousand books in three months, times that times two dollars, that twenty thousand in three months off one book, so you do the math if you get ten, fifteen, or twenty books published," Busta said. "Aw I didn't look at it like that," Twon said. "It's a lot of shit you gotta learn about book writing," Busta said . . . .

Chapter 9

"**M**om how are you doing," Twon asked his mom over the phone. "I'm good son, how about yourself," his mom asked? "I'm good to, I received the money order you sent, thanks, I don't know how I would've made it through this bide without you," Twon said. "That's what moms are for. I sent you some pictures of Angel, she done got so big," his momma said. "Is she home, I wanna talk to her," Twon said. "No, she at school, but she wrote you a letter, and sent it off yesterday, you should be getting it soon. You should see Angel's mom she out there bad, you wouldn't even recognize her, I seen her the other day on the stroll selling her body, it was so sad to see her that way. I'm glad I took custody of Angel when she was a little girl, because aint no telling how she would've turned out," his mom said.

"Mom I'm done, I finished writing another book," Twon said. "Here we go again with this book stuff," mom said. "You sound like the guys in here, every time they see me come around they just walk off, they already know I'm finna talk about some book writing stuff. If ya'll knew how much money book writers make ya'll understand why I always be talking about book writing," Twon said. "I'm proud of you that you write books, I hope you get out, and be successful, but you don't have to talk about it all the time," mom said as they both begin laughing . . . .

"What's going on with your appeal," mom asked? "The Supreme Court done denied another appeal, I'm done with appeals I don't got nothing but eighteen months left before I'm free," Twon said. "Eighteen months, that's it," mom said. "Yep, I'm at the end of the road. Hey mom they finna call us out for dinner, I'll call you back on a later date," Twon said. "Alright you stay out of trouble, and take care of yourself, always remember mom loves you," mom said. "Yeah, I know, and I love you to," Twon said . . . .

Eighteen Months Later(February 11ᵀᴴ 2012)

"The Greyhound bus will be arriving in Chicago in five minutes, please make sure to take all your personal belongings, Greyhound is not responsible for left items," the Greyhound bus driving said . . . .

After that five minutes Twon was stepping off the Greyhound bus with a box of handwritten manuscripts in his hand . . . .

His mom, his daughter Angel, and few more family members were already standing there waiting on him. Once he stepped totally off the bus the family begin cheering, and taking pics with their cell phones . . . .

Angel begin running towards Twon . . . . "Daddy, daddy," she said as she ran up and hugged him . . . .

I'm finally here, finally home after all these years, Twon thought to himself as he held Angel tightly in his arms . . . .

Twon then hugged his mom, then his other family members . . . .

The winded up getting into his mom new truck Twon couldn't believe how technology had change . . . .

While on the ride home her stared out of the window amazed. He noticed that everybody had cell phones, before he went to jail people was using beepers, the main people that had cell phones was people that was getting money . . . .

Once they made it to his mom house he stayed up kicking it with the family for a little while. Once the family went home he stayed up almost all night talking to his daughter Angel. He couldn't believe how much she had grown physically and mentally over the years . . . .

Within the next few days Twon begin to notice even more how technology had advanced, things he had seen in the movies about the future had actually came to reality.

A lot of Twons old homies tried to get up with him once they heard he was out, Twon had stayed his distance, he never started back fucking with them; he felt like if they were really his homie they would've been rotating with him while he was in jail, but they didn't.

Twon called his ex-pen pal Lisa Santana a few times to show his appreciation for her showing him love while he was in jail; she was engaged to be married so after a few times he stopped calling her, and just let her live her life.

Within months Twon's parole agent had found him a job at a construction company, the job paid fifteen dollars, an hour. Twon always thought that construction workers made more than that, some actually did depending on which construction company they worked for . . . .

Twon had decided to go through self-publishing companies to get his books published, because they'd process them much faster than regular publishing companies. With self-publishing companies you'd have to pay various prices, but once you pay your book would be published in the matter of weeks; contrary to regular publishing companies in which a large sum of them you'd have to have a literary agent for them to even look over your manuscript, then it'll be a process of three to six months for them to approval or reject your manuscript. Then even if they did accept your manuscript it would take nine to twelve months for them to publish, and print your book into actual book form. The main thing that was good about most regular publishing companies was that you didn't have to pay to get your book published, and that they utilized great marketing strategies . . . .

Twon's first book with a self-publishing company was erotica; the title of the book was Sex Demands. The book was a collection of all short stories written only by Twon. All the short sex stories consist of someone making a sexual demand . . . .

After Twon got his first book published through a self-publishing, he decided to take his hard earned money from construction working, and continue to get his books published. He was able to afford at least to get two books a month published . . . .

His first and second quarter royalty checks were small only about a couple hundred a piece. That was discouraging to Twon because by this time he had several books out . . . .

Through it all, Twon kept writing kept getting his books self-published . . . .

The third quarter was much better than the first two it was thirty five hundred which made Twon so happy . . . .

The fourth quarter royalty check came in the mail, Twon mouth dropped he couldn't believe it. It was twenty five thousand dollars . . . .

Twon begin jumping for joy, and immediately went, and showed his daughter Angel, and his mom . . . .

By that time Twon had almost twenty books published so twenty five thousand wasn't a lot of royalty payment for twenty books, but it was a lot of money for him, especially compared to the other royalty checks he was getting . . . .

Twon, and Angel moved from his mom house. Twon ended up finding him, and Angel a two bedroom apartment up north down the street from the lake front . . . .

Throughout Twon's freedom from prison he'd show lots of love to his daughter Angel; him and his daughter was close as if he never went to prison. From time to time he'd see Angel's mom on the ho stroll, she was so strung out on drugs that sometimes she wouldn't even recognize him . . . .

Every day as Twon looked at Angel he felt blessed that she didn't turn out bad like a lot of other teenagers. Angel had no boyfriend stayed in the house all the time studying . . . .

Angel is a perfect name for her, Angel is My Angel, that's what Imma start calling her My Angel, Twon thought to himself . . . .

"You're My Angel, you know that dad loves you," Twon said. "Yeah I know dad, and I love you to," Angel said. "Sorry that I went to jail, and missed out on majority of your life. But I'm here now, here for you, I'm never going back to jail. Imma keep writing books, and keep putting them out there so we can have things in life. Always try to stay positive, and stay focused on the right track and stay studying them school books so you can finish college, and be prosperous in life. Do you know what you wanna major in, in college," Twon asked? "I wanna study law," Angel said . . . . Twon got excited. "Study law, that's top flight, that's good sweetheart, but what makes you wanna study law," Twon asked? "Because I hate to see people go to jail, I'm always seeing on the news how people are being wrongfully convicted, especially the blacks, I wanna be a lawyer so I can help them be free" . . . .

Twon paused in a pleasurable silence proud of his Angel . . . .

Over time Twon continued writing erotica, and getting them published. His royalty payments started to enhance to a point where he didn't have to work anymore . . . .

Twon started doing charity work, and traveling to other countries to feed those starving in hunger, and those living in poverty . . . .

Twon felt that since God blessed him with the talent to write, and to receive large sums of money for his writings he should cast his blessings upon others, and he did just that . . . .

Twon begin taking a lot of trips with the corps across the world to help people living in poverty, but mainly to help people all throughout Africa . . . . Over time Twon got real cool with one of the kings within a small country in Africa, King Shariff . . . .

Twon begin to travel to Shariff's country quite often; not only to help his people, but to kick it with Shariff on a personal level. Shariff was knowledgeable, and would share his knowledge with Twon . . . .

"I'm most gracious that you dedicate sectors out of your vitality to help my people," Shariff said. "Your people is my people all of us are black, and beautiful," Twon said. "If you ever need anything feel free to let me know," Shariff said. "Naw, I'm good," Twon said. "My people manufacture some of the best heroin, that's flowing through the United States, and my cousin is a general in the U.S. army, I can get you dope, and brand new guns in through customs through my cousin," Shariff said. "What," Twon yelled out . . . .

Twon looked at Shariff in amazement couldn't believe what he just said . . . .

"I'm here to help people, not to create problems," Twon said. "You can help my people by selling some of our heroin in the states, and using the money to provide food, and shelter, as I do," Shariff said. "Naw I'll pass on that, but what I will keep doing is taking parts of my royalties and using it to help others," Twon said. "You a good man, but if you ever need heroin, guns, grenades, rocket launchers, flame throwers, or any other weapons just let me know, and I can assist you with getting them free of charge, and my cousin will get them through the United States with no problem," Shariff said. "Naw I'm good I don't need no guns or none of that," Twon said. "You should always keep at least a few guns you never know when trouble may occur, especially in the government you live in, filled with violence. Your governments law officials are some the cruelest people that ever existed. You never know when your government may come unjust with weapons drawn, you need to be prepared for the rapture," Shariff said. "Naw, I'm good man I don't worry about things of that nature because if I'm not doing shit, if I'm not committing crimes, then I don't gotta worry about it," Twon said. "But you never know when trouble may occur," Shariff said . . . .

Twon ended up getting on another subject, and later on that day he took a flight home contemplating on what Shariff told him, and missing his Angel . . . .

He arrived within his city late in the night. He debated if he should just go home or should he go over his mom's house to pick up his Angel. Normally when he'd take trips he'd have his Angel stay with mom. He decided to go pick up his Angel, after he'd stop by one his girlfriend's house . . . .

He went over to his vet house Teressa. He liked fucking with Teressa cuz she wasn't up with the drama, they never argued, she never complained about him being with other women, or him not spending enough time with her. Never complained about anything . . . .

As he entered her home there she stood in a see through lingerie set ready for whatever. As he closed the door behind himself she got on her knees unbutton then unzipped his pants and hungrily begin eating his dick like never before. She was eating the dick as if she was starving for it . . . .

Once he started busting a nut he let it go all over her face . . . .

She began begging for him to fuck her . . . .

He laid her on the floor took his pants off, and pulled her see through panties to the side. She held her on legs in the air as she continued to beg for the dick. He placed his rock hard dick in her pussy and begin slamming his dick in and out of her pussy.

She begin moaning painful sighs . . . .

She started rubbing her pearl tongue as he continued giving her the dick in the rawest form . . . .

"Oh yes baby, oh yes baby, keep giving me the dick like that, keep giving me the dick like that, keep giving me the dick like that. I'm cumming I'm cumming I'm cummming, Oh yes tear this pussy up, tear this pussy up," she said as she commence to cumming . . . .

For about thirty minutes they got it in sexually . . . .

After they finished fucking he washed up and went to his mom's house to get his Angel . . . .

Twon always kept a set of keys to his mom's house, so as he keyed the door, and then twist the knob, opened up the door Angel came running towards him with her arms open . . . . "Daddy, daddy," Angel said right before she jumped into his arms . . . .

"Daddy I missed you while you was gone, why do you have to take all those trips," Angel asked? "Sweetheart you know I be going on those trips to help people around the world. God blessed me with a talent to write, and all this money, so I cast my blessings amongst others," Twon said. "But dad I don't like being in the house by myself grandma is always over her boyfriend house," Angel said . . . .

Twon begin laughing.

"Girl you damn near grown you getting ready to be eighteen years old, you don't need no babysitter," Twon said.

"I promise I'm going to spend less time away from home, and more time with you," Twon said . . . .

Over time Twon stuck to his word, and spent more time with Angel, although he did do a little traveling mainly to Africa to help others . . . .

"Son, how is school going," Twon's mom asked? "It's a'ight. A lot people think college is hard, but it's really not, unless you going to law school, or med school. I know it's easy for me cuz I'm majoring in creative writing, and make up design, and I love writing, so creative writing is a walk in the park for me," Twon said. "Why do you have to take creative writing, you already know how to write books," Twon's mom said. "But I wanna make my skills better, and I took up creative writing so I can write screenplays for movie, that's when you get the big bucks when you write screenplays," Twon said. "Why are you taking up make up design, I can teach you how to put on make-up," Twon's mom said, as Twon begin laughing. "Naw make up design is like creating a certain look for characters in movies. Like for instance the movie Nightmare On Elm Street, the main character Freddy Cougar's look was done by a make-up stylist," Twon said. "Awww okay I understand, so you'll be doing things like putting on fake skin, and make up to make a character fit his role in the movie," she said. "Exactly, so when I start writing and producing movies I can design my characters appearance the way I want it to be," Twon said. "That's smart, I'm proud to have you as a son," his mom said as she gave him a hug . . . .

"I'm much obliged that you came to my country to help me, and my people," Shariff said. "Not a problem at all I enjoy helping others," Twon said. "Always remember if you ever need any weapons or heroin I can get it for you with no problem," Shariff said. "Naw I'm good thanks anyway," Twon said . . . .

For the next few days Twon, amongst others went out to the villages, provided food, and medicine for the people. Then after those few days were up Twon decided to go back home to his Angel . . . .

⁓

"Dad I don't like it when you be gone to Africa," Angel said. "You're not a little girl anymore you gotta get use to your dad being gone for a little while from time to time. Besides I'm going over there to help people, wouldn't you want someone to help you if you lived in a third world country and, was starving," Twon asked? "Yes, daddy, but I'm your daughter I need you here with me," Angel said . . . .

Twon got quiet remaining silent thinking about all the time he spent in jail away from her, then he started thinking of the people he seen in other countries starving, some living in huts, and some dying because of poor doctoring, and lack of the proper medicine . . . .

Twon walked out the room not knowing exactly what to say to Angel . . . .

He came back into the room, and stared at his Angel . . . .

"I'm sorry I went to jail, and left you. I'm sorry I be leaving you when I gotta go to Africa. I must admit I aint been to church in a while, but God talks to me, he tells me to get up go help them people, and when he speaks I listen, because thanks to him we have all these wonderful earthly things, and spiritual guidance, as earthly kings and queens," Twon said. "Yeah dad I know you gotta go to help those people, but I be wanting you here with me at all times. Dad it seems like someone be watching me through the kitchen window," Angel said. "Girl aint nobody watching you through the kitchen window, can't nobody even get through the back gate, the owners keep it lock," Twon said. "Dad somebody be watching me through the kitchen window," Angel said. "Girl it's all women live in this building, and one old ass man that live down stairs, so I know that aint no one of them watching you," Twon said. "Dad, and I been hearing rats in the house making noises in the night time. That's why I be needing you here with me dad," Angel said. "Girl you is tripping aint no rats in her," Twon said, as he left the room to go talk to his mom . . . .

"Mom this girl in there talking about it's a rat in here," Twon said. "I be hearing some strange noises to that's why I put down some glue boards the other day. I don't think it's no rats actually coming through holes in the walls or the vents I think they come in, and out that back door, because it be alot of rats in the back yard. Are you and Angel gone spend a night or are you, and her going home," Twon's mom asked. "We gone go home, she talking about I don't be spending enough time with her," Twon said. "You be with her every day, unless you're in Africa," Twon's mom said. "Yeah I know even the days when I go to school I still come home straight to her," Twon said . . . .

"Well let me check and see if she ready," Twon said . . . .

After Angel finished getting ready Twon, and her went home popped some popcorn, and watched some old black, and white movies on TV . . . .

Chapter 10

"Dad I know you gotta go to Africa, and help those people, but I don't like staying with mom, cuz somebody be watching me through the kitchen window, and some nights I be hearing noises from rats," Angel said. "Girl you been with mom damn near your whole life," Twon said. "But we never had rats living with us, and I know that somebody be watching me through the kitchen window," Angel said. "Girl you tweaking aint nobody be watching you through the kitchen window. But just stay over moms house this time, next time I go to Africa I'll find somebody else house for you to stay over. I really don't like you over nobody else house, cuz it be a lot of grown man around, and I don't want them to come at you, then Imma have to fuck them up. And people be smoking, and drinking, and I don't want you around that shit. Of course I smoke weed, and drink, but I don't do it around you," Twon said. "I be in the house by myself mom be gone with her lil young boyfriend, why can't I just stay at home," Angel asked? "Cuz I don't want you in our house for days, all by yourself, atleast at moms house she'll be there with you from time to time. You're a big girl you can handle yourself at moms house, but I promise that when I come back this time I'll find you somewhere else to stay while I'm in Africa, since mom don't be in the house that much," Twon said . . . .

All during his trip to Africa he worried, and missed his Angel. This time he stayed in Africa for five days, because the people there was in need of him. Usually while he was in Africa Angel would text him; throughout the whole five days he didn't get no text messages from her . . . .

Once he made it back to his city he went to the mall to go shopping for Angel, and then went to his mom's house bearing gifts for his Angel.

As he opened the door he noticed how nice, and clean the living room was as the sun glisten through the windows . . . .

He walked to Angel's bedroom, and there was no Angel so he went to the kitchen and seen her laying there half naked bleeding out of her face, as well as from various other places from her body, as a big rat ate away at her flesh. He immediately begin stumping the rat, putting it to death.....With his eyes he swiftly examined his Angel's body, he noticed she had been raped, and that her face, and body had been brutaly beaten; it was like a horrifying nightmare that had came to reality, as screams flowed fluently like a never ending echo from Twon's mouth.

He covered Angel's body with a blanket, lift her up, and it seems if her head almost fell of her shoulder, that's when Twon noticed that he throat had been slid from a to z, Twon got so scared, and nervous that he almost dropped Angel but didn't. As inner, and outer screams of turmoil, visions of Latisha lying in a casket in the past, demons, and demonic spirits emerged within his heart and mind he cried out for Angel to continue to live as he immediately rushed her to the hospital, but in reality he knew that his Angel's life had come to an end . . . .

Once he made it to the hospital with Angels blood dripping body in his hands, one nursed yelled out, "Oh my gosh, what kind of filthy animal would commit such violent offense on her, as one tear ran down her right cheek."

They rushed her to the emergency room. Twon knew she was died but he still cried out, and prayed to himself that she'd live, and grow old through the years . . . .

In a short period of time the doctor came out, and told him she was dead . . . .

"Twon fell to the ground as tears became like a sea of emotional torment, as his inner soul had died, he cried out loudly, "no, no, no." It was as echoes of pain could be heard throughout the hospital . . . .

Twon left the hospital in a blazing rage, not knowing where to go or what to do as tears continued to flow from his eyes. It was as he could see Satan's lake of burning fire as lost souls cried out to be released from Satan's burning layers. He could visualize gun shots ripping away at flesh as killers would kill, and then ask who's next, he could see camps were Jews would be lined up against walls naked, and slaughtered be firing squads. He could vision lions chasing down Africans, and catching them, and eating away at their flesh . . . .

As Twon drove down this seemingly lonely highway he snapped back to reality as he called his mom, and other family members, and told them the horrifying story, that his Angel was raped, and killed . . . .

As Twon told the family over the phone it was as if he could feel, and hear their painful cries, and screams . . . .

The same day the police came to his mom's house to do their investigation they came to find that there was no forced entry, only the back door was unlocked.

The police questioned everyone in the building, as well as neighbors, and came up with no leads . . . .

Twon stayed in the house for day's not answering nobody calls, but his mom; drinking, smoking, and popping pills to ease the pain.

Twon paid for the entire funeral he gave his mom the money for the funeral . . . .

Several days after Angel was raped, and killed the funeral was held.

Twon showed up to the funeral late couldn't bear to see his Angel in a casket.

Twon entered the church doors, as the pastor was preaching he seen Twon enter, and instantly got quiet. As Twon slowly maneuvered slowly up the aisle everyone stopped, and stared, feeling his pain.

As Twon made it to the casket, and bared witness to his Angel in it, he yelled out, "no", and stormed outta the church. His mom amongst others ran behind him, but couldn't catch him, as he made it to his car got in it, and burned rubber . . . .

The same day of the funeral homicide found out who had raped, and killed Angel. The police ran a check to see if it was any convicted rapist in the area that had recently been let out of prison. They came to find out that the old man that lived in the building had did time for a rape in the past, so they decided to question him . . . .

Once they made it to the old guys front door one police decided to twist the door knob to see if the door was lock or unlock, which wasn't proper procedure for the police to do. The door was unlock the police walked in to the bedroom in the back, and there the old guy was sitting there naked with his dick in his hand jagging off looking at a wall filled with pictures of Angel.

The police tackled him down, and fucked him up. They knew he was the one who did that to Angel once they seen all the pictures of her all over his wall . . . .

They searched his house found traces of blood on the clothes he had on when he raped and killed Angel; they took the clothes to send to the lab for testing.

While the old guy was held in police custody for a couple of days the lab testing came back that, that was Angel blood on his clothing.

The old guy was immediately sent to the county jail . . . .

Twon sat back in his house getting drunk, drinking bottle after bottle . . . .

Damn I should've listen when she told me somebody was looking at her through the kitchen window, it was that old ass man stalking her all along; I hope that old ass bitch die. When she was hearing rats she knew what she was talking about, it probably was the same rat she was hearing that was eating away at her dead body. I can't believe this shit happen, Twon thought to himself . . . .

Twon went straight to Africa to get up with Shariff . . . .

"What brings you to the motherland without the rest of the corp, you never come to Africa without the rest of the corp," Shariff said. "I need weapons, lots of em," Twon said. "Why what happen," Shariff asked? "They raped, and killed my Angel," Twon said . . . .

Shariff got quiet, and put his hand over his own heart, and feel to his knees . . . .

"You trying to tell me they raped, and killed you daughter," Shariff said slowly as his eyes started to get watery. "Yep they killed My Angel," Twon said as he broke out crying loudly . . . .

"Don't worry I can get you all the weapons you need," Shariff said as he hugged Twon for the first time ever . . . .

Twon left Africa, and went home, and began messing around with his design equipment making design of old people, white, black, and Mexican people . . . .

In no time Shariff cousin Uduma showed up to Twon's house dressed in his army uniform, with freshly polished black boots on . . . .

"Here go all the weapons Shariff told me to bring you. I'm sorry to hear about your daughter I know it's gone be some bloodshed. Take my number call me if you need somewhere to hide out," Uduma said . . . .

Twon took his number as soon as he left Twon begin loading up guns, in the process of doing so all Twon could vision was death, and destruction a land filled with no loving as firely flames were being inflicted to set earth on fire, as he himself would constantly put bullets in brains . . . .

Twon went straight to the ho stroll looking for his baby momma . . . .

As he pulled up to the ho stroll there she was, she was so high off drugs she didn't even recognize him . . . .

As he pulled up to her she pulled up her skirt showing him her pussy.

"Baby don't you want some of this tight pussy," she said. "Yeah I do, come to the car," Twon said . . . .

Once she made it to the car she stuck her head in the window trying to negotiate finance for sexual acts . . . .

As she talked he grabbed her shirt with his left hand, with his right hand shoved a big ass crone .44 revolver in her mouth knocking out her two front teeth as he pulled the trigger twice instantly taking her life line from her. He pushed her away from his car, and smashed off . . . .

Fuck that bitch if she would've been there for Angel, Angel probably a still be living, I heard the bitch didn't even show up to Angel's funeral, she probably was somewhere with a dick in her mouth, Twon thought to himself . . . .

Twon went straight home, and continued working on his old people designs . . . .

The next day Twon decided to get up with Q, and John, John. He didn't have Q's number so he decided to call John, John . . . .

"Hello," John, John said. "What's happening fam," Twon said. "Who is this," John, John asked? "This Twon, Antwon." "Aw what's up Twon, I aint heard from you since you first got out, you just stop fucking with a nigga," John, John said. "Naw it aint like that, I just be on some personal shit living my own life," Twon said. "Man, I know you heard what happen to kids momma last night," John, John said. "Naw I didn't, what happen," Twon asked? "She got killed last night on the ho stroll, I heard some nigga drove up she stuck her head in the window he handt her two in the mouth, because she gave him herpes," John, John said. "That's sad," Twon said. "Damn, Lord you lost your daughter, and your kids momma that's fucked up. I was at Angel's funeral when you came in, and ran right back out, I don't know what I'd do if my daughter ever got killed," John, John said. "I need you," Twon said. "What you need," John, John asked. "I'm working on writing my first urban novel, and need you, and Q's help," Twon said. "You trying to write a book, and your daughter just got killed," John, John said. "Yeah, even though my daughter is no longer with us I still gotta live my life," Twon said. "I feel you on that," John, John said. "I don't need ya'll to help me write it I just need ya'll input on it, I'll give you fifteen hundred a piece," Twon said. "Fifteen hundred can you come over right now, I'm ready," John, John said as Twon begin laughing. "I need you, and Q at the same time," Twon said. "I don't be seeing Q alot, I don't be hanging in the hood because they always shooting, the nigga Q don't never answer his phone, he be too high of shock. But this what Imma do I'm going to go, and find the nigga, don't worry Imma find him for fifteen hundred. Imma call you later, and you can meet us over my house," John John said . . . .

As they both hung up their phones Twon hoped that John, John would find Q . . . .

To Twon's surprise a few hours later John, John called him, and told him that him, and Q was over his house, and to bring their money, and that they was ready to get to work . . . .

Twon rushed straight over there . . . .

Twon pulled up to John, John's house, and there they was sitting on the porch.

Twon parked, and got out of the car.

John, John, and Q walked right up to him trying to shake his hand, as Twon upped the same big ass .44 and hit John, John twice in the mouth as Q tried to run Twon hit him four times, twice in the back, and once in neck, and once in the back of the head . . . .

Twon ranned back to his car, and smashed off destination unknown . . .

Fuck them bitch ass nigga's if they would've never went back to the hood and told people after I killed Abdula I could've been there for my Angel, she probably a still been living, Twon thought to himself . . . .

Where the fuck I'm a go what I'm a do I know homicide gone be looking for, I aint never going back to jail, I rather die than be sitting stuck in a jail cell, Twon thought to himself . . . .

As he continued to ride he remembered what Shariff's cousin Uduma had told him, that if he ever needed a place to hide out to call him. Twon called Uduma, and told him he needed a place to hide out at. Uduma told him the address, and that he'd be waiting on him to come . . . .

Twon drove to his house first to get all the weapons that Uduma gave him, he knew he'd be needing them. Then he went to his secret stash spot to get all the money he had stashed away just in case something like this ever occured. He had a hundred, and fifty thousand in big bills stashed away, not including all the money he had in his bank account . . . .

Damn this nigga live far from the city, Twon thought to himself on the long drive to Uduma house . . . .

Once he made it there he noticed that Uduma lived at the end of the block in a big white house.

Uduma begin to show him his high technology security system as he entered the front door . . . .

"The police can't even get straight through this door, and it's bullet proof so once it's locked it might take a hour or two for them to get in, if not longer. They can't get through none of the windows that fast neither it'll take them a while, and all the windows are bullet proof. Let me show you to the upstairs . . . . This is what I call the panic room, I got the name from the movie Panic Room, but this room is different from the one in the movie. The whole room is bullet proof, and as you see for yourself I got fully loaded guns everywhere," Uduma said. "You is a general in the army, what do you need with a house like this," Twon asked? "See that's why I got a place like this because I'm in the army, and I got a military mind, I never know, or from where trouble may come. Let's go back downstairs so I can show you my secret," Uduma said . . . .

Once they made it down stairs Uduma stoop down, and touched the wall, then on the other side of the wall a small panel opened up; there was a small shaped hand print. Uduma placed his hand over the hand print and a small part of the wall opened up like a sliding door. Twon stood there looking amazed.

This look like some shit out the movies, Twon thought to himself.

Uduma walked in the opened door on the wall as Twon followed him. Twon went in as Uduma hit the light. Twon instantly noticed a gang of T.V.'s which was used for surveillance around the house . . . .

"The only way somebody can get in here is if the program fits their hand. The program only fits my hand. But I'm a program it to fit your hand. But of course somebody can blow a hole in the wall, but let's be for real, who gonna come in a house looking for somebody, and think they're in the wall, and blow a hole in the wall. Army specialist, and the C.I.A. got equipment that can see through walls but the army, and the C.I.A. aint gone be looking for you, and besides if they was, about time they get in the house you'll be long gone. This long hallway leads to a big empty lot in which is filled with grass, and trees, nobody lives close by. On the other side of the lot is a car covered up, so if you ever have to escape you can make a clean get away," Uduma said. "What if they got road blocks set up," Twon asked? "I doubt it, and even if they do this tunnel leads you to the car that's blocks, and blocks away. I'll take you through the tunnel to the car later on," Uduma said . . . .

Once nightfall came Twon was anxious to go through the tunnel. Once nightfall did come, and Uduma took him through the tunnel he couldn't believe it how Uduma had all that set up . . . .

"I thought tunnel escape routes, and bullet proof rooms, and shit was only in the movies," Twon said. "No this real life, but the only reason I can do things like this is because I'm in the military, and I got a lot of money. Listen to me," Uduma said as he looked Twon in the eye. "Yeah I'm listening," Twon said. "Your daughter was killed so I can imagine the things you'll be in to, so if the police come here looking for you, which I doubt it because they don't even know you know me, but if they do come do what you do, even if you gotta kill some of them, don't worry about me, I am the law I know how to take care of myself. Well I done showed you around the house I'm leaving town for a few days, it's plenty food and liquor in the kitchen, make yourself at home, so I'll see you when I get back," Uduma said . . . .

Once he left Twon was like a little kid at a toy store playing with the weapons, and opening the secret passage to make sure Uduma program worked . . . .

Once Twon went asleep that night he begin having horryfying nightmares of lil kids being murdered, and sat on fire by militia men, and of his Angel, and that lil girl Latisha drowning in a ocean of insanity, while reaching their hands out to him screaming daddy, help me, help me, it was nothing he could do to save them, as he woke up out his dream . . . .

In the past Twon use to go to Mexico to help the people there, and along the way he met a few friends, he gave them a call, and told them in Spanish he'd be needing to see them, that he was going to some troublesome times, and needed there assistance . . . .

A Few Days Later

"Anthony Fox pack your shit you getting out on bond," the c/o said . . . .

What out on bond aint nobody bond me out, Anthony thought to himself.

Anthony wasn't going to tell them they fucked so he just packed his shit, and went with the program . . . .

As Anthony went through the process of being processed out he knew that once the county finger printed him they was going to see that they had the wrong person . . . .

Within a matter of time as Anthony stepped out the county gates in the middle of the night he noticed several cars wondering how he'd get a ride as this yellow cab pulled up and parked.

The driver got out the car and walked to Anthony.

"Your name Anthony Cox," The driver asked? "Yeah who are you," Anthony asked? "My name is Julio someone paid me to pick you up, and take you home." "Who," Anthony asked? "I don't know who she was some lady just walked up to me, and handt me a hundred dollar bill, and told me to come pick you up, and take you where you need to go," Julio said . . . .

Anthony got in the car, and told the cab driver the address of where he wanted to go . . . .

On the road to their destination Julio made a stop, and picked up two Mexican that didn't speak any English . . . .

Once they got in the cab, Anthony immediately felt uncomfortable, because all them were jammed in the back seat, and because Julio, and the two men continued to argue in Spanish . . . .

"Cab driver you taking the wrong road you suppose get off on Wolf road," Anthony said. "Don't worry I got you I gotta drop them off first," Julio said. "You could've dropped me off first," Anthony said . . . .

Julio gave Anthony some Vodka that was already in the cup. Anthony drunk it like it was water . . . . within minutes Anthony found himself getting dizzy, and weak, as his vision got blurry.

Outta nowhere Anthony felt a stun gun in his side the shock treatment felt horrible . . . .

The stun gun mixed the spiked Vodka left Anthony unconscious . . . .

Hours later Anthony woke up with his feet tied together, and his hands tied together behind his back, as he was laid out on his back . . . .

Anthony looked, and seen he was in a white basement fixed up like a regular apartment with Julio, and the other two Mexican standing over him laughing and speaking Spanish simultaneously . . . .

"What the fuck is so funny untie me right now," Anthony said in an aggressive manner . . . .

Twon walked up to Anthony, and took off his fake hair, and fake skin as Anthony eyes got big . . . .

"Hey man I didn't do that to your daughter, I didn't do that to your daughter, they got the wrong guy," Anthony said looking face to face with Twon.

Now all the laughter from Twon, and the two Mexicans was over it was nightmares of horrifying dealings, rapes, and killings had came forth to reality in all their minds . . . .

Twon, and the two Mexican grabbed Anthony, as two more other Mexican came out the back room to help, they turned him over, as he continued to plead that it wasn't him they pulled down his pants shoved a hoes up his ass held him down pour acid through the hoes. As the acid went up his ass he yelled, and cried like a little bitch, Twon, and the four Mexican remained silent loving every second of it, as they continued to hold him down firmly.

They turned Anthony around as he continued to cry, and scream like a bitch Twon cut his dick off and shoved it up his throat. Although he had his own dick in his mouth they could still semi hear his screams. It was like music to their ears . . . .

They left him as he bled to death . . . .

The four Mexican went back to Mexico . . . .

Twon had connects with the Mexican Cartel they took a liking for him when he use to come to their country to help their people genuinely. Twon learned how to speak Spanish fluently while he was in jail, so when he did travel to Mexico he could communicate with the people with no problem. The Mexican Cartel told him if he ever needs any assistance please let them know. Twon decided use them because they couldn't catch any cases because they'd come to America bogus with fake Visas; then once they got to America he found a way to get them fake I.D.'s and social security card so he could give them the money to bond out Anthony, and to buy the cab, and to rent the basement apartment to take Anthony to kill him. Everything went as planned . . . .

Twon went back to Uduma's home, and laid back plotting on his next move.

Twon ended up falling asleep, and for the first time since his Angel got killed he was able to get a peaceful sleep.

Twon woke up the next day to the sunlight shining across his face.

Twon went to the kitchen, and fixed him some turkey bacon, cheese eggs, and French toast.

After he ate he went back to the bedroom, and started back trying to design facial images with his head of a mannequin.

I like the way I made myself up to look like a Mexican, Twon thought to himself, as he commence to make images on the head of the mannequin . . . .

Twon felt his phone vibrating which was strange because he stop communicating with everybody since his Angel had got killed.

Twon looked at his phone, and it was a text from his mom: Son I am so happy, somebody bonded that bitch out, the same day somebody took him to a basement poured acid in his ass chopped off his dick, and made him eat it, the text read.

Twon couldn't believe that she used profanity she never use profanity.

Twon text her back: Sometimes when you do wrong it comes right back around, but mom I love, but I gotta go I'm busy . . . .

All day Twon experimented with his mannequin creating different images . . . .

I gotta go, I gotta leave homicide gone be coming here looking for me real soon, Twon thought to himself, as he visualized the first time homicide got him, and cracked him for a murder.

Twon started packing all his things.

Am a pack my shit, and if I need something while I'm still here I'll just get it out my laundry bag, cuz I'm a stay here to they come, when they do come I got a trick for they ass, Twon thought to himself . . . .

Twon stayed in Uduma's house eating up everything, getting drunk and steady making different images with the mannequin . . . .

Days later Twon woke up out his sleep in midday to the sound of the alarm of the security system. He looked at the monitor in the room that showed the homicide, and the feds everywhere.

They was trying to use a ram to get through the front door, but couldn't . . . .

Twon instantly begin smiling.

I knew you bitches would be coming, and I've been waiting on ya'll, Twon thought to himself . . . .

Twon opened the window and with no hesitation he unleashed a rocket launcher, and blew one police car up, it was two police officer near the car, one officer got set on fire the other one got hit in the eye with a piece of the car from the blast in which made him loose his left eye.

All the other officers panicked not knowing what to do.

Twon started throwing back to back grenades in the crowds of officers as they tried to run, and hide. Then he let go a roar of constant rounds from an A.K.

Within minutes Twon had killed seven police, injured four leaving one officer with one eye missing.

It happened so suddenly that the officer didn't get a chance to even shot back until Twon was gone running up the secret passage way with a garbage bag full of money, weapons, amongst other things.

As Twon ran up the secret passage way at full speed he felt as if he was going to have a asthma attack, and he didn't even have asthma . . . .

Once Twon finally made inside the car he couldn't even catch his breath to get the keys out his pocket.

Once he finally caught his breath he got the keys out his pocket, and tried to start the car up, and at first it acted like it didn't want to start, Twon heart dropped. He tried starting it up the second time, and it started straight up.

Twon pulled off scared to death.

The e-way was right around the corner. He bailed on the e-way, and got away with no problems . . . .

Uduma fled the country the same day, one of his neighbors called him as all the violence was going on.

Uduma didn't give a fuck about Twon killing those police, that's the reason he told Twon about all the secrets of his house, so if they ever came in which they did he could shot at them, and get away.

Uduma knew he had to flee the country because he was already under suspicion by the U.S. Army for selling guns to other countries they never court martial him because they didn't have enough evidence . . . .

Twon also fled the country . . . .

The feds, homicide, and A.T.F. wondered how did Twon even get out the country without authorities catching him. Later down the line they figured it out, he put on fake skin, changed his hair, and put on make up to look like someone else; and he found a way to get a fake passport . . . .

Overtime time the feds, homicide, and the A.T.F. assumed that Twon was somewhere in Africa, they was wrong. Then the feds, homicide, and the A.T.F. thought he was in one of the Spanish speaking countries, he still was never found . . . .

Years later the authorities never found Uduma, nor Twon. The only thing they knew about Twon was that almost every two or three months his mom would get another book of erotica published in her pen name, in which Twon wrote in the past. Every book she dropped hit the best sellers list . . . .

Until this very day Uduma, and Twon are nowhere to be found . . . .
BOOK WRITER.

Upcoming Urban Novel by
Alan Hines
Kidnapping

Chapter 1

It was noon time scorching hot summer's day as the sunlight from the sky lit up the streets, the public was tired of blacks being murdered by the police, and a shame of how black on black crime continuous increase.

It was madness in the city streets two unarmed black males were killed by the punk police; one was home from college pulled over at a traffic stop the police shot and killed him in cold blood, the police lied and said that they thought his cell phone was a gun, the victim had no gun no prior arrest, no criminal background; the other black male that was shot was one of their very own, he was an off duty seargent, the white cops walked up to him to search him assuming he was a street thug, as the off duty seargent went to reach for his badge the racist cops shot him three times in the left side of his chest instantly seperating life from death as the four five bullets ripped through his heart he instantly fell to the concrete visualizing stars as he life no longer existed organs torn apart.

People of all colors came together on and every side of town; north, south, east, and even the west. Through the city streets they marched, and protest only in signs and symbols of peace. Hoping the violence would come to an end, that it would cease.

On Madison street people stood on all four corners as if they owned it. They were together as one, White, Blacks, Mexicans, Puerto Ricans, and even a few Arabics were presents; they all wore t-shirts that displayed

Black Lives Matter, some were holding up signs that displayed honk you horn if you love Jesus.

Almost each car that rode past the crowds of people honked their horns; some yelled out there windows, "we love you Jesus," as others yelled out there windows loud and clear, "black lives matter.".....

Daily around the city meetings were being held in churches, unioun halls, amongst various other places but all on one accord to stop the violence.

Hundreds of protestors peacefully marched up to city hall with picket signs, telling those at city hall that the violence just gotta stop.....

The mayor of the city, and the police commisioner came together and made a statement on the news saying that he, and the Chicago police Department will be doing all they can to decrease the violence in the city streets.....

Mysteriously three black teenage girls came up missing, and had been missing for many months; the authorities had no leds to there whereabouts.....

After a innocent twelve year old black girl was killed by stray bullets, her mother was interviewed at the scene of the crime by the channel 9 news......

Running down her face drowning tears of sorrow knowing that her twelve year old daughter was dead wouldn't be here to live to see another day tomorrow.

She cried out on the channel 9 news in front of the camera for people stop the violence.

The grieving mother told the news, "the police don't give a fuck about us, if they killing our young black males, what makes everybody think they give a fuck about finding those missing girls. It wouldn't surprise me if they never find the bitch that killed my little girl."

Oh how her angry harsh words was so true.

The authorities searched and searched, did a thorough investigation, but no killer was found and charged with the murder of twelve year old Shante Smith.....

Chapter 2

"The niggas off the low-end been eating real good, them niggas been performing," Kuda said. "They been kidnapping niggas, they be trying to grab any nigga getting some real bread," Big Shorty said. "Awwww that's how them niggas been eating like that," Kuda said. "What they do is they kidnapp a nigga for a healthy ransom, or rob a nigga for some weight, and then whatever they get they invest it in buying more weight, flooding the low end with hella narcotics," Big Shorty said. "That's smart," Kuda said.....

Early one sunday morning Kuda sat in the park across the street, slightly up the block from where the shorties slang his rocks.

Big Shorty walked up to Kuda, as Kuda set fire to a Newport long, Kuda took a long pull off the square, as Big Shorty could see, and feel a sense of distress.....

"Man Big Shorty we got to hit us a lick, rob a nigga, kidnapp a nigga or something," Kuda said. "Your joint doing pretty good, why you wanna take some other nigga shit," Big Shorty said. "My joint only sell like a stack or two a day, it take me two or three days to scrap up the money to re-copp to go get another four and a baby, you feel me," Kuda said. "But you still eating alot of these niggas out here broke ass hell,"

Big Shorty said, "True, but look at the niggas off the low end they got joints selling 10 or 20 thousand a day, some of them even got two or three joints, selling weight and robbing niggas all at the same damn time, that's what I call getting money," Kuda said.....

Big Shorty remained silent for a brief moment knowing that Kuda was speaking the truth.....

"But Kuda it's so much chaotic madness, that comes along with sticking up. Them niggas off the low-end in constant danger," Big Shorty said. "I'm already in constant danger for all the shootings I've been doing over the years, representing the business for the hood, I deserve to be eating good, fuck the dumb shit I gotta hit me a lick," Kuda said.

Big Shorty remained silent again for a brief moment realizing the realization of what Kuda was talking about.....

Kuda joint started to get sweating more by the police because all ths shooting, that was going on in the area. It was hard for Kuda to work because of the police sweating his joint, and because the hood was in war. Now Kuda really knew he had to hit a lick to get some fast cash.....

More and more Kuda talked to Big shorty about hitting a lick.....

Kuda and Big Shorty ended up getting up with a few guys from the hood that was highly interested in kicking in some doors, and taking another nigga shit.....

A few guys from the hood knew of a few houses on the other side of town where niggas was holding drugs and money at.

Kuda, Big Shorty, and the few guys from the hood kicked in a few doors hitting licks. Each lick they came up on several thousands outta each house, which wasn't shit to them because they had to split it five ways each time.

Kuda was hungry to eat, he was tired of small time nickels and dimes he wanted to do it big.....

One of the guys from the hood that they went on the licks with seen how well Kuda, and Big Shorty performed when they ran in them houses, and decided to set them up to kidnapp his sister boyfriend. The guy couldn't do it himself because his sister boyfriend knew him, and he didn't want to send nobody else but Kuda, and Big shorty because other people was messy and would fuck shit up.

The guy sister would be the one to set her boyfriend up, she was tired of the nigga he was to cheap, but the nigga had long money.....

They planned on kodnapping him for thirty thousand, splitting it up evenly four ways a piece, therefore each individual would get seventy-five hundred a piece.....

Kuda was charged up, this is the kind of lick he was interested in hitting.....

Two in the morning as the streets lights lit up the sky, Kuda and Big Shorty set in the car parked several cars behind their soon to be victims car.

Kuda took a long hard pull of the last of his Newport long, inhaling, and exhaling the smoke out of his nose as if it was a blunt filled with loud.

Once Kuda was finish smoking the cigarette he threw the butt out the window.....

Outta nowhere comes this guy sister, and her boyfriend out the door walking down the porch.....

Her and her boyfriend made their way to the back of his car, and started tongue kissing him in which seemed so delghtful for the both of them.

As their lips and tongues disconnected he opened his trunk searching for a purse he had bought her.....

As he lift his head up trying to give her, her bag outta nowhere Kuda appeared instantly back hand slapping the shit out of him upping a big ass gun putting it to his stomach. As Big Shorty came from the back putting a gun to his head forcing him inside the trunk, as the girlfriend cried tears pleading with them to stop; she put on a great performance, she should've won a Oscar for.

As the trunk closed she started smiling, glad that they got his ass. But she continued crying and pleading with them to stop just in a case a neighborhood was watching.

Kuda drove the victim off in his own car as Big shorty followed Kuda in his car; the girlfriend ranned in the house crying as they pulled off.

Once she made it in the house she called her brother and told him, "they got his bitch ass".....

She left out the house went to her car and drove slowly to the nearest police station which took her approximately twenty minutes.....

She ran inside the police station crying emotional tears, that seemed really, real.

She told the police that her boyfriend was kidnapped, she gave up false identities of the kidnappers.

The police asked why didn't she call immediately after it happen. She told the police that the kidnappers robbed her for her phone and money so she couldn't call, and that she went to two of the neighbors house and they never answered their door bells.....

After finishing the police report she went home sipped some wine, relaxed in a hot bubble bath, thinking of the things she'd do with her seventy five hundred once she had it in her possession.....

Two days passed overlapping into nights; now it was crunch time. Kuda and Big Shorty had made arrangements for the kidnapped victims people to run thirty stacks,

They was supposed to leave the money in a trunk of a car parked near a shopping center that was closed, it was closed because it was the middle of the night, but during the day it would regularly be open.

Before they even made it there with the thirty stacks Kuda, and Big Shorty circled all around the area, there were no police cars or unmarked cars nowhere to be found.

Right before the victims people brought the money, Kuda and Big Shorty watched from a far distance with binoculars as some old lady came, bent down got the keys from under the left back tire as instructed.

As she opened the trunk Kuda, and Big shorty begin cheering, giving each other constant high fives.

She put the money in the trunk and the keys back under the left tire as instructed, and walked away disappearing into the night.

Kuda and Big shorty waited for approximately twenty minutes just to make sure the coast was clear, then they text the chick they had designated to go pick the money up.

She made it there in no time. As she walked up to the car bent down picked up the keys from under the left tire, opened up the passenger door.

As soon as she sat down, before she could even close the door, twenty unmarked cars surrounded her out of nowhere, all she heard was sirens and seen guns upped on her from every which way. It was impossible for her to get away.....

The police grabbed her by the neck slamming her face to the concrete, cuffed her up, roughed her up a little and put her in the back of one of the police cars.

The police drove her, and the vehicle that the money was in to the police station to further pursue their investigation.....

Kuda, and Big Shorty watched the whole thing their binoculars, shook the fuck up.....

Once the police left Kuda, and Big shorty pulled off confused not knowing what to do.....

Shortly after leaving the seen of the crime Kuda stopped at a nearby pond and threw his cell phone in it. From Big Shorties phone he called his phone carriers hot line, telling them his phone was stoling and had been missing for hours, he had insurance, so they'd definitely replace it. He threw his phone in the pond, because he text the chick that the police just grabbed from his phone, so if the police went through her phone and linked the text back to his phone he could say it wasn't him, that someone stole his phone.....

As they proceeded back driving home they both was worried, wondering if the girl would play fair ball, or switch up like a bitch and snitch.

Kuda was driving as Big Shorty kept looking back every two or three minutes to see if they was being followed by the cops.

"What the fuck, why is you steady looking back for," Kuda asked? "The police might be following us," Big Shorty said. "The police is not following us if the police wanted us we'd already been got. I hope the bitch didn't tell, I know she did," Kuda said.

"Straight up," Big Shorty said.

Once they made it to the police station at first she played like she didn't speak any English.

She was Boricua, Kuda had nicknamed her the thrill seeking Puerto Rican, because she was adventurous loved violence. Even when the police grabbed her and roughed her up, she loved it.

Months prior to her arrest Kuda, and Big Shorty use to fuck her at the same time; she loved two dicks at once she preferred one in the mouth, and another in her pussy at the same time as Kuda, and Big Shorty would choke her and slap her around in the midst of sex.

She was a bad bitch she just got an adrenaline rush off hardcore shit.....

As the police proceeded questioning her even when they went to get her an interpreter she winded up speaking to them in English.

The cops came to find out her name was Maria Rodriguez. She had been to the joint before twice, once for a kidnapping, and the other time for robbery, and was still on parole for the robbery.

She lied and told the cops that someone paid her to go pick up that car, only because they was pulled over by the police for driving with no license, and once the police left they came back to leave an additonal set of keys under the left tire so she could pick the car up since she had license. To assure them that she had no knowledge of a kidnapping.....

The police knew her story was bullshit, so they asked her who didn't have license and sent her to pick the car up for that reason. She told them she couldn't give any names, because she didn't know what was going on.....

The police pleaded with her for hours to give up a name or names, she didn't tell them shit.

They ended up fingerprinting her processing her in and charging her with kidnapping and sending her to the County Jail.

Of course she didn't want to be locked up, but she wasn't worried at all, on her bus ride to the County she'd vision all the pussy she'd be eating once she made it within and started mingling and getting to know the other girls.

After a few days rolled around Kuda, and Big Shorty didn't know what to do with the victim. Normally in a situation like that the individual that had been kidnapped would be put to death since the people got the police involved.

Kuda, and Big Shorty contemplated long and hard about killing the Vic, but decided not to, because if they did they could possibly give Maria a conspiracy to murder, and she could start singing the blues to the police telling them everything.....

After about a week in the middle of the night they dropped the vic off and left him in a abandon building still blindfold and tied up, called his people and the police and told them where to get him from.

Kuda and big Shorty wasn't worried about the vic sicking the police on them; he didn't even never see their faces, they had on masks, and even if he did see their faces he didn't know them or there whereabouts because they were from different sides of town.....

After a few weeks Kuda, and Big Shorty was able to get in touch with Maria, she'd call them collect continously.

Come to find out, she was a down bitch, didn't tell the police shit; they kind of figured she didn't snitch because she knew where Kuda, and Big Shorty lived, and if she would've told the police would've been at their house by now.

Kuda and Big Shorty wanted to bond her out, or atleast put up something on her bond, but she couldn't bond out because she was on parole, she had a parole hold.

Kuda and Big Shorty started sending her money orders constantly to make sure she was straight in there.....

The vic they kidnapped continued dating, fucking around with the chick that set him up to get kidnapped, never in his wildest dreams would he even assume that she was the one that set him up to get kidnapped. Later in life he even ended up getting the bitch pregnant with twins.....

Chapter 3

Black lives matter was getting to be an even more major issue. Peaceful protest even seemed to get violent. The black politicians and even black cops was sick and tired of being sick and tired of all the killing blood spilling of the black population.....

More and more teenage black girls would mysteriously come up missing. More and more gangs were waring harder throughout the city, North, South, East, West.....

The black people begin to have meetings quite often mainly at churches, and Union halls.....

One night they had a meeting to their surprise unnumbered white people, and Latinos showed up to support black lives matter; they wore shirts and buttons displaying all lives matter.

The meeting became slightly hostile as not the blacks or Latinos, the white people started snapping out saying that racism does exist, and they were tired of blacks losing their lives by gun-fire, especially from white-police officers that gets paid from tax-payers money to serve and protect the community, when all along they were causing the deaths and destruction within the community, it so much killing and hate, seemed as if it was no-love, nor unity.....

They allowed this one white lady to approach the front to get on the stage onto the pulpit, to preach the bullshit.....

"If we study our past history blacks were hung, lynched by white mobs, shot down by angry white fire squads, and even killed by the police as they same way today. With the 1900's many white that committed hate crimes against blacks were either investigated by the police, some even were put on trial and as documenting they were liberated of their crimes. History does repeat itself in a way. Now technology is advance and I've seen with my own eyes on video, shown white police killing black men, and even after shown on video surveillance, the officer still gets acquitted of all charges someway somehow.

If a black man kills another black man he'll immediately be placed in prison until trial, and in large unnumbered cases he'll get found guilty. And if a black man kills a white person in most cases that black man will eventually get found guilty, and sentenced to excessive time in prison possibly until he dies of natural causes. That's one of the main problems with the police brutality and unjustified murders of blacks they know they can get away with it because they are the police. What need to happen is that the police need to start getting persecuted and sent to prison for their crimes of hate. Until they start getting convicted of the crimes the madness won't stop," she said.....

As she dropped the mic tears flowed freely from her eyes. Knowing that racism was still alive. Lucifer's legacy of racism and hate wasn't decreasing any, but instead it begin coinciding with his sick enterprise.

Everyone in the church begin clapping, and cheering impending her speech.....

This one lady sat in the back all the way in the corner dressed in black with a veil over her face as if she was going to a funeral; she cried silently of sorrow drowning watery tears that shall forever shed throughout her lifetime of years wishing it never happen, wishing her son was still living, still here.....A few years prior to that date her son was wrongfully shot down, murdered by the nation, better known as the police; the two officers that killed her son did stand trial, and was acquitted of all charges against them of her sons murder.....

Soon as the second individual stepped to the pulpit to voice his opinion, gun shots rang out, five of em, sounding like a canon was outside.....

Everyone in the church got frightened, and then within rage everyone ran out the church, not scared of the gun-fire, but pissed the fuck off.

They ran out the front door in a rage eagerly trying to see who was standing, and what for.....

As majority of the people had exited the church it was still more rushing out the front door, one woman spotted a guy up the block laid out on the sidewalk.

She yelled out to everyone, "it somebody down there laid out on the sidewalk."

Everybody rushed to the individual that was laid out.

Come to find out it was a teenage boy that was still breathing, living. He had been shot once in the ass, and once in both of his legs.....so that meeting was officially over for that night.

As they approached him they seen him shot up as blood ran perfusely down the sidewalk he'd repeatedly keep saying, "I can't believe that pussy ass nigga shot me;

I can't believe that pussy ass nigga shot me; I can't beleive that pussy ass nigga shot me," he said. "Who shot you son," one of the gentlemen in the crowd of church people ask? "I don't know who shot me," he said.

He was lying like a motherfucker, who knew exactly who shot him.

"They called the police already, they should be here soon, it's a police station nearby," the gentlemen said.

In no time flat the police arrived first, and the ambulance arrived shortly after.

The guy that had got shot told the police he didn't know who shot him, although he did. He didn't want the nigga that shot him to get locked up, he wanted to kill the bitch.....

Several days later the guy was let out of the hospital but had to be in a wheel-chair, not for a long-term, only to his ass, and legs were well.....

The same day he was let out of the hospital, the same night the guy that shot him was killed, somebody shot him with a double barrel shotgun taking half his face off.

As homicide started their investigation they called it the face off murder. They never found any witnesses or suspects, so no one was never convicted or even charged with that murder.....

It seemed as if day by day the city streets, begin to be filled with madness, killings, mournings, sirens, and sadness.

It was clicks within the same gangs waring against each other. Rivals was waring against each other even harder. You had certain gangs that was into it with two different gangs at once. Then it was certain gangs that was into it with their own gang and into it with the opps all at the same time.

Part of the reason why gangs was tearing it up with each other was because years prior, and even to the present date the feds was locking up all the heads of gangs; everytime a new head would step up and get in play the Feds would find a way to lock his ass up to, leaving no law and order within the streets amongst; just like a body once you cut the heads of the body will fall. It was uncontrollable anarchy within the city streets.

Throughout the city streets it was constant gun-fire, like it was New Years Eve.

Some of the rappers changed the nickname from The Windy City to The City of No Pity.

Shit got so fucked up they start killing niggas in broad daylight on purpose.....

On one side of town two gangs was waring so hard they just start shooting ata ny and everybody that was affiliated with the oppositions.

One time they caught one of the opps main-girl walking the dog; they shot her and the dog. She lived the dog died.

The same nigga that girl and dog they shot, in return he caught an opp grandma-ma walking home from church with her bible in hand. He walked up to her upped a black .44 automatic to her stomach. Her smile instantly turned into a frown as she said, "praise the lord son," whole heartidely.

As he walked in the alley by gun point she didn't say a word, she wasn't scared at all not one bit, she feared no man but God.

As he walked her to the middle of the alley he seen a car slow down by the alley, he thought it was a detective car; he made her get on her knees on the side of a garbage can, he stood on the side of the garbage can faking like he was pissing. He immediately notice that it wasn't the police.

He looked down at her, she was on her knees praying. She wasn't worried about herself, she was praying for him, praying to the Heavenly Father that he would forgive him for his sins, and that someday he'd convert his life over to the Lord.....

Three shots ripped through her head, leaving her for dead, more blood to shed.

After the third shot many people came out on their back porches, not witnessing the actual murder, but witnessing seeing him fleeing from the scene of the crime.....

What the killer didn't know was that she was more than happy to die or be killed, because she knew that upon death she'd finally meet the king of kings, the lord of lords, God, and his only begotten son Jesus Christ to have eternal peaceful life in Heavens paradise.....

The same day the opps found out who killed his grandmother, him and his guys tore the streets up. The niggas from the other side tore it up as well they went round for round.

It was like a riot in the hoods they were from. They burned down houses, and cars, niggas from each side got shot up bad or killed.

They even burn up some houses waited until the opps came running out and shot them up murdered they ass.....

A few days after grandma was murdered homicide apprehendid the killer taking him to jail charging him with that murder. What the killer didn't know was that is that many people witness/saw him running up the alley after he shot her, and that he'd never see the streets again, he'd spend the rest of his natural life rotting away in a jail cell.....

All the violence brought forth more police harrasement of blacks.....

More protesting about Black Lives Matter.

In various places on each side of town you'd see large numbers of people on corners, holding up signs saying honk your horn if you love Jesus, some of the people had on Black Lives Matter T-Shirts, as others had on All Lives Matter T-Shirts. Almost every car that road pass honked their horn, some hollered out "we love you Jesus, Black Lives Matter." A small percentage of passing cars parked their cars joining in on the peaceful protest.....

A few guys in the crowd dipped off to the alley, all you heard was 3 gunshots from a .45 sounded off as the crowds on the streets immediately dispursed. The guys in the alley ran back to the crowds blending in running away as if they didn't know where the shots were coming from, but simply trying to get away from the danger like everyone else. They did that because they joint was right up the street and they couldn't sell their dope with protesters on location, so that quick smart way to get rid of them.

As time progressed along more and more black girls were being kidnapped in various places around the United States; the situation begin to strike controversy, because all of them black.

In the past the black community slightly lost focus on the girls that were being kidnapped, because they found out that a hand full of the missing girls that they thought had been kidnapped, had ran away from home, for different reasons and stayed gone for long periods of time, but eventually returned on their own free will.....

Upcoming Urban Novel
by Alan Hines

Black Kings

Chapter 1

It was the middle of the night as the blue, and white police car drove swiftly up the block. The car slowed down as it reached the end of the block as the passenger examined the address of the house to make sure it was the correct address they were looking for.....

Inside the police car was two white police officer's.....

"Is the address 4955," the driver asked the passenger? "Yes it is," the passenger responded.....

The officer's parked their squad car and they bailed out of it swiftly. As they walked up the stairs before they even got a chance to ring the door bell five shots of gun fire rang out....

Two gun shots hit one of officer in the back of the head twice. The other three shots hit the other officer in the back of his head twice, and once in the neck.....

The got shots had came from across the street from the third floor of an abandon building.....

Within seconds Will, and Black was gathering up all their shit trying to swiftly exit the abandon building.....

"Hurry up," Will told Black. "Hold on I drop the banacolus," Black said.....

Once Black picked up the banacolus off the floor, they ran to the stairs, and start running down the stairs at top speed.....

They made it their car which was in front of the abandon building.....

Black made it to the drivers side of the door reached in his pocket, and couldn't find the cars keys, he panicked, and started searching all his pockets......

"What the fuck unlock the door," Will told Black. "I can't find the keys," Black said, as he continued searching all his pockets, even the back pockets of his pants. "Look in your front pocket, the left one," Will said.

Black stuck his hand all the way in his left pocket and came up with the keys, unlocked the door got in the car reached over and unlocked the passenger side of the car. Started the car up, and got in it, and smashed off with the pedal to the metal, burning rubber......

At top speed Black was putting forth his best effort to get away......

"Slow down," Will said. "Slow down, we just killed two police officer's I'm trying to get away," Black said. "Man slow this car down," Will said in a demanding manner......

Black started to slow down a little......

"Man slow this car down, you gone get the police to start chasing us. When you do dirt like that you got to leave the scene at ease, that way the police don't get on to you. I'f they see you driving fast that automatically know what it is. Now if they see you driving regular with your seat belt on blending in with the hundreds of cars passing by they are less likely to try to get at you. Even if you drive right pass them after doing dirt, as long as you're driving regular nine times out of ten they aint gonna fuck with you, becuase they'll think you a regular car just driving past," Will said......

Black slowed the car down driving at regular speed......

They drove to a secret hide away only to stash the guns. Then they drove to another secret hide away where the usually have meetings......

Once they made it there Will begin to think about what they just had did, and the mistakes they made......

"You did a good job, but the way we did that was messy, we got to make it better next time. We can't slip up and drop things like we did the banacolus, and we definitely can't misplace car keys. You keep it in your mind exactly where the car keys are at. Just think if we wouldn't have found those keys we'd probably had to make it home on foot, chances are we would've been chased by the police or even caught. We would've looked real suspicious walking down the street dressed in all black carrying large equipment concealed in bags," Will said......

"You know that no matter what happens whenever you do dirt like that you must not tell nobody not even those that's part of the Black National family," Will said.

Black remained quiet staying attentive listening to Will as Will would feed his brain powerful knowledge.....

Will, and Black were part of an organization called Black Nationals. Will was the founder of Black National, Black was the co-founder. Some may would've considered them a gang, but the Black Nationals considered themselves to be an organizations that was in existence for the upliftment of black people.

The Black Nationals was a small organiztion that consist approximately thirty members. Every once in a while they'd accept a new member. Only in meetings they'd wear all black. They did a little protesting, and preaching in schools, and churches. But mainly they focus on trying to get blacks education, on a higher level of higher learning so that blacks would be successful on a positive note. When they did their protesting, and preaching they didn't represent Black National, they represented for the black people. Black National was like a secret society.

The Black Nation was against crime, and any usage of drugs, alcohol, and tobacco usage. The only crimes that the Black nationals was up with was violent hate crimes against white people.....

The next day after they killed them two police Black Nationals held a meeting in one of the members basement that was made up like a church. Will led the meeting as usual.....

"It's about the growth, and developement of the black community. We are black, and beautiful, black beauty's. It's time for change, and improvement, and we must do what it takes to change, and improve. We were once kings, and queens we ruled the place we once lived in before the white devils came in. We governed, and control our own lands. Our women even walked around bare chested showing of their beautiful black breast not as a sex symbol to men, but as a way of being. The women did this until the white devil came along, and made it seem wrong. As we go back the Alpha in bible the snake Satan tricked Adam, and Eve into thinking nudity was an impurity, and abnormal the white devils did the same to us. Every black brother, and sister in the divine area right now hug one another, as a form of undying love unity for your black brothers, and sisters" Will said to the Black Nationals as they all stood at attention dressed in all black unlocking their hands from behind their backs to tightly hug one another listening vividly to Will as he continued to preach.....

Overtime the Black National's membership slightly grew, as the Black Nationals terror of vicious hate crimes dramatically increased.....

One late cold winter's night Ruby ran up to an parked squad car occupied by two white officer's with her coat open, and her shirt slighty torn with her big beautiful brown breast bouncing.....

"He tried to rape me, he tried to rape me," Ruby said to the officers.....

The officer was so mesmerized by the sight of those big ole titties, that they wasn't able to respond right back it was as they were in a trance.....

Within no time the officer's came back to reality.....

Both officer's got out of the car.....

"Who tried to rape you," one officer asked with his eyes on her breast. "Where he at," the other officer asked with his eyes stuck on her breast. "He in this alley," Ruby said.....

Ruby ran back to the alley as the police got in the squad car to follow her.

As they made it to the part of the alley were Ruby was at they wondered why she didn't get in the car with them instead of running back to the alley on her own.

They rushed out of their car before they could say a word Ruby sprayed them in the face with Mace. Then she begin cutting one in the face back to back, as he grabbed his gun busting shots unable to see due to the Mace in his eye he accidently shot his partner in the eye twice. The bullets went to his brain instantly leaving him for dead.

The Mace in the officer's eyes made him feel as if he was blind, as Ruby stabbed in his throat a few times he dropped his gun, as he himself collapsed to the ground Ruby got on top of him stabbing in both his eyes, his face, and his head, as he squealed like a pig, Ruby snatched his life away from him.....

After the short period of drama Ruby vanished away from the scene of the crime.....

Ruby was a member of the Black Nationals, she was thoroughbred, had more heart then most of the members in the Black Nationals, and she knew how to do her dirt smart, and kept her mouth shut.....

Days later Ruby walked up to some of the Black National members as they were discussing the two police getting killed. Never in their wildest dreams would they have imagined that Ruby was the one who killed the two police.....

Didn't nobody know what Ruby did, she had learned from Will to do dirt, and to keep your mouth close, that way you wouldn't have to worry about no one telling the police.....

Sometimes members of the Black Nationals would do dirt to white people by themselves, and keep their dirt to themselves; other times they'd get together in numbers to do dirt, they called it war games.....

One late quiet night Will, Black, Ruby, and two other members of Black National, Dennis, and Tody, all decided to play war games.

Sometimes they'd split up to play war games. This time they decided to do it together, but in two different cars that would be right behind one another.

They'd use the women as driver's so that way after they did their dirt the men could duck down in the cars as if the women were in the car driving by themselves; that way it would be less likely the police to bother a car only occupied by one woman.

Will, Black, and Ruby was in one car. Tody, and Dennis trailed behind them in their car.....

While driving on a quiet side street unexpectedly they spotted a black prostitute just finished performing hardcore erotica for a white trick in a white Sedan. Black whom was sitting in the back seat of the first car signaled Todie, and Dennis to pull over.

Both cars pulled over on the other side of the street a short distance from the white trick in the sedan, and cut their lights off swiftly. The prostitute exited the car, and walked swiftly anxious to spend her earned money on buying her some dope.

He was so mesmerized by the sexual experience he just had with the prostitute that he sat in the car smoking a cancer stick oblivious to his surroundings and what was soon to come.....

Outta nowhere three shots sounded off like canons, "dooock, dooock, dooock." One bullet hit the white trick in the bottom part of the back of his head the other two hit him in his back.

Will felt wonderful after he shot the man up three times, as he ran back to the car the sounds of victorious trumpets sounded off in his head.....

As Will made it to the car all three men in both cars duck down, as the ladies smoothly coasted off as if nothing never happen the way Will taught them how to do it.....

"Did you get him, did you kill him," Ruby asked excitedly? Will begin slightly laughing. "I don't know I hope so," Will said.

About an hour later they found another victim. A white guy dressed up in a three piece suit walking down the street as if he owned the street with a briefcase in his hand.....

They pulled both cars around the corner Will got out and walked up to the man. As Will approached him the white gentleman looked up at Will with a smile upon his face on verge of greeting him. Will upped on him hitting him three times in the forehead the bullets ripped through his skull pushing half of his head off. The sight off it made Will so happy.

Will ran back to the cars jumping for joy.....

What Will didn't know was that the man he had killed was a homicide detective whom was coming home from work. Thw detective decided to walk home from work instead of driving, because his head was clouded by the constant murders, and secretive racism that was going on in his precinct, and around the world in general. The detective was on his way home to be with his black wife, and his two bi-racial kids.....

Later that night both car loads were mad, and jealous that Will had did all the killings himself that night. It was almost daybreak, and they had decided to call it a night. Ruby spotted this older white guy standing a bus stop on a main street.

She pleaded with Will to let her kill him. Will told her no the women were only used in war games to assist the men to get away. Ruby debated with Will that men, and women should be as equals especially the black men, and women. Although Ruby, and Will only debated for a short period of time Will decided to let her free to commit murder.

Both cars pulled around the corner, and parked, Will reloaded the gun handt Ruby the gun, and told her to be careful. Once Ruby got out of the car Tody, and Dennis looked at her stun with no clue of what was going on.

As Ruby started to walk to her destination Will got out the car, and told Tody, and Dennis that Ruby was getting to kill the white chump at the bus stop.....

As soon as Will got back in his car, and slammed the door he heard six shots go off. The shots was so loud that it was if the were coming from only a few feet from him.....

Ruby had walked up to the white guy on the bus stop, and asked for a cigarette the white guy made a racial slur, as Ruby upped on him shot him up six times unloading her .38 revolver as the bullets ripped through his flesh she knew he wouldn't live through tips of hallows to see a better day tomorrow.....

In no time Ruby made her way back to the car got in the driver's side, and smoothly coasted off.....

As they drove away to their secret hide away they all visioned Ruby taking away that white chumps life.....

Right then, and there Will knew Ruby was a winner, and a proud member of Black National's.....

Overtime Will wondered, and wondered how would it be possible for his dream of Black Nationlism to come to reality. He wondered how would blacks begin to govern politics in their own communities, how would blacks become more book smart through education, and how would their be more blacks becomming business owners.....

Will, Black, amongst others in the Black National worked for the white men. And those that didn't work for the white men were either mechanics or beauticians whom didn't have their own shops yet. But all of the Black Nationals had one thing in common they all long for the day to come were they all lived like kings, and queens on earth legitimately without any crimimal grinding.....

"Black beauty's I'd like to thank each, and every one of you for showing up today it's my privilege to be part of this organization. Since we first started it's been all talk, and not enough action. We gotta figure out a way for improvement," Will said as everyone started to clapping, and cheering.....

Everyone started clapping and cheering because they'd been feeling the same way.....

Within the next meeting Will had came up with a plan to make black people slightly advance. He told them that were mechanics, and beautician to train other blacks those trades; not just the blacks in Black National, but black people in general. Will told them to do that so that they would be able to make extra money outside of their day jobs, and eventually be able to take their trade and earn money, and be able to open up small shops. Will also told the Black Nationals to go to libraries, and attend college to study politics, that way they'd be able to slightly advance on a political level. The Black Nationals followed instructions.....

Within only weeks Will would talk to members of Black National, and he could tell by their conversations that they'd followed orders. Will felt good that he planted mental seeds of growth that was slowly starting to grow.....

Over time the Black Nationals continued to play war games. The war games had slowed down dramatically, most of Black National was more interested in the knowledge of being book smart.....

Ruby, and Will feel in love with war games, most of the time when they played them it would be just them two.....

One night after playing war games Will, and Ruby decided to go over his house to spend a night simply because it was late, and both of them were to sleepy to drive far. Will lived closer to where they was at than Ruby did so that's why they decided to go to his house. It was cool because Ruby's husband was a part of Black National, and Will girlfriend whom didn't live with him was real cool with Ruby, and her husband.....

Once they almost made it to Will's house it started to rain. When they made to Will's place they couldn't find a park therefore they had to park all the way up the street, and get out and run to his house in the rain in which left they clothes all wet up.....

"You can go in my bedroom, and look in the closet my girlfriend left some clothes of hers in there, you can get a pair of her clothes, get in the shower, and change clothes. You can sleep in my bedroom I'll just sleep on the couch," Will said.....

Will sat the couch feeling uncomfortable because of the wet clothes, and because he was fighting his sleep he wanted to wait until Ruby was done so he could get in the shower.....

Within a few minutes Ruby came out the bathroom ass hole naked with only a towel drying off her hair.

Will stood to attention looking at Ruby as if he'd just seen a ghost.....

"Ruby what are you doing," Will asked? "I'm drying my hair," she said calmly, and innocently. "Ruby where your clothes at," Will asked? "They're in the bathroom. I remembered what you had said at a meeting one time that we were free to walk around naked in Africa before the white man came, and poisioned our minds," Ruby said.

Their stood this naked beautiful black young lady. She stood five feet, chocolate super thick with such a cute face, and naturally curly hair.....

This girl on some bullshit, she know she married to one of our black brothers, and she want to put me in this situation, Will thought to himself.....

She stopped drying her hair off dropped the towel on the floor and walked up to Will, and gently hugged him around his waist, as he didn't attempt to reject. She looked him in his eyes and told him, "I love you." "But you're married," he said. "But I'm only human, and I love you, and I want you take me as your queen, and do whatever you want to me, I belong to you," she said.

Will begin smiling, and laughing right before their lips connected, as they began playing the French kissing game that seemed like forever.....

Eventually Ruby snatched her lips away from his and fell to her knees. She looked up at him, and asked him, "can I suck your dick." "Go ahead," he said.

Ruby eagerly broke the button off his pants, and then unzipped them.

Once she pulled his dick out of his underwear she paused speechless she couldn't believe how long, and fat his dick was, she had never seen or had a dick that big.....

She wrapped her left hand around the back of the dick, then she tried putting it in her mouth she almost couldn't open her mouth wide enough to put it in but she finally did.

She stroked the back of his dick with her left hand as she ate his dick up as if she was hungry craving for it. She was sucking it vigorsly as if she was trying to suck the skin off of it, and shove it down her throat, and stroking it with her hand, all at the same damn time.

I love Ruby, I hope she never stop sucking my dick, Will thought to himself. At that instant moment she stopped took her mouth off his dick, and spit on his dick five times. Will couldn't believe she had just spit on him. She immediately started back sucking his dick. Will immediately felt how better it was after the moisture of the spit. Within seconds she paused and spit on his dick three more times back to back. Once she started back sucking on it the spit ran down her face which made her look like a sick dog foaming at the mouth.....

In no time flat Will was unleashing nut in her mouth as she drunk, and swallowed all of it like a champ.....

Afterwars Ruby laid on the couch on her back with her eyes shut thinking to herself like this guy getting ready to kill this pussy with that big ass dick, and he did just that.....

Will had her hollering, and screaming half the night. Before the night was done he even bust her the ass.....

After that night they promise not to let their sex interfere with their personal lives.....

Chapter 2

Black entered Will's home.....

"Guess what happened," Black said. "What happened," Will asked? "I've been drafted to go fight in nam," Black said. Will paused, he couldn't believe what his ears were hearing.....

"That's sad," Will said in low tone of voice.

"Everything we've been through, all the efforts we put forth to be black powerful superior to the devils, and they pulled this stunt. They don't want to treat us as equals but now they want you to fight their war," Will said. "I aint going Imma skip town," Black said. "You can't skip town, that's a case, you gone to have to do a prison term when they catch up with you, that's a federal case I think they call it draft dodging or something like that," Will said. "So what would you do if they drafted you for war," Black asked? "I don't know, that's a good question. I might just go and kill up some of them Orientals. I think I'd rather try my luck on the battle field, than spend a long term in prison," Will said.....

Will, and Black paused for a moment in time as their minds was flooded with alot of unanswered questions, as they visualized the battle fields in Vietnam, death and destruction, and the past history of the white men hate, instead of loving.....

Within the upcoming days Black decided to go to fight the war in Vietnam.....

"Good evening my black, and beautiful people," Will said to the Black National Organization. "Good evening," the Black National Organization said back to Will simultaneously.....

"We were all design, and taught to be warriors to live, eat, and breed, on a militant mind settings, we have military minds. That comes from ancient African tribes that's the way we survived and ruled our lands as soilders of war. Right now the white man has his own personal war going on, and forces us to fight it, due to their laws we have no other choice if called upon. No matter what happens don't let the white people tear you down mentally nor physically. Stick your chest out, and hold your head up, and concur all obstacles.....To the devils we are ugly to me we're all black, and beautiful," Will said full-heartedly.....After that meeting the Black Nationals begin to think more about the art of war.....

A couple weeks later Black was shipped of to Vietnam nervous, and worried about if he'll make it through alive. At this time Black was only twenty one years old, Will was only twenty years old, Ruby was twenty three. Majority of the Black Nationals were young, but they had the brains of people twice their age.....

Will decided to quit his job working for the white man. He felt as if he should practice what he preach. Will knew how to cut hair so he started cutting hair, as a hustle, and it paid of instantly.....

———————————

Once Black first made it to the U.S. soilders overseas he noticed that the soilders had to do extreme workouts. And he knew that his turn on the battle field was soon to come.....

After a period of training Black was sent to the battle field for war. He was nervous like never before in life, but he didn't let it show.

During his first few times on the battle fields he was lucky they didn't come across any enemy troops.....

His first time coming across enemy troops was one late night as the mosquitos constantly ate away at the soilders flesh as the hot dreary night seemed endlessly they walked across dry land as Black, as well as the other soilders hoped that they didn't step on a land mind which would be a painful death they made it to a small body of water which was only approximately two feet high.

They crossed the water, and made it to these short bushes. As they stood still in the water in which seperated them from dry land they looked in them, and seen a small camp of enemy troops.

The general gave signal with his hand for everyone to remain silent. Then the general used his fingers as a sign language giving orders in the way to attack.....

Black became even more nervous each second. He knew it was time for war, time to seperate the boys from the men.....

In no time the soilders were attacking enemy troops the sounds of on going rapid gun fire that flooded the sound waves of ears as grenades sounded off like rocket launchers. You could hear crying, screaming, yelling in different languages as death, and destructions became one.....

Once that battle was over the U.S stood triumphant, their was casulties of war on both sides. Majority of the casulties was that of the enemy troops. Those that the U.S. didn't put to death fled the camp.....

That night Black seen how prosperous the art of surprise could be......

Overtime Black experienced more episodes of being front line on the battle field, as soilders were constantly getting killed, Black started to like war fair.....

Overtime the other soilders begin to call Black, God. They nicknamed him God because everytime they'd go onto the battle field it seemed as if he had God on his side.....

Will, and Black stayed in constant contact mainly through letters, occasionally over the phone they'd talk.....

Black would tell Will how intense the war in nam was, and that it made their war games seem like a joke. Will told Black that the Black National were starting to rotate with the ViceLords. Black didn't like it, Black knew the ViceLords was a street gang.....

Will had met some of the outstanding members of ViceLords by cutting hair. Will had came to find out that they had some of the same exact concepts that Black Nationals had. They were even getting funded from the goverment to help uplift the black community, as a sign of thanks and reparation for blacks helping building this country which was long overdue.....

Will had been introduced to the minister of ViceLords. The minister instantly took a liking for Will because he was smart, and he showed the qualities of a leader.....

Overtime Will had did alotta dirt for the minister, Will would bring nightmares of death, and blood shed to reality for the minister.....

Within time Will, and majority of the Black Nationals became ViceLords, the minister made Will a five star universal elite.....

The king of ViceLord kept hearing good things about Will, and decided to start rotating with him a little. The king didn't rotate with to many people heavy; He loved people, but didn't trust no one.....

The king of ViceLord rotated with Will a little turned into alot. The king had never met someone so young, so thorough, and so dedicated to the upliftment of ViceLord, and the upliftment of the black community.....

At this point in time the ViceLords wasn't very deep but they we're on fast uprise. They mainly resided on the west side of Chicago. Their were a few in the surrounding suburbs, but they wasn't that deep.....

Will would go out, and do recruiting, and go out and provide knowledge, and finance, and whatever assistance he could to the black community.....

In no time flat Will was a supreme elite, and had jurisdiction to create gang literature that the ViceLords had to abide by. He also had the kings blessings to start his own branch of ViceLord if he decided he wanted to do that.....

Will worked on the literarure of ViceLord with the king, and the minister, and now had expectations in becomming the king of his own branch of Vicelord.....

Within the matter of months Will finally decided to start his own branch of ViceLord, his branch would be the Traveler ViceLords, T.V.L.....

Mainly but not all branches of ViceLord name derived from ancient African tribes.

The Traveler tribe was an ancient tribe from Africa that traveled to conquer other tribes but not in war, but using their brains to manipulate them to became as one. The traveler tribe would find out were slave ship were and go to kill white slave traders, sometimes they'd became successful, other times they'd come up unsuccessful slaughtered like animals, but those that would survive would continue on, on their missions.....

Their were many other ancient African tribes; the Mandego's, the Zulu's, the Shabazz, the Ghosts, but Will decided to use the Travelers name because they were more in the likeness of himself, and his beliefs.....

Will became the youngest king of any branch of ViceLord that ever existed.....

Chapter 3

After a year, and a half fighting in Vietnam Black's tour of duty was over, he was sent back home. He couldn't wait to touch the city streets again.....

Will went to pick up Black from the airport in one of his new cars. As they drove, and reminisced Will took Black through the areas were ViceLords dwelled Black was impressed.

Will took Black through the areas were they Travelers was, and Black couldn't believe how Will had blossomed in the streets while he was gone.

Black was impressed by Will's street growth, but still had the Black National concept embedded in his mind frame in which he didn't believe in Will's committing crimes.....

As the day turned to night Will took Black through one of his spots were they sold his dope at.

The spot was inside a small building, the dope fiends would go into the front door, and walk shortly to a door with a slot in it where the mail man would stick their mail in. The dope fiends would slide their money through that slot, and tell the people on the other side of the door exactly how many bags of dope they were interested in purchasing.

Will had someone in the front of the building on security so when the police come they could get rid of all the drugs, the money, and the gun. They'd get rid of it by quickly taking the front part of their vent off, and giving it to the neighbors, or they would just give it to one of the neighbors up stairs; the upstairs neighbors would drop a long cord down for them to load up their merchandise in when, and if the police ever came.....

Will, and Black sat across the street on top of the hood of Will's car checking out the business. Black couldn't believe how many customers were constantly coming, and how much money Will had to be making off all them customers.....

Many of the Black Nationals became Travelers. Those they didn't become Travelers still did things to uplift the black people in their on way, and time.

The Black Nationals never told anyone, about their involvement with Black National, or the war games they played. They all kept it secret, they didn't even tell the Travelers that wasn't initially Black Nationals, about Black Nationals.

From time to time the ex-Black Nationals continued to play war games.....

After they left Will dope spot they went to see all of the ex-Black Nationals. All of them was more than happy to see Black home from the war.....

The last ex-Black National member they went to see was Ruby. Tears of joy ran down Ruby's face; she was so happy that he made it home safe, because so many people was getting killed in that war.....

Will ended up dropping Black off at his moms house, and went to meet Ruby at his own house.....

Will went, and jumped in the shower, as Ruby sat on the couch with the tip of her finger in her mouth, sucking on it as if she was a shy teenage girl.

Will came out of the bathroom wearing a robe.

As Will robe dropped to the ground Ruby took off her dress in which she had no panties, no bra. She dropped to her knees, with purple lipstick on she gently placed Will's dick in her mouth begin humming and bobbing back, and forth doing her best to make him fill pleasure, and love through the art of dick sucking.....

Ruby, and Will had got real close, but they kept their loving a secret. Ruby loved Will as if was he an angel on earth. Will loved Ruby, adored her sex, but loved his real girlfriend even more.....

The next morning Will went to go pick up Black. Will took Black shopping for clothes, and took him to the car lot, and brought him a brand new Cadillac.....

As Black started driving the area in his new lac with Will in the passenger seat a dude named Smurf spotted them, and flagged them down. As they parked Smurf ran to the passenger seat, and Black easily raised down the window.....

"William, Dirt robbed me," Smurf said. "Don't never call me William, call me Will. My Dirt, Traveler Dirt robbed you," Will said. "Yep, he robbed me last night, I was looking for you all night, you was no where to be found. I was gone took care of my business, but I can't bring no hurt, harm, or danger to one of the ViceLord brothers, that's just like doing something to one of my family members," Smurf said. "How much he rob you for," Will asked? "A bill, and a quarter," Smurf said. "One, twenty-five," Will said, and then reached in his pocket pulled out a roll of money, counted out a hundred, and twenty five dollars, and gave it to Smurf.

"That's good the way you went about the situation. By us being black men, and ViceLords all of us are like family, well atleast we suppose to be like family. But T.V.L. is like my immediate family. Like I just said it's good that you went about it the way you did, 'cause if you ever cross me, and do something to anybody claiming T.V.L. it's gonna be killer clowns, guns that explode, and burning of eternal fire all at once as a rapture you must feel," Will said. "Come on William, I meant to say Will you know I wouldn't never do nothing to none of the Travelers," Smurf said. "I heard that slick shit you said out your mouth, talking about you was gonna handle your business. As long as I'm living, and breathing you or nobody else aint gone do shit to no Traveler, and if you do you aint gone get away with, so don't let me hear nothing like that come out your mouth again. Just meet me in the pool hall tomorrow around twelve thirty, or one, we gone enforce law on dirt," Will said. "Alright, I'll be there," Smurf said as he stepped away from the car, as Black pulled off.....

"I been knowing you for umteen years, and you make everybody call you Will. Whats wrong with calling you William, thats your full name," Black said. "Yes, you have known me for umteen years, and you been calling me Will for umteen years so just stick with it," Will said. "Well from now on call me God," Black said. "I'm not calling no other man God," Will said. "That's my name, they gave me that name while I was at war. They gave me that name because each time I'd go to battle I'd always stand triumphant, and I'd always make it back safe," Black said. "Okay then God," Will said possessing a big smile on his face.....

The next morning Will, God, and some of the ViceLords were in the pool hall shooting pool. Some where smoking cigars, while others were sipping cheap wine, while others were doing both. Will, didn't smoke or drink.....

While shooting pool Will kept looking out of the window to across the street. Will had a dime bag powder spot across the street. He kept looking over there observing the customers in, and out the indoor spot.....

Will winding up sending someone to get Dirt.....

About an hour later in comes Dirt through the pool hall door with one of the other Lords by his left side.....

"Will you was looking for me," Dirt said, as everyone in the pool hall stopped what they was doing, and got quiet.

Before Will answered Dirt, Dirt noticed Smurf standing over in the cut. Dirt immediately put his hand on his gun which was tucked in the waist of his pants. Then he gave Smurf a mean mugg, a cold stare, that of a villing from a nightmare.

Reality immediately came forth Dirt now knew what Will had wanted him for.

Although Dirt wasn't at all worried about Smurf pulling a stunt in the presence of Will he still clutched his gun just to let Smurf know if he got out of his body he'd be feeling the pain of bullets.....

Dirt step closer to Will as everyone including Smurf surrounded him.....

"This brother said you robbed him," Will said to Dirt. "Yeah I robbed him so what he aint no Traveler, he a Renegade, fuck 'em," Dirt said.....

All the other ViceLords that wasn't Travelers, and those that was frowned up in disgust.

"So what he aint no Traveler, he still a ViceLord. That's why I be telling ya'll to learn ya'll lit, then ya'll will know how to conduct ya'll self as ViceLords. Now if this brother would've came back and did something to you the Travelers would've had to murder the Renegades making them extinct going against the laws, and policies of ViceLords, and killing of our own black brothers," Will said as everyone remained speechless.....

"You gotta learn your lit, you in violation for baring arms against a member of ViceLord, disobeying the laws of ViceLord unity, and jeopardizing the body of ViceLord. Normally you suppose to get a minute for each charge, but by this being you first time in violation you gone get one minute from head to toe. Big C collect all the weapons from all the brothers in this room," Will said.

Big C was a Conservative ViceLord..... Always at meetings, or when a brother was in violation there was to be no weapons, because meetings, and violations were considered to be somewhat spiritual, sacret, and uplifting.....

Once Big C collected all the weapons from the brothers they all tucked in their shirts faced the east, bowed their heads closing their eyes, lifting their palms up.....

God stood in the cut watching everything amazed about how the ViceLords orchestrated things.....

Big C started to read the Statement of Love, "For you my brother my love begins at birth that has manifested itself throughout our heritage for the color of our skin which is black. For I am you, you are me. Our minds are for the same cause. Our efforts are for the same goals. Our souls bound for the same destination. Our lives are for the same new nation. For you my black brother I give my unity, my vitality, my undying love, almighty."

Once Big C was done reading the statement they all opened their eyes, and lifted their heads up.

Dirt stood against the wall.

Will looked at his watch then in a matter of seconds he gave Big C the go ahead, to violate Dirt.

Big C hit dirt in the face once, Dirt fell to the floor as Big C continued violating him for a minute.

After the violation Dirt stood to his feet body aching in slight pain, he shook each ViceLord hand, and then hugged them.

He shook hands, and hugged Will last. As he hugged Will, Will whispered in his ear, "learn your lit."

Afterwards Dirt, and the guy he came in the pool hall with left, and everybody started back playing pool, smoking, drinking, and laughing as if nothing never happen.....

God started to fall in love with the way the ViceLords did things.....

Will and God left the pool hall.....

"That was raw the way you did things back there, what was that, that guy was reading," God asked? "That was the Statement of Love, that's a piece of ViceLord literature, I'm the one that wrote it. Alot of ViceLord literature I wrote. I took alot of Black Nationals concept, and turned them into ViceLord concepts, and wrote it up in literature. Me or none of the others that was once Black National told the ViceLords about the Black National, I'll take that secret to the grave with me," Will said. "Literature I didn't even know gangs had literature," God said. "We not actually a gang we're a nation of people that's about the upliftment of black people. ViceLord is design to uplift the black people," Will said.....

God stopped at a stop sign and pulled out a cigarette, and set fire to it, and begin puffing.....

"You smoke cigarettes, you digging yourself an early grave. Black Nationals, are not to use drugs, alcohol, or smoke tobacco," Will said. "Black Nationals, don't suppose to commit crimes, unless they were hate crimes," God said, and then inhaled, and exhaled cigarette smoke. "But I commit crimes, for the uplifting of the community. I sell alotta drugs, but I take the money, and invest it into good things within the black community," Will said. "You tearing down the black community, selling them drugs," God said. "But if I don't sell it to them it's many others that will. But I promise you majority of my money is being invested into positive things that will make blacks prosperous in the future," Will said.....

Within the upcoming weeks God noticed that Will was serious, because he seen with his own eyes how Will helped blacks with the money he made off drugs. Will would give black churches large sums of money, provided blacks with places to live outside of the ghetto, help people with their bills, and donate money to schools for better, advanced books, so blacks could get a higher learning.....

God start to see with his own eyes how the goverment would help fund ViceLord; and that the ViceLord would do many things for the black community, such as help blacks find jobs, provide after school programs so that the kids could come there to study, and have fun, amongst other things.....

God started to spend time with ex-Black Nationals that had become Travelers he noticed that none of them were in the streets selling drugs, or committing crimes they were working in places of after school programs, drug treatment centers in the black community or in college working on degrees.....

In no time God became a Traveler. He went from having no status to a branch elite, that dictated only to Traveler ViceLords, to a universal elite that dictated to all Vicelords, then to the prince of T.V.L. And he earned his way up to that title......

The Traveler ViceLords, amongst other branches of ViceLords rapidly grew, and spreaded throughout the city, and to the surrounding suburbs.....

Will, and God both became amazed with numbers of membership growth. Many all through the westside of Chicago wherever you went you seen guys with their hats broke to the left flagging ViceLord.

God started to apply his military experience in Vietnam to the ViceLord structure. In the military when soilders were punished for minor things they'd only have to do a harsh workout. God put within ViceLord law that if a representitive of ViceLord did something minor to break law they wouldn't have to get violated physically, but they would only have to do a harsh work out. The king of all ViceLords, and the minister liked that concept.

The minister of ViceLord put Will and God in play to be his personal assistances with creating more diplomatic ViceLord literature.....

God wrote his first piece of Vicelord lterature called ViceLord Life:

ViceLord Life

In the scriptures of life let it be of the creators will and might to project and show liberty and disadvantages of life.
But let life be a test and delight.
Always honor, guard, and protect brothers and sisters of ViceLord life.
Let it be done here and on a positive note uplifting to show growth to others in life.
Be forever real, be forever ViceLord with-through, upon a ViceLords life.

God's second piece of literature he wrote was called Concepts of Men:

Concepts of Men

Policies, concepts, and the conduct of men.
Honoring the five points of the golden star to withstand.
Love, truth, peace, freedom, and justice to the blackmen.
Utilizing knowledge and intellect to advance.
Remain sane dealing with circumstances.
Uplifting the brothers as much as you can.
Obey the unity, policies, concepts, codes, and conduct of being a black man.

After God wrote those first two pieces of lit, and put them in ViceLord literature the king of ViceLord, and the minister depending on God for more knowledgeable lit to add within ViceLord literature.....

The king of ViceLords, and the minister was honored to have Will, and God as outstanding members Of ViceLord; the king, and minister was amazed on how young, intelligent, and dedicated to uplifting the black community Will, and God was. What the king, and minister didn't know that Will, and God thrived off Black Nationalism long before they became Vicelords. What Will, and God didn't know was that the king, and minister was grooming them to be the king, and prince of not only the Travelers, but of all ViceLords.....

Chapter 4

Once Dr. Martin Luther King was killed the streets was filled with rage. Will, and God came up with the notion that if the ViceLords wanted to commit hate crimes against white people than go ahead, but ViceLords were not to burn down business, and buildings in the black community, no matter if a white person owned them or not. The king of all ViceLords, and the ministers, and supreme elites of other branches of ViceLord shared this notion, and told the ViceLords not to tear down the black community by destroying business, and buildings in the black community, no matter if a white person owned them or not.....

Although most of the ViceLords obeyed the orders it didn't matter because black gangs, and those that wasn't gang affiliated tore the city up......

Shortly after Dr. Martin Luther King Jr. was killed the ViceLords amongst other gangs had stopped getting funds from the goverment. The goverment claimed they were embezzling funds. So now drug dealings and black, on black crimes instantly started to reach an all time high.....

The original king of ViceLords, and the minister step back, and let the supreme elites govern the mob; they step down because they were being investigated by the feds.

The entire ViceLord nation became more needy of Will, and God's leadership.....

Will, and God started to open up more dope spots so they could use the money to fund growth, and development within the black community.....

With their owned dope money they were able to keep open some of the drug rehibilatation centers, and a couple of the centers that helped blacks get jobs amongst other things.....

Will, and God opened up with dope in the projects that made them start to see more money than they had ever did before in their lives; the projects was a gold mind.....

Since the Renegades was the deepest branch of ViceLord in the projects they started going through Smurf to sell their dope, Smurf was a three star universal elite.....

As the money grew, more people wanted to become T.V.L.

Smurf, and majority of the Renegades ended up flipping T.V.L. It was good for them, because they was still ViceLords just a different branch. Will made Smurf a five star universal elite.....

Daily more, and more of all branches of ViceLord depending on Will, God, or some of the other travelers for assistance, and guidance, and the Travelers extended their hand, as a sign of love, and support.

More, and more the Traveler mob grew. Other people that were from different branches of ViceLord started to flip Traveler, as well as oppositons wanted to be part of T.V.L., and even those that wasn't gang affiliated became T.V.L.

Other gangs in the city forced people to become members, or forced oppositons to flip. The Travelers, and the other branches of ViceLord didn't, people wanted to be down 'cause the ViceLords were thoroughbred.....

Within time ViceLords everywhere honored King Will, as the King of Kings.....

Chapter 5

W ill, and God started to have problems out of their main girlfriends, more, and more their main girlfriends wanted more time together, instead of space; they'd often be questioned about creeping with other women; one time God's main chick even threw his clothes out on the front porch, and poured bleach, and paint all over them.....

Will, and Ruby decided to take a trip to Indiana to rotate with some people to attempt to lay down a foundation for T.V.L. Ruby's husband told her while she was in Indiana he'll be leaving the state as well to go visit a sick, dying family member.....

God drove Ruby, and Will to the airport. Right before Ruby, and Will got out of the car Ruby gave God the keys to her house told him that her husband would be out of town, and that she had forgot to call an electrician, and then asked him if he could go over her house to do some electrical work. He gladly accepted the keys, and said yes.....

God learned how to do electrical work when he was younger, from his uncle.....

The next day God went to Ruby's house, as soon as he stepped a foot in the door he could see clouds of smoke, as if the inside of the house was slightly on fire as he smelled the reefer smoke he paused for a fifteen seconds not even closing the door behind himself, but loving the smell of burning reefer, and wanting to smoke some of it.....

God stepped in the house closed the door, and locked it. Walked to the bedroom, and there Ruby's husband was giving some lady's pussy all of his dick in the rawest form.....

Ruby's husband was on top of this lady, as she had her legs on his shoulder choking her neck with both of her hands as if he was really trying to choke her to death slamming his dick all the way in, and out of her pussy as if he was mad at the world, she moaned, and pleaded with him, "stop, stop, don't, no, no." As Ruby husband kept giving her the dick God became pleased with the action. Ruby's husband begin slamming his dick in her pussy harder and faster as his grip around her neck became firmer his nut exploded within her pussy. At that very moment it was as God could actually feel the intense pleasure that Ruby's husband had acheived.

Ruby's husband, and the lady didn't know God was slightly in the room with them, they was to busy fucking.

As Ruby's husband finished nutting, God seen the woman's face.

Damn Ruby's husband fucking Will's main girl Thunder, God thought to himself as he quickly vanished out of the room.....

God left the room, but stood to a distance where he could still see the action, but they couldn't see him unless they got up, and looked directly that way, and even if they did look that way he'd try to move swiftly so they would'nt see him.....

Ruby's husband took his dick out of her pussy, grabbed a little tube out of his pants pocket that was on the floor. The tube had raw cocaine in it. He opened the tube sprinkled cocaine on both of her titties nipples, then snorted it off. Then he put a little cocaine on his tongue, and went down, and started eating her pussy as she laid there on the bed loving every second of it.....

Once he stopped eating her pussy, she stayed laying on the bed, he began fucking her mouth like it was actual pussy, feeding her the dick, and choking her with it.....

What God didn't know was that she loved being choked while having sex, rather it was hands around her neck, or with a dick in her mouth.....

God rushed out of the house closing the front door behind himself, but making a mistake, and leaving it unlock.....

God left not knowing what to do. He couldn't tell Will what he seen Will loved Thunder, and Ruby loved her husband; and also God knew that Will was creeping of with Ruby although he never caught them in the act it was still obvious.

Thunder, and Ruby's husband started creeping 'cause they both new that Will, and Ruby was creeping although they was never caught in the act it was still obvious, because they spent to much time together.....

Once Will, and Ruby came back from Indiana God was there to pick them up from the airport.....

God immediately told Ruby that he didn't get a chance to go over her house to do the electrical work, she told him no problem she'd just call an electrician.....

Excitedly Will told God about the ViceLords that he had rotated with in Indiana, and that they wanted to become Traveler ViceLords, instead of Conservatives, and they had potentials on pushing alot of dope, weed, and cocaine for him so that he could now help the black community in Indiana. All the while, while Will talk all God could think about was Ruby's husband slamming his dick in and out of Thunder. God decided to keep what he'd seen a secret although he wanted to tell his right hand man Will, about Thunder.....

God dropped Ruby off at home. Then him, and Will went over to Will's house.....

Will came out the kitchen eating a sandwich drinking on a pop out the bottle, and seen God on the couch looking like he was getting ready to fall asleep.

"Why is you always so sleepy all the time," Will asked God? "I been up all night fucking around with this new chick, the one I was telling you about from out south. The bitch got a mouth piece that's, that of another planet. I been smoking reefer to that's what got me a little sleepy," God said. "You need to stop smoking reefer, and cigarettes, it's no good for you, that's what I miss about Black National we was against all that," Will said. "I'm T.V.L., don't get me wrong Black National gone always be in my heart, but I'm T.V.L.," God said. "I wish I could of put no drug usage in ViceLord lit, I could but I know it'll never work, to many of our black brothers, and sisters love to get high, that's why I can't wait til the day come when I don't got to sell drugs to our black brothers, and sisters, when I have enough money to retire from the drug game, and focus on rebuilding, and uplifting the blacks. Although I'm T.v.L. til the death of me Imma always have Black Nationalism in my heart," Will said, and finished the last of his sandwich, and sip of pop.....

"I'm getting ready to shit, shower, and shave, and go to sleep. Once I wake we gone go check on Smurf to see what the projects been doing.

Did you check on the other spots while I was gone," Will asked? "Yeah, I only got seventy six thousand, and a few odd hundreds the few days you was gone," God said. "Only seventy six thousand, you said that like it aint nothing," Will said. "It aint nothing compared to what we usually get in a few days," God said. "Yeah you right about that. But that's cool I can re-up, and still have enough to put some money into the blacks after school programs, and re-habs center," Will said. "You are a good brother, and it's good that you do what you can to uplift the black community, but that's not normal for a guy to sell all that dope to blacks, and then open re-hab centers for blacks," God said. "Yeah I know right, it's my only hope, the only answer to my prayers to uplift the black community. That's the only way a black guy like me can get so much money, so fast to use to uplift our black brothers, and sisters. As God, not you the real God is my witness if everything go as plan one day real soon I'll be done selling dope, or doing any criminal activities. Imma be so rich that I can spend all my money, and time bringing forth a change in the black community. But when it's all said, and done Imma be Black National, and T.V.L. til I reach Heaven or Hell," Will said, as he walked away from God, going to the bathroom to shit, shower, and shave.....

Once Will shitted, shaved, and shower he went and looked at God laid out on the couch sleep. He walked over to God and slighty lifted the sleeve of his right arm that showed the marks on his arm.....

This guy is the co-founder of Black National, and the prince of Travelers everywhere and a straight dopefiend. How he think that I don't know he shoot dope with all them marks on his arms always trying to cover his arm up with all them long sleeve shirt, when it be hot as hell outside, always talking he been smoking reefer, you been shooting dope, Will that to himself.....

Once Will, and God finished sleeping they went to see Smurf.....

As they pulled up to the projects they seen a mass amount of dopefiends walking up, and pulling up to buy dope as the workers would tell them that they wasn't working. As soon as they parked their car in front of the building Smurf came running out of the building as if someone was chasing him and bailed in the backseat.....

"I been steady calling ya'll, we been out of dope since yesterday morning," Smurf said. "You sold all that dope that fast," Will said. "Yep the building been tipping, I think it's a drought on good dope," Smurf said. "It aint no drought, they just don't got a good connect like I do,"

131

Will said. "You need to start selling weight I gotta alotta people driving down on me trying to buy large pieces of dope. Some the Lords off the ave. trying to buy two-hundreds grams. We should start selling weight, we can start taxing people for our good dope," Smurf said. "Okay I'll front you a hundred grams to sell in weight," Will said. "How much I gotta bring you back," Smurf asked? "I don't know I'll give you a price later. Right now I'm all outta of dope, I been out a town wasn't able to re-up, but I'll make sure you get some work later on tonight. Imma send you those hundred grams, and Imma send fifty bundles, Imma turn the bundles into two thousand bundles, and put an extra bag in each pack for the workers can get an extra sawbuck. How much you owe me already, fifty five thousand right," Will asked? "Naw it's fifty six, when they brought the bundles they thought it was fifty five but it was fifty six somebody musta miscounted," Smurf said. "Alright thats cool, Imma send somebody to pick up the money and bring you the dope. A'ight get out I gotta go I'm in a hurry," Will said. "Take me right down the street so I can get me something to eat," Smurf said.....

What's taking this guy so long, Will thought to himself as Smurf finally came out the restaurant with his food in hand.....

Smurf got into the car slammed the door hard, ripped open the paper bag, and started eating. Will, and God looked at him in digust.....

"Uhhh you eating that pork," God said. "I should get you violated, even if you do eat pork atleast don't do it around the brothers," Will said. "I eat pussy, pork, jello pudding pops, and all type of shit. I snort dope, shoot dope, and cocaine, shoot people, and a bunch other shit. Don't get me wrong I do honor ViceLord law but I'm not trying to hear nothing about not eating pork," Smurf said. "You betta be trying to hear it before you get violated," Will said.....

They dropped Smurf off at the building and went their seperate ways.....

Chapter 6

More, and more the Travelers, amongst other branches of ViceLord grew. They started to migrate to other towns, cities and states.

God begin writing more lit for the ViceLords.....

One late night God sat home alone treating his veins to heroic heroin as he begin to vision the past war games the Black Nationals use to play, the war in Nam he survived the street wars of gangs, and the gangbanging that ever took place, he wrote some literature:

Love and Respect

For those that's a representation of ViceLord we must, honor,
love and respect, never neglect.
Stand by each others side even under the threat of death.
Never deny ViceLords or ones self.
Be forever real, forever viceLord from the alpha, until death.

Holy Divine

On this holy divine day our praises go to Allah father of the universe.
On this holy divine day we thank the founder of all ViceLords for bringing
ViceLords to the west.
On the this holy divine day we say a special prayer for those that sacrificed

their very own lives for the upliftment of ViceLords.
On this holy divine day we vow to honor the laws of ViceLord that's
from guidance of the most merciful one, the most gracious one.
We shall honor these laws as an upliftment for the black community,
always keeping the hope alive as continious growth
with the abundance of love and unity.
On this holy divine day we shall pray that Allah guides us not to go, or be
lead astray, never letting Satan the dragon of the beast have things his way.
We must always safeguard, provide protection within our
community, utilizing talents, crafts, and intellectual minds to
be beneficial to yourself, and the community as a whole.
On this holy divine day we solomnly devote our
undying love, unity, and vitality
to the ViceLords, and the entire black community.

As time grew Will, and God had to stand on more nation business for ViceLords. Each branch of ViceLord had their own leaders rather it was a king, a prince, or some sort of elite brother, but some of them wasn't rightous, and/or couldn't think on Will's, and God's level. Those that had power within ViceLord that wasn't righteous Will would
make attempts to get them right but if they didn't get right he'd have them murdered.

Will, and God started to rotate with other gangs under the five point star to form an alliance with them. They'd rotate with the Black P. Stone, the Latin Lings, and the Bloods. When the rotated with Bloods it had to be in other states because it wasn't any Bloods in their city or state.

They took a liking to the Black P. Stones, and the Gangster Stones which was small branch of Stones that derived from B.P.S. Actually Will, and Black got cool with the Black Stones through the Gangster Stones.....

On a hot summers day Will, God, and one of the prince of the Gangster Stones pulled up in the heart of Black P Stones area on the south side of Chicago called Mo-Town.....

Will, and God mouth dropped they had never seen nothing like this in Chicago.

Once they made it to Mo-Town it was like they was in another state. Everybody roamed the streets with the colors red on one way or the other, with their hats broke off to left. From red hats, to red shirts, to red pants, to red shoes, to red shoe strings.

In Chicago and throughout Illinois they did draw off colors a little as gang representation, but not like the Black Stones did, they was serious about they colors they would wear something red every single day. In Chicago those under the fin wore they hat to left those under the six wore their hats to the right, that's mainly how they showed which gang they was affiliated with.....

They drove to this vacant lot in the heart of Mo-Town on one of their main streets.

They got out the car, and seen the Stones on each corner of the vacant lot standing silently with their head up chest poked out with right hand over their left hand seemingly dignified as military soilders.....

Before they could actually make it into the lot the guys on the corner of the vacant lot yelled out to this older gentlemen standing in the middle of the lot leaning on a car, "All well sir." "All is well," the older gentlemen said swiftly.

Fox, Will, and God walked to the older gentleman.

As they actually approached the older gentlemen he stood to attention as a soilder on the verge of greeting his superior officer with his right hand over his left hand; through symbolic signs and symbols the left hand meant Satan dragon of the beast, the right was a reflection of father of the universe so they'd held their right hand over their left hand as a sign of crushing Satan dragon the beast.

Once they made it all the way to the car they seen light smoke, and smelled the burning reefer. It was one guy in the drivers side smoking a fat ass joint, as the guy on the passenger side was speaking something Arabic sounding like a beast, Bismillah ar-Rahman ar-Raheem Al.....

They all stood their silently as the gentlemen in the passenger seat finished speaking Arabic, and the drivers smoke the last of the reefer.

The passenger, and the guy in the drivers side got out of the car.

"This is two of my newly titled generals, and I was teaching them to speak the Al-Fatihah in Arabic. Yourself is looking real superior, and divinely. I can bear witness that you've been drawing of the signs, and symbols, the code of conduction, of Black Stone," Cheif said. "All well sir, yourself looking divinely as well," Prince Fox said.

135

The two generals shook up with the prince; one by one they looked him straight in the eye connected hand touched each others index finger together as making a pyramid, then gave each other a high five then lifted their hands high as if they was throwing the fin in the sky, and then balled up their fist and hit it own there chest across the left side, the heart....

"It's truly an honor in meeting yourself, I've heard so many good things about one self you're truly emperors on earth that represent for the blackmen, the five points of the golden star, and of the most important most gracious, and merciful one Allah father of the universe," Cheif said to Will and God.

Will could look at Cheif and could tell he was drug free, and tell from the way he talked that he was a serious dude, but Will didn't understand the Mo's slang way of talking in which later on down the line would come to life vividly that they way of talking came from the Koran, and the Al-Islam faith.....

"Nice meeting you to," Will and God said.....

Will, God, Fox, and Cheif spent off from the generals, and started to talk about the
structure of the fin ball, and about the things they could do to provide more structure
and unity for those under the fin, and for the black community as a whole.....

Will, and God came to the realization that those under the fin did things similar to each other but still had a slight difference which was good that would be beneficial to each other.....

Will took a liking to Cheif he seen how thoroughbred, and serious about uplifting the black community he was.....

Will started to rotate with Cheif alot by himself on personal level. Will seen that Cheif was real knowledgable and that he could gain from that; cheif felt the same way about Will.....

When Will first started hanging with Cheif he noticed that the Mo's never looked as if they used drugs, that's because Cheif had put it in Black Stone lit, that any member of Black Stone must not use any drugs other than weed. Cheif put in Black Stone law that Black Stones were not allowed to sell any drugs other than weed on Black Stone land unless that have to give up have of majority of the profit to him in order to rebuild and uplift the black community.

Will loved the concept of black brothers not being allowed to get high off anything other than weed. Will wanted to apply that law to the ViceLords he knew it'll never work because to many ViceLords loved the dope, even his own prince was a dopefiend.....

Cheif would go more into religious side of the concept of the fin ball with Will which mainly came from the Koran, and a small portion came from the bible King James version, amongst other religious books. Will had slightly studied the Koran but wasn't familiar with it as deep as Cheif was.....

Chapter 7

K ing Will started looking for more growth and expansion for the Traveler ViceLords. Will started to network with the peolpe he knew in other states. Once he got to other states he noticed that it was already ViceLords there, and few cities had a descent amount of just different branches of ViceLords including a small amount of Travelers. Will was amazed on how ViceLords migrated and blossomed.....

As Will continued within his journey he noticed that every state he reached it was many different gangs he never even heard of; but in every state it was many different gangs but in every single state it was atleast Bloods or Crips or ViceLords, or G.D's, and Latin Kings. ViceLords, G.D's, and Latin Kings began in Chicago. Some places Will reached had never even heard of ViceLords until will turned them out to be ViceLords. At first will didn't even know that Bloods was under the fin.

Some places the ViceLords, Bloods, and the Latin Kings drawed as a whole as fin ball in other places they didn't. In some places blacks, and Latino didn't click together at all it was all about what race you was in. Some other city or states gangs stuck together off which hood you was from, in the cities within the state of California they called their hoods sets......

One week in Chicago the police was sweating the shit out of the Travelers, because they was getting to much money, and creating to much bloodshed within the streets, and the police wanted them stopped. Will and Black decided to skip town for a little while so they wont get twisted in some bullshit, and end up in jail.

Black took a vacation to Los Angles to enjoy the weather, and have some fun. Will on the other hand took a trip to Florida to visit some family.....On this particular trip Will took his girl Thunder with him, because she had been complaining that Will was neglecting her, and never spending no time with her, which was the truth.

Once they first made it to Miami Will wanted to go see the family, but Thunder wanted to go get some rest at the Motel room.....

As soon they made it to the room as the suitcases fell to the floor Thunder undressed, under her clothes she wore see through lingerie. Without a smile on her face she stepped to Will looked him in his eye, and said, "thank you for bringing me on this trip, thank you for letting me be your queen, for you I'll do anything."

In 0.3 seconds Will undressed dick hard as ever before anxious for hardcore erotica.

As Will stood straight up Thuder fell to her knees stuffing his dick deep down her throat chokikng herself but at he same time eating his dick thoroughly and using her right hand to jag him off all at the same time. Will was pleased with the action, all this time they'd been together she'd never sucked his dick this good before.....

In no time flat Thunder felt Will's dick getting hard in her mouth, that's how she knew he was getting ready to nut. Usually when she knew he was getting ready to nut she'd take it out her mouth. For the first time she let him nut in her mouth sucking it even better as if she was thirsty for to taste more nut as she swallowed the entire load. Will couldn't believe she swallowed his nut for the first, and how great of a pleasure he'd just receive.....

Thunder stood up, and will fell to his knees. Thunder took off her see through lingerie set as Will commenced to sucking licking, and eating her pussy with his whole head in her pussy. As she began to cum she started sucking, rubbing, and kissing her own tittie nipples for the first time ever in life.....

Will stood up and pushed her on the bed as if was made at her. He made her hold her own legs up grabbed his dick, and rammed it in her, and began beating the pussy up. As she moaned in the midst of pleasure, and pain, Will enjoyed the tightness and moisture as he'd fuck harder he began talking to her, harsh, and loud as if she was a prostitute he met off the streets, Thunder loved every second of......

Will bust a few nuts, and both Will, and Thunder fell asleep.

The next day as sunlight gleamed upon their faces through the window which curtains was wide open the both awoke to a pleasurable morning kiss although both had the bitter taste of morning breath within their mouth.....

They went into the washroom together brushed their teeth, and showered together as Thunder couldn't stop staring at Will's dick admiring the size.....

Once they finished showering she sucked his dick for little while, brushed her teeth again, as they dressed, and went out to eat breakfast.....

After breakfast they went to see Will's family it was like a small family renioun, a lot of Will's family was there to greet, and welcome Will, and Thunder to Miami.

All that day Will, Thunder, and Will's family had a ball going shopping, chilled at the beach, and hit the dance clubs after hours.....

After being in Miami for a few days Will noticed in some areas he'd pass it would be small groups of guys with their hats broke off to the left. So Will investigated to see if it was ViceLords in Miami. Come to find it, it was alot of ViceLords in Miami, majority of them was Insane viceLords, I.V.L's. That was strange to Will because the Insane's wasn't that deep in Chicago in which ViceLord started from, but had numbers in Miami. Will came to find that the original king of the insnaes went to Miami in the past because the money was plentiful, and it wasn't many ViceLord in Miami so he left Chicago, moved to Miami, to let his hair down......

Will, and Thunder stayed in Miami for a few weeks they really enjoyed themselves. Once it was time to leave Will's family was disappointed wanted them to stay forever.....

Once will made it back to Chicago, he dropped Thunder off at home which was sad for her because she knew that Will would go back to the streets to take care of nation business and that she wouldn't be seeing him that much.....

Will drove through the areas in an unmarked car he noticed that everywhere he turned the police had nigga's jacked up. He went through the projects and seen the building tipping with no police in sight.....

The same night he got in touch with everybody that was in charge of his dope spots and flooded them with more than enough dope to last for a couple weeks.

By this time Will had smarten up he didn't touch any dope at all; he had people in play to do everything, from going getting it from his connect, to having a table crew to go to the table and bag it up, and someone who was in charge of each spot to hire, and fire workers, and to make sure everything was ran correct. The only thing Will did was collect the money from those in charge of each spot......

The next night after Will came from Miami he met up with Ruby. Ruby and Will went to his house. Ruby insatntly begin saying shit letting Will know that she was jealous of Will, and Thunder being together. Will wasn't trying to hear that shit because she had a man at home.

Ruby's feelings for Will started to grow more. Will feelings had been started to grow for Ruby.

After it was obvious to Ruby that Will wasn't interested in the shit she was talking about Ruby grabbed Will's hand led him into the bathroom, and closed the door behind them.....

What the fuck is she bringing me in the bathroom for, and closing the door for, Will thought to himself.

Ruby hugged him around the waist, as Will slowly hugged her back tightly. She looked up at him with the low bedroom eyes, and whispered to him, "I love you, and I missed you so much, I hope we be together until we die." Right then and there she slapped him on his neck, and the bottom part of his face, but not real hard, but it was hard enough for him to feel it. Before he could react she pulled down her pants and bent over, on the sink and told him, fuck me real hard.

Will was pissed off because she slapped him, so he pulled his pants to his ankles,

shoved his dick in her pussy grabbed her hair with his left, and started fucking the shit off her while pulling her hair with one hand, and slapping her ass cheeks with the other hand, and talking dirty to her all at the same time; that was what she wanted to be treated like his bitch, that's why she slapped him first, she knew that would bring forth rough hardcore sex.....

What Will didn't know was that although both of them were in relationships with someone else Ruby was his bitch, and she'd do anything for him. Ruby felt as Will was her king of all kings.....

After sexing Will told Ruby that she bet not never in life put her hands upon him, or on any other member of the ViceLord nation, and that she bet not never let nobody find out about them being secret lovers......

The next day Will decided to go pay cheif a visit. Sometimes, but not all the time Will would have security on him, but everytime he rotated with cheif he went alone; he wasn't worried at all about nobody doing shit to him, because he knew if they did the ViceLords would tear the city up.....

"How was your trip to Miami, yourself looking real happy got a presidential smile upon face," cheif said. "It was good, I enjoyed. I came to find out it's ViceLords in Florida, and it's large numbers of them, majority of them Insanes," Will said. "Yes sir, Chicago gangs blossomed plentifully in other states, you'll be surprise on how many cities within through the map got followers claiming T.V.L. I landed myself in other states, and seen that it was B.P.S. that honored the literature of Stone Love, but they proclaimed to be Black P Stone Bloods. I come to find that some of my most loyal generals had migrated to other states and formed alliance with the Bloods; which was a divine usage of knowledge since the Bloods are under the fin they national color is red. Although I never sanction that orchestration, myself is pleased with leadership and brain power that was used by the generals. My respect for the generals are highly because the generals made sure that all the Blood Stones knew and honor the original Black P Stone literature, and honored myself as the founder of B.P.S, and as the chosen one set forth by the father of universe to divinely lead the brothers in the path of righteousness. The generals could've started their own branch of Black Stone or did something else under their names but they didn't they respected me as their leader," Cheif said.....

Cheif went on to provide Will with knowledge of the structure of fin ball, ancient African history, and of the bible, and the Koran, on how everything coincided with fin ball.

"Many of seeded people don't understand the concept of the fin points of the golden star, love, truth, peace, freedom, and justice. Love is because ourselves should love one another is if we were actual seeds that grew, and conceived from the same mother, and father. Truth shall never be over looked or misinterpreted in our eyes. Peace is because we shall always try to keep peace amongst or black brothers and sisters to inspire prospeity through growth by utilizing knowledge as power. Freedom is because we

142

must attempt to remain free mentally, and free from the prison system, the beally of the beast," cheif said.

"History has repeated itself; the white men didn't come and bondage us into slavery the white men came and influence other black men to trap slaves, and bring them to the ships, you even had kings of tribes that was literally selling their own people into slavery for crumbs. That goes on today blacks will work with the white men to enslave blacks in this unjust systematic systeming of prison," Chief said.

"Let me read to you this scripture out of the bible," Chief said.

Cheif begin to read parts of the bible, and then switched over to read scriptures from the Koran. Cheif vividly explained how the bible and the Koran had it's similarities, and how alot of stuff that went on in ancient time before Christ had repeated itself to that present day.....

More and more King Will's knowledge expanded as the Traveler ViceLord mob grew......

Chapter 8

Will, and God was riding through the hood on there way to the pool hall when they heard sirens. Will was driving. Will looked in the rear view mirror, and immediately asked God, "are you dirty," Black told him no.

Will pulled over thinking to himself what could they possibly want I havent broken any law.

Once he pulled over completely and put his car in park the detective car parked directly behind him.

One big tall chubby white detective got out the car with a cup of coffee in his hand. The other detective got out the passenger side he was a short fat white guy, that wore a tight fitting shirt, and jeans that looked as if they belonged to his little brother.

Both detectives ease their way to the car.

The detective outta the driver side stepped to Will's window. The detective outta the passenger side stepped to God's window with their hands on their guns.....

They demanded Will, and Black to step out of their vehicle.

"Is everything okay did I commit any crime," Will asked through his slightly opened window. "No just get out the car right now," the detective said to Will as he sat his coffee on top of Will's car with his left hand, with his right pulled his gun out his holster.....

As Will, and God stepped out of the car both detectives forced them to their knees, slightly repeatedly pushing their heads, and kicking their legs telling them they would have to pay them to sell dope in this area or they'd continue harrasing, and locking up all the Travelers in the area, Will, and God remained speechless mad than a motherfucker.....

Crowds of ViceLords grew on each side of the streets yearning to slauhgter them punkass pig police. Will repeatidely shock his hand no telling the Lords not to react. Will knew that if he wanted to he could have those two detectives murdered right then, and there; but that would only cause rage, and madness amongst the brothers of ViceLords in which he devoted his love, life, and unity to. If those two pigs would've got murdered right then and there alot ViceLord would be going to prison, and getting murdered in return by other cops......

The detectives begin to get nervous seeing the crowds of ViceLords, and decided to let Will, and, God go but told them they better start making arrangments to start giving them large sums of money from time to time if they planned on continuing selling drugs in that area.....

Will and Black got into the car, and smashed off.....

They immediately left the hood outta no where Will snapped out, "I'm T.V.L. I am a motherfucking black king I'm not paying them pigs shit," Will said.....

Will, and Black immediately left the state. Black decided to go to visit some of his family in the west coast. Will decided to take a trip back to Florida he took Ruby with him this time.

Will's girl Thunder wasn't to please that Will was going on a trip without her, but she knew what came along with being with a king of a large organization.....

Once they made it to the hotel in Florida Will could sense racism going on because they didn't give him the room he had previously made reservations for after they seen he was black which they didn't know when he made reservations over the phone.

Will and Ruby left the hotel, and checked into a motel nearby.....

Once they made it in the room they silently relaxed for approximately ten minutes.

Will begin to snap out about how the detectives mistreated him, and how the people in the hotel acted when they seen he was black, Will was pissed off.....

"I commend brother Malcolm, and Martin for sacrficing their lives for the equality, and uplifting of the black community. Although by law thanks to Martin we do have equal rights, but to the white devils we will never be equals. They say you gotta fight fire, with fire, that's a lie. You fight fire with water to put out the fire. When you got a problem with someone you gotta deal with it accordingly, you gotta put fire under they ass, and make them feel it. You gotta make them pigs feel it. All you doing is talking about it, talk is cheap, so stop being so motherfucking cheap," Ruby said as she passionately begin tongue kissing Will in his mouth.

Will picked her up, and took her to the bed, and slammed her on it. Took her clothes off, and then took his own clothes off.

With the tip of his dick he played with her pussy until it got super wet. Commenced to slamming his dick in and out of her pussy taking out all of his anger and frustration on it, and she screamed and hollered as if he was killing the pussy......

When he felt hisself getting ready to nut he pulled it in her mouth as she ate and swallowed all of it.....

She ate his dick repeatedly on and off through the night to allow him to inherit pleasure, with attempts to momentarliy take away the pain he felt within his heart, and mind, and she did such a good job in doing so.....

A burning of religious crosses were set on fire in front of both pigs house the next night.....

An across a street neighbor that had just finished watching a late night talk show, cut off the T.V. stretched, and yawned, and seen three people dressed up in Klu Klux Klan outfits settng fire to a cross on one pigs lawn. She was shock didn't know what to do or didn't understand what was going on because they lived in an area where only whites lived. As the three Klan members got into their car, and fled the seen. She stood their momentarily confused staring at a firely blaze.

She snapped back to reality reached for her phone book frantically, and nervously opened it searching for the pigs number.

The pig answered his phone in anger mad at whomever was on the other line calling his home so late at night. The lady told him that it was a cross burning in front his house.

He couldn't believe it. He instantly dropped the phone and looked out of his second floor bedroom window, and seen that she spoke the truth.

He ran down the stairs grabbed a fire extinguiser, and ran outside with only his boxers, t-shirt, and a pair of socks on and put out the fire.

A few of the neighbors including the neighbor that witness it came running out there homes.

After the lady that witness it told everyone what she had seen, they couldn't believe it that KKK members sat fire to a cross in a all white area, especially since majority of them was racist as hell.

Meanwhile on the other side of town the pigs partner was going through the same thing, putting out a burning fire from out in front of his home; afterwards coming to find out the fire of burning crosses was started by Klan memebers.

The same night both pigs temporary relocated their families to other areas to live with other family members until they got to the bottom of what was going on.....

Neither one of the pigs informed the other police of what ahd happen, they wanting to deal with it unprofessionally, and violently like a criminal once they found out who did it.....

They next day both pigs went to work without a clue of who set fire to the crosses, and why.

They harrassed any everybody they seen walking down the streets in the black ghetto the patroled.

They pulled up on one of the main blocks where the Travelers dwelled. They started searching some of them being straight ass holes. One Traveler walked up to them out of nowhere, and told them, "King Will said you honkies betta find ya'll somebody to play with the crosses was just a warning."

The two officers snapped out and started hitting him with their billy clubs. After they hit a few times a piece they bust his head open, as he took flight, and started running. The pigs gave chase but they never caught him. While they was chasing him everybody else took of running as well.

For the rest of that day they harrased the Travelers, from planting drugs on them then arresting them, to just walking up beating them with billy clubs, to making racial slurs, they even stripped one Traveler of his clothes, and made him run up the street naked.....

The next night the two pigs was found in a alley in their detective cars that had been sat on fire while they was still in it, as their bodies had been burn to a crisp. Their no witnesses or evidence on that incident.....

The autopsy showed that they had been sat on fire while still living; their cause of death was being burned to death.....

King Will sent somebody to tell them to meet him somewhere to pick up the money he'd give them to stop harrasing the the Travelers. Once the made to the location, the was ambushed by many men with guns, so they couldnt reach for their guns. The men robbed the pigs of their guns, tied them up in their detective car, and sat it over fire. He took Ruby's advice and he put fire under their ass to make the feel the wrath, and to kill them, and to abolish them as a problem.

King Will was smart he was outta town while all this was taking place so he wouldn't be a suspect in the murder. King Will had some people from another state handle that business because they was unmarked faces.....

The authorities never understood what was the two cops doing on that side of town way out of their jurisdiction in which they shouldve been at work, and their entire car being set on fire with them in it, and someone even put out the fire without even calling the fire department. The first thing that came to the authorites mind was that the Italian Mob had something to do with.....

The police worked hard to find out who did it, and even brought the federal bereau of investigation in to help them, but they never ever found out who did it, or even had any leads. The investigation would be an on going cycle that would last many years until they would finally give up.....

Will stayed in Florida for a little while rotating with the Insane ViceLords. Will found away to recruit a few guys into becomming Traveler ViceLord, although the Insane ViceLord had Miami sewed up as far as ViceLord was concerned.

Will begin to rotate with other cheives of gangs. At first Will was kinda nervous to be in Miami rotating like that being that he was a king, and didn't have the manpower, and respect like he did in Chicago. But yet and still, he still wanted to plant a formulated knowledge, power, and understanding in the black community through embedding the concept of viceLords.

Some of the heads of other gangs in Miami some he even never heard of until touching Miami, didn't mean him no harm; although he never heard of them they had heard of him,

and the Travelers. They liked the concept of ViceLord, and the uplifting of the black community, although their gang policies, and concepts were totally different.....

The gangs cheives in Miami Will rotated with wasn't interested in becomming Vicelords, but they did adapt some of the laws, and concepts of ViceLords, and treated Will with the upmost respect for being so young, so intelligent, and so courages.....

Will decided to stay in Florida for a little more while; he sent Ruby back to Chicago to be with her lover although she didn't want to leave Will forced her to go, only to be with her lover......

Will and Thunder would talk over the phone each day. Thunder really missed him; but Will really missed Ruby.

Will came in acquaintance with this beautiful young black lady that had the smoothest caramel skin, and chestnut brown eyes. She was standing in line ordering food, a cheeseburger, and fries, as she reached in her pocket she noticed her money disappeared.

Will stood right behind her in line noticed that she was searching in each pocket so it became obvious to him that she lost her money. Will stepped up to the cashier and paid for her food before she could tell him no. She told Will, "thank you," in a low soft tone. Will ordered the same thing she did and paid for his food which came fast, as him, and her walked off together.

Will paid for her food genuinely wasn't trying to get with her at first. But once they walked off and begin talking they became highly interested.

He could immediately tell from her accent that she wasn't from America. He came to find she was from Haiti her name was Stephanie; and that she studying Political Science in college.

Will questioned about the concepts Political Science. She told him graphically about the way potical science worked; it was the law of the land used to govern to form laws to use those laws the way goverment works, and how they use power to gain even more power.

Will feel in love with concept of Political Science, and knew beyond reasonable doubt he could use that to empower the black man.....

Days to follow Will, and Stephanie would go out during the days to enjoy the weather laid on the beaches. During the nights they'd go out to dance clubs and out to dinner. Will didn't dance but he enjoyed watching her, and the other ladies dance it was a blast.....

More and more Will found himself wanting to sex Stephanie, but waited patiently because she was a classy lady, and he knew it would take a little time for him to finesse....

After dinner one night, Stephanie invited Will back to her home; Will was excited knowing he was getting ready to get some pussy.....

Stephanie lived in her home with her parents, her parents was gone on a trip to Haiti.....

Once they made it into the house Will instantly begin tongue kissing Stephanie. After seconds Stephanie seperated her lips from his, and started showing him around the house. She first showed off all the black, and white photos of herself when she was younger, and of her mom, and dad in which he had never met yet; she then showed him the kitchen, and then led him to the basement.....

Once he got to the basement there twelve people where have dressed, women, children, and mostly men whom look as if they hadn't shaved in months.....

Stephanie introduced him, and told him they were Haiti immigrants that had came over here on a boat they had made themselves. "One of her neighbors had found them down by the shores laid out on the grass; she took them in found out the were Haitians, and turned them over to us since she knew we were from Haiti. My family, and I don't know what to do," Stephanie said.....

Will paused not knowing what to do or what to say. He sat in a chair against a wall while everybody stared at him looking for an answer.

"Do they speak English," Will asked? "Yes they do," Stephanie said. "First thing I'm going to do is get them some fake indentification so they can get them some jobs, and attend school. I'm going to get them some clothes as well, they need to be presentable to the public," Will said. "Aren't they going to get in trouble with the law with fake indetification," Stephanie asked? "No, as long as they don't get in trouble with the law, by committing any crimes they'll be good," Will said.

Will had Stephanie to walk him upstairs to the front door, and gave her a long passionate kiss before he left her house.....

The next day he went over to take pictures of them for the indentification, and to get their sizes for clothes, and shoes.

After a few days he came back with the fake indentification, and clothes, and shoes.

He took the Haitians out through Miami streets to find jobs, it wasn't easy. He ended having to go through one of the gang cheives he rotated with in Miami that helped him find Jobs for the Haitians.

Days to follow Stephanie invited Will over to her home. On the trip over there Will thought Stephanie needed more help with the Haitians, oh how he was wrong.

As soon as he stepped in her home she begin tongue kissing, sucking his bottom lip, and went back to tongue kissing him again. She unbutton, then unzipped his pants stopped kissing him, and snatched his rock hard dick outta of his pants. Her eyes got wide open she couldn't believe how big his dick was.....

Will slowly undressed her, and then undressed himself, he stood up admiring the view to him her body was flawless.....

Will paused, and asked her, "where is everybody at." "I'm home alone," Stephanie said.

Will made Stephanie lay flat on her stomach on the couch. Will then played with the ass cheeks momentarily squeezing, slapping, and rubbing them. Will then begin finger fucking her with one finger two fingers, and then three, Will came to see that her pussy was extremely tight.....

Will took his fingers out of her laid on top of her wrestled to get his dick in her tight pussy, and then tore the pussy up, as she begged him to stop because she couldn't withstand the pain, he didn't stop or show any mercy.....

For a short period of time he gave her great sex......

Will knew that soon he'd have to go back to the Chi, but before he left he helped the small amount of Travelers he formulated in Miami by teaching them ViceLord literature, and helping them with jobs. He didn't want to supply them with dope he wanted them to do bigger, and better things as far as getting an education, and for them to someday to became black business owners to help the black community.

Before he left Miami and sexed Stephanie a few more times, and did some other things to help those in Miami.....

Alot people he rotated with in Miami didn't want to see him leave but knew he had to go, especially Stephanie but she understood she knew he had a woman, and a life in Chicago.

Chapter 9

Will had been gone to Florida for several months, once he made back Thunder was there to greet him. They went straight home, and in bedroom Thunder showed how much she missed, and loved him. She'd get her knees and he stood straight up she'd suck his dick looking up at him straight in his eyes thinking to herself how much she loved him, and missed him, and didn't want to lose him. Majority of the night their sex consisted of her sucking his dick, and his balls for the first time.....

They next morning Will took Thunder shopping spent tons of money on her. During the rest of the day they enjoyed the sights of Chicago's downtown area, and went out to dinner, and a movie.....

Once they day was complete that ended up home. Will had his mind on the streets, Thunder had her mind on being a freak.....

Will laid on the couch eyes wide open visioning his life as a whole, past, present, and the future; outta of the back room came Thunder wearing see through lingerie set

he had bought her earlier.

Will just laid there looking at her amazed, and pleased. He laid in shock as if that

was his very first time seeing her half naked. As he laid there and didn't move she walked over to him looking straight at him with those low bedroom eyes bent over, and begin tongue kissing him like never before.

After finishing kissing neither one of the two said a word as he continued to lay there she got on her knees unbutton, unzipped his pants, and pulled his dick out stared at it for a few seconds smiling. She left her eyes open wrapped her lips around it, and starting sucking it as she positioned herself side ways so she could look him in the face as she performed. She sucked the dick like it tasted like sweet nectar, as if she was eating it continuously hungry for more and more.

I love this girl Will thought to himself as his nut begin unload she took the dick out her mouth as a large load of nut shot in her face; they both loved every minute of it.

Will told her to take off her see through panties, and she did just that leaving her see through lingerie top on. Will get up as she laid on the couch he held her legs up, her ankle by her eyes, locked her legs with his arms so she couldn't get away once he start giving her the dick.

He told her to put his dick in her pussy herself and she did just that like a pro. He eased his dick within her a few times slowly until the juices got to flowing within her. Once it got juicy he started slamming his dick in and out her pussy as if he was mad at her, and the world, as he hollered loudly feeling the affect of pleasure, and pain, as she'd holler, calling him king dingaling......

Will and Thunder fucked, and sucked each other all night.....

The next morning Will awoke, as Thunder remained sleep, he crept out of the bed so he wouldn't wake her. He went into the bathroom to shit, shower, and shave.

After showering he crept back into the room to get his clothes, and shoes. He quietly got dressed. Right before he was able to leave out the door Thunder softly called his name, he looked back and there Thunder stood as naked as the day she was born. "What time you coming back," Thunder asked, with a pleasant smile on her face. "I'm unsure maybe real late tonight, I got alot of business to attend," Will said.....

Will walked over to Thunder hugged her, and gave her a long passionate kiss, and then departed out the door to the streets.....

The first thing Will did was to go check on his money. After he collected all his dope money from everyone that was in charge of selling his dope it totaled out to 1.5 million. Will was disappointed he knew it was suppose to be more money than that. Will knew some people was scheming, and double juggling since him and God was gone out of town for that short period of time. Even Will's connect whom he never let no one know until him and God went out of town he had to, to keep business flowing said that his workers was playing games they wasn't coping as much work like he did, that's because they was buying their own work from other connects to put on the joints so they could check a bag while Will, and God was gone.....

After Will put his money up he'd roam the streets standing on ViceLord business in many areas. In a few areas he rode through around the time school was letting out he noticed that the Black Panthers would be standing out being self made crossing guards for the kids, and giving up free after school lunches for the kids. Will loved the sight of what the Black Panthers was doing, and promised hisself that once he had some free time he'd do whatever it took to help them.....

As Will continued on to his journey through Chicago city streets had came to find out the bad news that one of the Kings of one of the branch of ViceLords were trying to extort money from some of the supreme elites within his own branch of ViceLord which led into death, and destruction. The supreme elites that the king was trying to extort caught the king and few of his guys on the e way rode on the side of them exploded gunfire outta guns, killing their own king, and everybody else in the car with him. The supreme elites tried to flee the scene as a state trooper get behind them they opened fire, and murdered him. Crashing into a wall the driver was instantly killed from the accident, as another supreme elite were injured but still living unable to get out of the car because of injuries, and because the car doors would'nt open because the accident was to bad. In no time flat the police, ambulance, and the fire truck arrived prying the supreme elites out of the car finding all the guns that they did the murders with. The story brought water to Will's eyes he knew that those brothers would never ever see the streets again, and those brothers that was killed could never be brought back to life. Will wished badly that he could've been in Chicago to prevent the whole ordeal.....

Will went home to Thunder, and hugged her tightly as if he hadn't seen her in years, as if he was a soilder coming home from a war, or had been release from prison after doing a long term.....

There Thunder stood ass hole naked smiling for him. He unhugged her looked her straight in the eye, and told her, "I love you."

They started kissing, and ended up on the bed as he ate her pussy she ate his dick at the same damn time.....

Damn this girl suck dick much better than usual Will thought to hisself as she continued eating his dick. Damn he eat pussy better than he normally do Thunder thought to herself as continued eating the pussy. What Will didn't know was that Ruby's man was giving her the dope dick while he was gone, and teaching her how to eat dick better. What Thunder didn't know was that Will had learn to eat pussy better because Ruby taught him to do better.....

The rest of the night was sexual pleasure for the both of them......

The next morning after Will stood on a little nation business for the ViceLords, he went solo by himself to get up with the Black Panthers. He was able to get up with the actual leaders of the Black Panthers. The Black Panthers knew of the ViceLords, and respected some of their concepts; but the Black Panthers didn't like that the ViceLords would flood dope into the black community, and would commit black on black crimes.....

Will pleaded with leaders of the Black Panthers to accept large sums of his money to use to uplift the black community. The Black Panthers thanked Will for his kindness but told Will that in no shape form or fashion could accept even one cent from Will because his money came from flooding drugs into the black community. Will continue to plead with them, as they continued to say no. Eventually Will came within grips of reality knowing they'd never accept his money.....

Will was smart though he just waited days later get in touch with a Black Panther that wasn't a leader and started flooding her with fat checks, to donate to Black Panthers. Of course she knew the checks was coming from Will but she lied and said they was coming from elsewhere. Know Will would devote large sums of his money to the Black Panthers as long as they exist, or until his death, which ever one came first.....

Will decided to spend more, and more of his money on the community; after school programs, building agencies that would help blacks get jobs, denoting it to black organizations that helped with blacks college tuition, and doing whatever it took to uplift the black community.....

About a week after Will came back to town God came back from out of town, as well.

Will was in the pool hall shooting pool, he glanced out of the window to make sure his security men was tight, all ten of his security was on point outside, and the other eight security men was on point inside of the pool hall. It was Will turn to shoot pool, and he made a mistake and shot the eightball in. One of the guys in pool hall yelled out, "loser," as everybody in the pool hall started laughing.....

Will glanced out the window again and seen God, and Frog park right in front of the pool hall, and jumped out Frog's old black Cadillac. God was driving Frog was in the passenger seat.

As they bailed out of the car Will instantly noticed that God was wearing army fatigues, and that both God, and Frog looked sleepy as if they hadn't been to sleep in days.

As they slowly entered the pool hall, Will seen that they wasn't simply sleeping they was drunk off dope.

They slowly stepped to Will scratching, and nodding to a point as if they were sleep walking.

Once they finally reached Will, Will immediately smelled the odor as their clothes reeked of reefer smoke.....

God was so drunk off dope he could barely stand up or even talk.....

It was no secret that Frog was dopefiend, Frog didn't give no fuck, even though it was in Black Stone literature not to use drugs other then weed Frog wasn't trying to hear none of that.....

Later on that night God admitted to Will that he was a dopefiend; it was as no surprise to Will because he already knew that.

God explained to Will that the reason he was wearing army fatigue was because he was a soilder willing at anytime ready to battle for safety of ViceLord, and for the safeguard of the community......

At times when God would be drunk off dope he'd be shell shocked from when he served in nam; he'd visualize the soilders getting suited, and booted for war, as some would say their prayers before stepping on the battle field as inner souls cried out for the war to be an ending ordeal. God reflected on the soilders he seen that lost their lives, at home it could be no husband for the dead soilders wives, fatherless kids no more seeing dads in eyes still alive.

Sometimes God would wake from his sleep that had him hearing the sounds of bombs, and gun fire, seeing the other soilders shooting dope as a way to be free, a way to be higher.

God would never go to war and fight for a country that in reality had no love and respect for blacks, but God felt he'd forever ever be a divine soilder for the nation of ViceLords; would live and die for ViceLord, the lord of the lords.....

Will told God about the chaos that was going on amongst ViceLord in just the little time they were on vacation, how the brothers had lost their life, and some even caught cases.

God instantly got pissed off he knew that the problem was from the leaders of different branches of Vicelords that was corrupt mainly interested in a profit rather than uplitfment.

Although God was a dopefiend he never let his habit interfere with ViceLord.....

Will, and God sat down, and wrote a new piece of lit together called Giving All:

Giving All

I shall give my entire livilyhood to usefulness of African descendants,
not some but all.
Together we shall stand never divide never fall.
Giving the black's love, and loyalty in it's entirety, all.
Understanding imperfections, but continuing to work on flaws.
Concept of ViceLord honoring all laws.
Be the best you can be not just for yourself but for the community
Of blacks as a whole, all.

Will, and God decided to write that piece of lit, because they honestly felt that,
those claiming ViceLord should give it their all not just a percentage.....

157

Chapter 10

W ill, and God would see how the Black Panthers rotated, and loved their style. The Black Panthers didn't sell any drugs in the communities, or committed any other crimes, although the media would falsely paint pictures of them as being bad guys.

Will, and God seen with their own eyes how the Black Panthers would provide food, shelter, clothing, love, and guidance to the Blacks without seeking any profit, their profit was seeing the black community advance.

Will, and God wished the ViceLords could be more divine like the Black Panthers.

Will, and God continued to donate thousands of dollars at a time to Black Panthers through secret sources, because the Black Panthers wouldn't accept any of their money knowing it came from drug sells.....

Will, and God started to see how the ViceLord nation was continuing to grow, and grow. The more the ViceLords grew the more they became needed of Will, and God.

The other branches of ViceLords had their own kings and princes, but Will was the king of kings.

They became aware that endlessly they had to ride on ViceLords to stand on the business making sure everything was in order. It was a headache but they had no problem in doing so they did it outta love.

Will and Black never lost focus of the true concept of Black National, and of ViceLord which was to uplift the black brothers, and sisters.

Will and Black seen with their own eyes that some of the brothers with status, and without status wasn't righteous they was more interested in personal gratification within gaining finance through drug dealing, but not giving back to the community.

Will set up a meeting with the king, and princes, of each every branch of ViceLords, and had a long talk to them about doing more to uplift the community by provide my finance to assist the black. Each, and every king, and prince agreed with everything Will had said, and even voiced their opinions on how they all could do more to donate, and provide more money for the community. Although everyone agreed, and knew Will was correct, Will knew it wouldn't work; simply because most people are more interested in financial gain for themselves not for others.....

Will would walk around the hood with a few of his guys trailing him on security mentally in distress trying to figure out a better way, a better plan, a better future for the black brothers, and sisters.....

One way that Will figured out to help the black community was flood it with more dope so that could make more money to spend it on the black community.....

Will got up with God and told him his plan on how he'd start slanging more dope in the community to provide more money to uplift the community. God was drunk off dope as usual, and instantly begin laughing.....

"So, tell me again how is putting more dope in the black community gonna help the black community," God asked with a smirk on his face, nodding, and scratching. "I'm a sell more dope so we can have even more money to spend on the reconstruction of the black community," Will said.....

God paused remaining silent, thinking to himself, now knowing Will had a valid point.....

Will's first step was putting the five star universal elites that has boss mentalities in play not to sell dope for him, but to sell dope for themselves with the primary objective to gross more income for the community, and to teach some how to survive own their owns without having to work for the whitemen, and how to be their on bosses, and rulers of their domains just as the ancient Africans was before the Satanic ships came, and kidnapped them of their glory. Although the ancient Africans didn't sell drugs of course Will wanted to teach his people to be more like the ancient Africans.

One of the first guys Will put in play was Shake Bag. They called him Shake Bag because he use to sell brown bag dimes of reefer, the reefer was potent just all his bags was small full of shake. Shake Bag was arrogant, and rude as fuck but knew how to stand on business, and would take no shorts or loses, and he honored the concept of ViceLord......

Will fronted him a four and half of cocaine, and told him what block to set up shop on.....

Days to follow Will would go through, and check Shake Bag, he'd see Shake standing the corners talking rude as fuck to his workers, and to the few customers make sure business was ran right; that's why Will put him in play because he knew he'd stand on the business.....

In no time flat, which seemed as if it was over night, Shake bag was building clientale, so Will decided to give him some heroin to, to see what it do. Once Shake Bag got that herion in no time flat Shake Bag had his joint doing numbers.

Although it was actually Shake bags joint, Will still would check a bag from it to use to uplift the community because he was the one fronting Shake the C and the D.....

Once Shake Bag got in play, everybody else wanted their own joint.....

Will started putting the five star universal elites in play giving them joints in the hood, fronting them work.....

In no time flat the hood was infested with every drug known to men. In due time all the joints starting rolling hard.

Then Will started open up joints in many other hoods, mainly where the Travelers dwelled.

Back then Will was one the first ones that started the dope network. The dope network consisted of Will giving somebody that had a joint alot of dope already bagged up, they'll sell it under their names on their joint but bring Will back majority of the cash; like for instance if somebody was selling approximately 10,000 a day on the dope Will would give them 10,000 worth of dope bagged up, and tell them to keep three for themselves and bring him back seven, It was easier that way for the individual whom joint it was because they didn't have to bag up the dope nor did they have to spend money to cop the dope either. It was good for Will because he didn't have to stand on workers, or even worry about what was going on, on those joints all he had to really do is sit back, get paid like a boss. He had people in play to bag up the dope take to them, and even come back collect his money, and those joints wasn't even under his name people didn't even know that, that was his dope on those joints.....

One day Will met this bad bitch, yellow bone, natural brown hair, hazel brown eyes. So he made arrangements to spend a night with her, in both of their on silent minds they was interested in hardcore erotic fucking.....

Will had his security men follow his car trailing him to her house. Once he made he checked the address, and then parked. His security men which were all in the car that trailed him they parked right behind him. They all got out and escorted Will to her door step.

Will rang the door bell she instantly opened the door smiling wearing nothing on but a gown that was open that showed her matching black panties, and bra set. She thought Will would be alone she instantly seen his security got nervous, frantically closing her gown, and tying it up. Will told his security to leave.....

Will stepped in, and tried locking the door behind himself, in which the door seemed as if it didn't want to lock. She stepped to the door bumped it a little, and then locked it. She stepped away from the door dropped her gown to the floor, and took her bra, then panties off, and dropped them to the floor.

Will started kissing, and then went to her titties, and sucked them one by one. Then her took her big ole titties, and put both nipples in his mouth at the same damn time and sucked them as if he was actually breast feeding.

Will snatched his mouth away from her titties reached in his pants and upped his rock hard dick on her, she couldn't believe the size of it.....

Will, and her already knew what time it was because they had been talking pornographic over the phone earlier that day.....

"You dick so big please let me suck that big ass dick, please let me suck your dick, please let me suck that big ass dick," she begged.....

Will didn't say a word. So she kneeled down and placed his dick in between both of her titties as he commenced to tittie fucking she started eating his dick vigorously. The pleasure felt so good to Will that he knew beyond a reasonable doubt in his mind he definitely be going back to her for seconds on a later date.

In no time flat was Will letting his nut go on her big pretty yellow titties as she rubbed the nut on her titties as if it was lotion.

She stood up looked him dead in the eye he spinned her around bent her over, and rammed his dick her pussy, and started beating the pussy up. She tried to run away from the dick, but Will had a lock on her that wouldn't let her get away. The more she tried to get away the more he give the dick to her.....

Throughout the night she scream and holler Will's name in the midst of pleasure and pain. She'd scream, and holler Will's name so much the next door neighbors would forever know Will's name.....

Will awoke and called his security over. Once his security pulled up honking their horn Will locked out the window, and seen them, and noticed his car was gone.....

Will ranned out to them telling them his car was gone.

At first Will was confused thinking to himself maybe somebody else he was close to

had a set a keys, and pulled off in it; within seconds he came within grips of reality that someone had stole his car.....

He had security to take him to the hood so he could get in one of his other cars, and go home. During the entire ride to the hood he remained silent, mad than a motherfucker.....

Once they made it to the hood they dropped him off right on the side of the pool hall where he had some of his other cars.....

As he keyed open the door, one of his security man raised down the passenger windows and asked him, "Do you need us to follow you on your security." "No I'm okay man ya'll can leave I got to go take care of some personal business," Will said as he opened the door got in the car started it up put it in gear and smashed off.....

Will destination was to go home to Thunder. Will never used security when he went home he didn't want nobody to know where he lived at.....

During the drive home he was pissed off because somebody stole his car. Money wasn't a thing to him, he could get a new car whenever he got ready it was the point that someone stole something that belong to him.....

Once he made it to his home he parked right in front of it and started to visualize the past racism burning of crosses, by the KKK little black boys and girls lives took, and lost. Dogs and water hoses of cold water, hearts of frost. Prejudice statements flowing freely from ones mouth. In a vivid vision he seen Lucifer cheering, clapping, and begin to shout as blacks was being led by the mountain top by those in white sheets eyes literally been blinded by bleach, as they was being pushed off the mountain tops into the lake of fire, the burning lake of sin, of deceit.....

I gotta do something, I gotta do more to uplift the black community. We need black doctors, more black lawyers, and more black business owners. Not more black drug dealers, and gang members. I gotta move faster on getting more money from selling dope, so I can quit selling dope, selling dope is tearing down our black community, Will thought to himself, as his eyes begin to get teary.....

Will slowly walked to his front door, keyed his way in and there Thunder sat on the couch looking as if she was mad at the world.....

"Where were you last night," Thunder asked? "I was standing on nation business, you already know that I devote my livelyhood to uplifting of the black community," Will said. "All that's fine but you got to make time for yourself, for me, I love you, and I need you," Thunder said. "I love you, and I need you to," Will said. And then they started kissing as the french do as their tongues, and lips continuously connected allowing love and pleasure to be felt with no rejections.....

Thunder was actually interested in a arguement with Will, but once they started kissing all that was over with.....

Will snatched his lips away from Thunder, and then pushed her on the couch and angrily snatched her clothes off.

She wanted to suck the dick first but before she could Will remembered that the lady from last night pussy had a slight odor to it, and that he didn't even wash his dick after last night he knew Thunder would smell the scent of pussy on his dick or even taste it, so he decided to fuck her first.

He rubbed vaseline thick on his dick, and gently worked it in her pussy as she instantly started moaning he begin slamming his dick in and out the pussy and talking dirty to her at the same time until he begin nutting in her as she begin cumming on his dick all at the same time.....

They sexed only for a little while, afterwards showered together and laid up in the bedroom watching t.v. and chilling out around the house for a few hours.....

After a few hours overlapsed Will told Thunder about his car being stolen and he had to go investigate the matter.

He left home wondering how he was going to deal with the issues of his car being stolen.....

After a few days overlapped he figured it out. He got up with one of the black kings of one of another branch of ViceLord that dwelled close by the area in hopes of finding out if someone in that area stole it or knew he stole it.

Will wasn't actually interested in simply getting his car back, he wanted blood to shed behind those whom took, stole something that was his.

The black king of the other branch of ViceLord was named Rufus. Rufus introduced Will to Row.

Row was going to be the one to investigate on who stole the car, and if Row found out whom stole it he'd also be the one to take care of the business of making blood shed through gun-fire of lead.....

Row was cool with some of the local major expert car theives, so he hung out with them treated their veins to some good dope.

After a minature investigation Row found out the dude who did it. One late night Row got him in his old black van treated his veins to some dope pulled off in an alley as if he had to piss upped a small .38 shot him twice in the side of the head and twice in the heart open the door pushed him out the van shut the door and road off like nothing never happen; before the gun shots even took place the dude never even seen it coming he was to drunk off dope.

The next day Row told Will, and Rufus that he address the business. Will was pleased that he did it so fast, and wasn't messy with it.

Will started to rotate with Row. Eventually Will had Row to take care of some more business for him. Will liked that after doing killings Row would keep his mouth shut unlike others that would brag to some of their closes friends.

Will never understood how this guy that was young but thoroughbred on killing wasn't selling dope or being flashy with money, Row didn't even have a main girl didn't even date alot didn't have no kids or no type of family ties. All Row wanted to do was poision his veins with dope as a way of being free, and commit murders of death. That's why the ViceLords named him Death Row, but they shorten his nickname to simply Row.

In no time Row flipped Traveler, and Will gave him a glove made him a five star universal elite, and made him cheif enforcer of law.

Will never knew Row's story until he heard it from someone else.

Row was from a small town down south where racial tension was at an all time high.

One night Row's mom, and dad had been arguring because Row's dad was being unfaithful.

So Row's mom took a short walk through the woods and witnessed from a distance the KKK beating, torchering, than hanging of two black men, she took off running scared to death she assumed they didn't see her but they did one KKK member stepped away from the action because he had to piss real bad, and seen her frantically running away.

She ran home to tell Row's daddy his mouth and heart dropped. As she continued telling the gruesome story they both went back and forth looking out of the window, scared, confused not knowing what to do.

She told Row's dad that they didn't see her, well that was what she thought.

Row's mom and dad sat on the couch for like fifteen minutes trying to figure out what to do.

Row's dad decided to get up, and go to the back to load up his shot gun. Before he could even get off the couch the KKK memebers kicked in the door like villings with torches, and riffles in hand. They grabbed Row's dad and swiftly beat the shit out of him with riffles, and then tied up his seemingly dead body on the floor. They then snatched off Row's mom skirt and panties, and raped her in the ass repeatiedly as screams never left her mouth.

Row's dad laid on the floor almost unconscious, but slightly conscious to sit and watch his wife get raped and feeling the immense pain of being beating with the riffles; laying there he felt like a straight bitch.....

Row was only a few years old but he was old enough to understand the violence. He stared out of the crack in his bedroom door witnesses everything as permenant tears fell from his eyes. He never left the room as he was to scared and confused.

After the KKK finished raping his mom they stripped her all the way naked and beat the shit of her with riffles and she cried, and screamed they beat her worser.

They tied her up including her mouth took her and her husband to their truck tied them to the end of the truck and dragged them on the dirt road for almost an hour. Took the remains of their bodies to the river tied bricks on their bodies through them in the river and left for dead.

Days later their bodies were found by accident while a fisherman was fishing.

The family was devistated. They immediately went to the house looking for Row. Row was there halfway dressed laid out on the his bedroom floor just had finished eating bologna as dried up tears surrounding his face.

When the family first came to his rescue he laid there on the floor as if he was lifeless as if them or nobody and nothing else even existed to him.

As his uncle lifted him off of the floor tears of joy ran down his uncles face, as never ending tears sorrow starting run down Row's face as he had constant flashes of what the Klan had did to his mom and dad.....

Row told his uncle what happen vividly; his uncle went to report it to the authorities. The authorities told him he had no case because the accusers wore white sheets, and white hoods. Also that they couldn't go off the statement of a kid that was only a few years old.

What Row's uncle didn't know was that the police he was talking to was one of the ones that was under the white sheets that did the killing of Row's, mom and dad. The officer didn't give a fuck no way, to him it was two less dead nigga's he had to worry about.

Row ended up living with his uncle and his wife. They didn't have any kids so Row was like the son they never had.

Row's uncle and his wife treated him like he was their very own in the beginning.

Over the years they started acting funny, treating him like a step child.

Row would notice that alot of times when he was in the bathroom his uncle would make up an excuse to come in there. His uncle was a closet fruit cake that lusted for the penis of little boys.....

Around the time Row was ten years old one morning Row woke up outta his sleep and instantly noticed he had no underwear on. He jumped up and there his uncle stood ass hole naked jagging off. As he arose from the bed his uncle looked at him in disgust and kept jagging off as if he didn't even exist.

Row immediately put his underwear and clothes on and ran out the house. His uncle didn't give a fuck he just kept jagging off.....

Row's uncle didn't actually touch him when he was asleep. His uncle just gently slipped his drawers off to see his dick, balls, and ass, so he could get aroused while jagging off.

His uncle really wanted to have sex with him, but he knew that would cause a major problem.....

Later that night Row's uncle's wife stayed late at the church to help some of the church members with extra work details within the church.

Row never told any one what happen earlier that day he just crept in the house to get some of his clothes so he could run away from home.

Row stepped in the house quietly and slowly in hopes his uncle being asleep. To his surprise his uncle was asleep snoring loud as hell.

Row crept in the room filled his laundry bag up with clothes swiftly.....

On his way out the door he passed up his uncles room as he came closer to the door the snoring got louder. Row rushed to the front door, and put his clothes and the front came back inside grabbed a bat went into his uncle room hit him three times on the back of his head busting his shit wide open. Blood ran everywhere as his uncle jumped crying and screaming like a bitch Row ran out the front door. Snatched his clothes off the porch and ran away fast as he could without looking back.....

Row's uncle had to get many stitches in his head. His uncle never told anyone that Row did it. He lied and said members of the Klan did it.

Although Row bust his uncle head wide open, his uncle felt guilty for pulling that gay as shit with his nephew, his uncle knew that shit was bogus.

After a few days Row's uncle begin to questions Row's whereabouts. Nobody knew where Row was.

Row didn't want to go over none of his family members house he didn't fuck with them he been knew they was phony as hell. He went to live with his little homie Choncey.

Coincidently Choncey's family would be leaving to start a new life in Chicago. Row had told them what happen so they felt sorry for him and took him with them.

After a couple weeks Row's family found out he'd move to Chicago with Choncey's family. So they didn't worry about it anymore. They didn't tried to inform the police or anything, they allowed him to be free.....

Immediately after they moved to Chicago Row got addicted to the fast life. Only ten years old but loved the street life.

Row stayed in trouble so much that Choncey's family had to kick him out.

Now Row was all alone, had no place to call home. Now it was time to seperate a boy from a man within himself.

At only ten years old everyday he had to hustle to survive. He did whatever took from stealing lunch meat and bread out of stores, to washing cars, to standing on the ho stroll with the prostitutes begging the tricks for change.

Normally he'd sleep in abandon cars, a garage, or on a park bench. Every once in a while when business was slow for the prostitutes a few of them would invite him home or to motel because he was only a baby and didn't have no place to call home they'd teach him how to smoke reefer in the process eat his dick for him free of charge. The prostitutes couldn't do it often because their pimps didn't like it. The pimps didn't give a fuck about his situation all they was interested in was the ho's making money for them.....

Row started to rotate with the young Vicelords. They was a few years older then him but they had game like grown men.

That taught Row how to steal cars and take them to various places to sell the parts. They'd also do a little sticking up. They even introduced him to some of the Lords in which he could work for them selling a little drugs.

Row started to like the ViceLords they treated him like family. In no time flat he became a ViceLord.

Once he became a ViceLord he never had to sleep in abandon cars, garages, park benches or none of that. He never had to beg strangers for money or steal food outta stores just to eat, his pockets stayed decent, and each night he'd have various places to lay his head, with no problem.

By the time he was eleven he was straight killer. When the ViceLords got in street wars the others would have shoot outs and wouldn't even hit shit, or in some cases if they did it would be from a distance.

Each time Row would handle nation business for the ViceLord Row would bring death to reality. That's why they started calling him Death Row, but later on shorten it to Row.

At only eleven years old King Rufus feel in love with Row. Because Row was youngest killer he ever met or even heard of in life. Row wasn't messy the killings he'd do dirt and keep his mouth shut. On the killing side Row was more thoroughbred than most grown motherfuckers.

By the time Row was twelve he was straight dopefiend he love treating his veins to herion, and taking swift back to back puffs of the reefer. To him being high was a way of being free mentally.

Each time he'd shoot dope into his veins he'd visualize the bad things, the company of miserable things, this world of nightmares that came to reality awaken from sleeping dreams; he'd see the Klan tormenting his mom and dad he'd break out into sweats interact the incident over and over again as if it was actually taken place repeatedly but the exact same way.

Row never smile that much, he never cried at funerals it was as if he was emotionless. The only time he'd cry was when he was super high all alone in a zone he'd shed tears for his mom and dad that was dead and gone.....

By the time Row was thirteen King Rufus gave him status made him a five star universal elite. At first Will once was the youngest universal in ViceLord history until Row came along to become the youngest universal elite in ViceLord history.

Although young and a dopefiend the ViceLords honored and respected him to the fullest.....

At the time when he was seventeen that's when he became a Traveler/ cheif enforcer of the ViceLord mob.

He'd stand on his function to the fullest with a iron fist.....

Previously Published Urban Novel

Queen of Queens

Chapter 1

"You sure this the right spot, man?" Slim asked.

"I'm positive this is the right spot. I wouldn't never bring you on no blank mission," Double J said.

With no hesitation, Double J kicked in the door and yelled, "Police! Lay the fuck down!"

Double J and Slim stormed into the crib with guns in hand, ready to fuck a nigga up if anybody made any false moves.

As they entered the crib, they immediately noticed two women sitting at the table. The women were getting ready to shake up some dope.

One of the women laid on the floor facedown, crying out, "Please, please don't shoot me."

She had seen many TV shows and movies in which the police kicked in doors and wrongfully thought an individual was strapped or reaching for a gun when they weren't, and the police hideously shot them, taking their lives from 'em.

The other woman tried to run and jump outta the window. Before she could do so, Double J tackled her down and handcuffed her.

Double J threw Slim a pair of handcuffs. "Handcuff her," Double J said.

As Slim began to handcuff the other chick, he began thinking, Where the fuck this nigga get some motherfucking handcuffs from?

The woman who was on the floor, crying, looked up and noticed that Slim wasn't the police.

"You niggas ain't no motherfucking police," she said.

Double J ran over and kicked her in the face, and busted her nose. "Bitch, shut the fuck up," Double J said.

She shut up, laid her head on the floor. As her head was filled with pain while tears ran down her face, with blood running from her nose, she silently prayed that this real-life nightmare would come to an end!

Simultaneously, Slim and Double J looked at the table filled with dope. Both Slim and Double J's mouths dropped. They'd never seen so much dope in their lives. Right in front of their eyes were one hundred grams of pure, uncut heroin.

Both women laid on the floor, scared to death. They'd never been so scared in their natural lives.

Double J went into the kitchen found some ziplock bags, came back and put the dope in them, and then stuffed the dope in the sleeves of his jacket 'cause it was too much dope to fit in his pockets.

"Man, we gotta hurry up. You know the neighbors probably heard us kick the door in," Slim said.

"The neighbors ain't heard shit 'cuz of all the fireworks going off. That's why I picked this time to run off in here, while the fireworks going off, so nobody won't hear us," Double J said.

"Shiit, they could've still heard us. The fireworks ain't going off inside the building," Slim said.

"Don't worry about it," Double J said.

"Lord, let's search the rooms before we leave. You know, if all this dope is here, it gotta be some guns or money in here somewhere," Double J said.

"Yep, Jo, I bet you it is," Slim said.

Double J walked over to the woman whose nose he busted, knelt, put a .357 to her ear, and clicked the hammer back. The woman heard the hammer click in her ear. She became so scared that she literally shit on herself.

"Bitch, I'ma ask you one time, where the rest of that shit at?" Double J asked in a deep hideous voice.

She began crying out and yelling, "It's in the closet, in the bottom of the dirty clothes hamper."

Double J went into the closet snatched all the clothes outta the hamper and found ten big bundles of money. He saw a book bag hanging in the closet, grabbed it, and loaded the money in it. Double J went back into the front room. Without second-guessing it, he shot both women in the back of their heads two times a piece.

Double J and Slim fled from the apartment building, got into their steamer, and smashed off. As Double J drove a few blocks away, Slim sat in the passenger side of the car, looking over at Double J, pissed off.

"Lord, why the fuck you shoot them hos?" Slim asked with hostility.

"Look at all the money and dope we got," Double J said.

"What that gotta do with it?" Slim asked.

"You know that that wasn't them hos shit. They was working for some nigga, and if that nigga ever found out we stuck him up for all that shit, he'd have a price on our heads. Now that the only people who knew about us taking that shit is dead, we don't gotta worry about that shit," Double J said.

Yeah, you right about that, Slim thought as he remained silent for a few seconds. "You just said something about dope and money. What money?" Slim asked.

"Look in the book bag," Double J said.

Slim unzipped the book bag, and it was as if he saw a million dollars. His mouth dropped, amazed by all the money that was in the book bag.

They hit the e-way and set fire to a lace joint as they began to think of all the things they'd be able to do with the money and dope.

Double J and Slim were two petty hustlers looking for this one big lick, and they finally got it. They had various hustles that consisted of robbing, car thieving, and selling a little dope. All their hustles revolved around King Phill. King Phill was a king of a branch of ViceLords, the Insane ViceLords (IVL). They'd rob, steal cars, and sell dope through King Phill, one way or the other.

Double J and Slim were basically King Phill's yes men. Whatever Phill would say or wanted them to do, they'd say yes to.

After forty-five minutes of driving, they parked the steamer on a deserted block where there were no houses, only a big empty park.

Double J began wiping off the inside of the car. Slim began to do the same.

"Make sure you wipe off everything real good. We don't wanna leave no fingerprints," Double J said.

"You ain't gotta tell me. The last thing I wanna do is get pinched for a pussy-ass stickup murder," Slim said.

Double J put the book bag on his back. They left the car, wiping off the inside and outside door handles, and they began walking to Double J's crib, which was about thirty minutes away.

"Lord, fire up one of them lace joints," Slim said.

"Here, you fire it up," Double J said as he passed the joint to Slim.

Slim instantly set fire to it. They walked swiftly to Double J's crib, continuously puffing on the lace joints. Once they made it halfway there, out of nowhere, Double J stopped in his tracks.

"What the fuck you stop for?" Slim asked.

"Lord, we gotta get rid of that car," Double J said.

"Why?" Slim asked.

"'Cuz like you said, we don't wanna get pinched for no stickup murder. If somebody seen that car leave the scene of the crime and they tell the police and the police find the car and dust it for fingerprints and find one fingerprint that matches one of ours, we booked. We'll be sitting on death row saying what we should've, would've, and could've done," Double J said.

"How we gone get rid of it?" Slim asked.

"Here, take my gun and bookbag and meet me at my crib. My girl there, she'll let you in," Double J said.

"You still didn't answer my question," Slim said.

"What's that?" Double J asked.

"How we gone get rid of the car?" Slim asked.

"Don't worry about it. I got it," Double J said.

"Let's get rid of it together," Slim said.

"Naw, man, we need to make sure the money and dope is safe, and we need to get these hot-ass guns off the streets," Double J said.

"Where is the dope?" Slim asked.

Double J reached into his sleeves, pulled out the dope, and handed it all to Slim as they departed and went their separate ways.

I hope this nigga don't get caught fucking around with that car, Slim thought.

Double J went back to the car, looking for something to use to set it on fire. He ended up finding some charcoal fluid in the trunk of the car, squeezed all the fluid out of the bottle all over the car, struck a match, and threw it on the car as it instantly began burning. Double J took off running. He ran halfway home and walked the other half.

Once Double J made it home, before he could even knock on the door or ring the doorbell, Slim opened the door. Double J rushed in nervously and slammed the door behind himself and frantically locked it.

"Nigga, what the fuck took you so long?" Slim asked.

"What took me so long? Shiiit, I ran halfway back, but anyway, I took care of the business. I burned the car up," Double J said.

"How much dough we got?" Double J asked.

"I don't know. I ain't even open the book bag up, I was waiting to you get here," Slim said.

"See that's why I fuck with you. Anybody else would've played me for some of the money and dope," Double J said.

"You my nigga. I wouldn't never try to get over on you. To keep it real, you didn't even have to take me on the lick with you," Slim said.

They went into the bathroom, locked the door, and began counting the money. Each bundle of money was a G.

"Damn, Lord, we got ten stacks and all this dope," Slim said.

"How we gone get rid of all this dope?" Double J asked.

"We gone sell it in grams," Slim said.

"Naw, man, we need to sell it in bags. We'll make more money selling it in bags. The only problem is where we gone sell it at. You know anywhere we try to open up at, they gone close us down," Double J said.

"We gone sell it in the hood," Slim said.

"Stop playing! You know damn well we dead in the hood. You know if we open up in the hood, they gone close us straight down," Double J said.

"We gone have to go through Phill," Slim said.

"Yeah, we'll get up with Phill tomorrow," Double J said.

"Man, don't tell nobody where we got the dope from."

"Nigga, do I look like a lame to you? What the fuck I look like, telling somebody about what we did," Slim said.

"I'm finna go to sleep. You might as well spend a night," Double J said.

"Yeah, I might as well spend a night," Slim said.

"I'll holla at you in the morning. I'm sleepy as hell," Double J said as he started to yawn.

Slim went and lay on the couch in the living room. Double J went into his bedroom, undressed down to his boxers and T-shirt, and got into bed with his wife, who he assumed was asleep. As Double J pulled the covers back, he noticed that his wife was in bed asshole-naked. I'm glad I married her, Double J thought while enjoying the view.

Slim and Double J stayed awake for a little while, thinking about the money they had and the profit they was going to make off the dope. As Double J closed his eyes to go to sleep, he felt his wife's hands gently slipping into his boxers, rubbing his dick.

"I thought you were asleep," Double J said.

"I ain't sleep. I was just lying here thinking about you," she said. She continued rubbing on his dick.

"Now you know you can't be rubbing on my dick without any lubrication. That shit don't feel good when you do it with dry hands," Double J said.

She got up and squeezed a little Jergens in the palm of her hand as he slipped his boxers off and lay back on the bed. She grabbed his dick firmly, began lathering it up with the lotion, and jagging him off at the same time.

As she thoroughly jagged him off, he pumped her hand until his nut unleashed on her titties, and she began rubbing the nut around on her titties as if it was baby oil or lotion. She then took his dick into her mouth, gobbling it and the lotion in all, swirling her tongue around it and sucking on it as if she was trying to suck some sweet nectar out of it.

Once it got rock hard, she began deep throating it, choking herself with his dick while rubbing on her own clitoris roughly while humming. In no time flat, he was releasing a load of nut down her throat. She stood, wiped her mouth, and slightly began growling. She then got on top of him and played with his dick for a few seconds until it got back hard.

She looked him in his eyes, as she grabbed his dick firmly and shoved it in her pussy, and began smiling. She began riding it slowly to get her pussy totally wet, while he grabbed her ass cheeks, guiding her movements.

Once her pussy got wet, he began slamming his dick in and out of her, enjoying the tightness of her moist pussy. She clawed his chest, moaning in the midst of pleasure and pain; she liked when it hurt.

It felt so good to him that every time he'd slam his dick up in her pussy, it felt like he was actually nutting.

As Double J began to nut, she was cumming simultaneously. As he began to slam his dick in and out her pussy rougher and harder, she began fucking him back. It was like a rodeo show as their orgasms exploded.

"Get up. Get on the bed so I can hit it from the back," Double J said.

She got on all fours on the bed. Double J got on his knees right behind her and began squeezing and rubbing her big brown pretty ass cheeks.

"Tell me you love me before you start fucking me," she said.

"I love your hot ass," he said. Double J then rammed his dick in her hot pussy, gripping her ass cheeks and slamming his dick in and out her pussy hard and fast while admiring the way her ass cheeks bounced. In no time, he was letting another nut explode in her pussy.

"Let me suck it," she said in a low seductive tone.

"Hold on, let me roll up a joint," Double J said.

"You know that I don't like the smell of lace joints. Why you got to lace your weed with cocaine? Why you can't smoke regular weed like everybody else?" she said.

Double J began smiling and looking her straight in the eyes. "Well, I'll smoke a regular joint just for you," Double J said. He rolled up a regular joint with only weed in it, set fire to it as she got on her knees with an aim to please.

As he inhaled and exhaled the potent weed smoke, she simultaneously sucked his dick, utilizing a suction method sucking mainly the tip thoroughly. The potent effect of the weed combined with her superb suction method and the moisture of her mouth felt so good that within seconds he released a glob of nut in her face.

He finished smoking his joint, and both of them lay on the bed. "You must really been wanting to fuck," Double J asked.

"I been thinking about you all day at work. I had to take off work because I creamed in my panties daydreaming about your dick going in and out my pussy and mouth. I been sitting in the house all day waiting on you," she said.

I done married a freak, Double J thought

They began to tell each other how much they loved each other and how their lives wouldn't be the same without each other, before both of them fell into a deep sleep.

The next morning, after Double J's wife had gone to work, Double J and Slim sat at the kitchen table eating breakfast, reminiscing about the stickup and the murders.

They glorified and celebrated the stickup and the murders as if they were professional athletes who just won a championship game or as if they had won the lottery.

It's sad how bloodshed make others glad. But this life some live in as thugs consist of no love. Other people were brought up to increase the peace and strive to earn college degrees, and live the American dream. But those who live the street life thrive on death and destruction. They rob, steal, and kill with no discretion, and glorify others' names who do the same.

"Hurry up and finish eating so we can go holla at Phill," Double J said.

"I'm already finished," Slim said.

"Well, empty the rest of that shit that's on the plate in the garbage and put that plate in the sink," Double J said.

Slim emptied the rest of the food in the garbage, put the plate in the sink, and went and grabbed the book bag.

"Naw, we gone leave the dope and shit here, unless you wanna take your half to your house," Double J said.

"It's cool, I'll leave it here," Slim said.

As they rode up the block in the hood where Phill was, they noticed many of the Insanes on Phill's security as usual.

Once they made it to where Phill was, Phill began smiling, 'cuz he was happy to see them. He needed them to take care of some business for him.

King Phill was a pretty boy. Stood about six feet five, half-Latino, half-black, with naturally curly black hair in his midtwenties. Those who didn't know Phill personally would've never believed that he was a king of a large street gang. King Phill looked like a pretty boy college student.

"Park the car. I need to holla at ya'll," Phill said.

They parked and got out to holla at him.

"I need ya'll to get some steamers for me," Phill said.

"We ain't on no car-thieving shit right now. We need your assistance on some other shit," Double J said.

"What ya'll need?" Phill asked.

"Let's step away from everybody. It's personal," Slim said.

As they stepped away from everybody else, Phill began trying to figure out what Double J and Slim wanted. Maybe they finna ask for some shit, Phill thought.

"Phill, we got some dope we need to get off," Double J said.

"What you talking about?" Phill asked.

"We need to pop it off in the hood," Slim said.

"What ya'll talking about, opening up a dope spot in the hood?" Phill asked.

"That's exactly what we're talking about," Slim said.

"You know ya'll can't work in the hood if ya'll ain't a five-star universal elite," Phill said.

"I told him," Double J said.

"Well, make us universal elites," Slim said.

Phill began laughing. "I don't just give out status like that. I ain't one of these phony-ass niggas that let people buy status. You gotta earn it fucking with me," Phill said.

Slim looked at Phill like he was crazy. "Earn it? All the shit we do for you and for the hood while them niggas you made universal elites be in the Bahamas some-motherfucking-where! We be doing all the shootings for the hood and all type of other shit for you and the hood," Slim said.

"Yeah, you do got a point, 'cuz ya'll do stand on nation business. This what I'm going to do for ya'll. I'ma let ya'll work in the hood under my name, but ya'll gotta pay," Phill said.

"How much we gotta pay?" Slim asked.

"That depends on how much dope ya'll got," Phill said.

"We got ten grams," Double J said. He was lying.

"Ten grams? That ain't shit. Ya'll work them ten grams for two or three weeks outta Argale park. In two or three weeks, ya'll should've at least doubled or tripled them ten grams. Once ya'll do, ya'll gotta give me a stack every week," Phill said.

Double J and Slim looked at each other smiling, knowing it was finna be on.

"A stack a week. We got you. We'll holla at you. I gotta go pick my girl up from work." Double J said. He was lying.

As Double J and Slim got into the car and rode off, listening to Al Green's "Love and Happiness." They were happier than a kid on Christmas Day.

Chapter 2

Three Days Later

"How much is that small black digital scale?" Double J asked the cashier.

"That one right there is a hundred dollars. But I'd recommend this white one right here if you're going to be weighing things over twenty-eight grams. A lot of customers usually buy that small black one, then later on down the line, the same customers come back and buy a bigger one, which is a waste of money to me," the woman cashier said.

"How much do the white one cost?" Slim asked.

"Two hundred," the cashier said.

"We'll take it," Slim said.

"Will that be it?" the cashier asked.

"Naw, we need five bottles of Dormin and a bundle of them little black baggies right there and two of them mac spoons," Slim said.

As other customers walked into the small record store, the cashier paused and began covering up the small area where contraband was being sold.

"Thomas, can you service the new customers?" the female cashier said to her coworker.

"Wait 'til these customers leave, then I'll give ya'll, ya'll items," the female cashier said to Double J and Slim.

"Ya'll sell scales, baggies, and all type of shit to everybody in the city, and now you wanna act like it's top secret," Slim said.

"Yeah, we do supply a lot of people with contraband, but those are only the people that come in here asking for it. We can't have contraband on display, because it's all types of people that come in here. A person might come in here with their kids. Or an off-duty police officer might come in here to buy some records. And if they see all this contraband on display, they'll report our ass to the city. We won't lose our store or anything like that, but we'll have to pay a healthy fine," the cashier said.

Within minutes, the other customers purchased their records and left the store.

"Your total will come out to three hundred seventy-five dollars," she said.

Slim paid her, and they left the store.

Once they made it to Double J's crib, they immediately weighed the dope for the first time.

"Damn, Lord, we got a hundred grams! I thought it'll be about fifty grams," Slim said.

"Yeah, me too," Double J said.

"Aw, we finna put up numbers if this shit is a bomb," Slim said.

"Showl is," Double J said.

"Why did you buy baggies instead of aluminum foil?" Double J asked.

"'Cuz we gone put the dope in the baggies. We don't need no aluminum foil," Slim said.

"But we need to put it in the aluminum foil so it can stay fresh," Double J said.

"Once we put it in the baggies then put some thick clear tape on the baggies, the dope will stay fresh," Slim said.

"We need to find us a connect on some quinine," Double J said.

"Naw, we ain't gone put no quinine or none of that other crazy shit on the dope. We either gone use dorms or sell it with no mix on it at all. We gone put three pills on each gram of dope," Slim said.

"How many grams we gone bag up the first time?" Double J asked.

"We gone bag up ten grams first and put it out there and see what it do. You know we can't bag up to much, 'cuz if it don't sell quick enough, it'll fall off," Slim said.

"That's my point exactly. That's why I ask," Double J said.

Double J weighed out ten grams on the scale. Then Double J and Slim opened up thirty dorms, which were actually capsules. Double J and Slim then grabbed two playing cards apiece and began mixing the dope with the dorms.

"How many mac spoons we gone use?" Double J asked.

"We gone give up two macs for a sawbuck and see how that go first. If the dope is a bomb, we gone drop down to one mac spoon or a mac and a half. That all depends on how good the dope is. And if it's real good, we gone put more dorms in it," Slim said.

Double J and Slim grabbed a mac spoon apiece and began measuring the dope and putting it in the bags.

"I got some thick clear tape in my room, in the closet," Double J said.

"Wait 'til we get finished before you go get it," Slim said.

After about an hour and a half, they'd finally finished bagging up the dope.

"Let's count it up to see how much we bagged up," Double J said.

"We gone put twelve blows in a pack. Whoever sells the pack gets twenty dollars and turns us in a hundred," Slim said.

"How much we gone pay people to run the joint?" Double J asked.

"We ain't worried about that right now. We gone run the joint ourselves. Once it picks up, then we'll put people in play to run the joint. We'll worry about what we gone pay them when that time comes," Slim said.

As they sat at the table counting up the dope, Slim began to wonder who they were going get to work the packs.

"Shiiit, who we gone get to work the joint?" Slim asked.

"My lil cousins gone work the joint. They been sweating me for the last couple days about when we gone open up the joint so they can work. They juveniles, so if they catch a case, they mommas can just sign them out from the police station," Double J said.

Once they finished counting the dope up, it came out to twenty packs and seven odds. They bagged up $2,070, not including the two blows in each pack for the pack workers to get paid.

Slim began doing the mathematics in his head. "So if we got two stacks off ten grams, then we gone get at least twenty stacks off of the whole hundred grams," Slim said.

"Shiit, we gone get more than that if the dope is a bomb and if it can take more than three pills a gram," Double J said.

"Yep, showl is. Go grab the tape outta the closet," Slim said. When he came back with the tape, Slim examined it. "Yeah, Joe, this tape perfect," Slim said.

They put twelve bags on a strip of tape then put another strip of tape over the bags. They put the tape over the bags in order for the dope to stay fresh, and so none of the workers wouldn't dip into the bags.

Double J and Slim grabbed the dope and a .45 automatic and went to pick up Double J's cousins and set up shop in Argale Park. They posted up at the corners and in the park. One of Double J's cousins walked through the hood, telling all the dope fiends that they were passing out free dope in Argale Park. They dope fiends rushed to the park and spread the word. Two niggas who stood in the park, Double J's cousins, were passing out the samples to the dope fiends. A couple of hours later, the park was filled with dope fiends shopping for dope.

Double J and Slim couldn't believe how fast and how many dope fiends were coming to buy dope. Judging by the large amount of dope fiends who were coming to buy dope so soon, Double J and Slim knew they had some good dope.

"Damn, Lord, look how many dope fiends waiting in line to shop," Slim said.

"That's 'cuz the dope fiends that we gave samples to went and told everybody that we got good dope. Word of mouth travels," Double J said.

Within two days and one night, Double J and Slim sold the whole hundred grams.

"Lord, who we gone buy some more dope from?" Slim asked.

"That's a good question," Double J said.

As they continued to smoke and ride through the hood, they remained silent, trying to figure out who they'd start buying weight on the dope from.

"We gone have to start buying from Phill," Double J said.

"Phill got good dope, but it ain't a bomb," Slim said.

"How you know? You don't even use dope," Double J said.

"I can tell from the numbers his dope spots put up. His spots put up little numbers, but they ain't all that," Slim said.

"Who else we gone buy dope from? We gone have to get it from Phill," Double J said.

"Ride through Lexington and see if he out there," Slim said.

As they made it to Lexington, they saw Phill standing on the corner with a gang of niggas standing around him for his security.

"A Phill, check it out, Lord," Slim said.

Phill walked toward them smiling.

"Where's my money at?" Phill said.

"What money?" Slim asked.

"My g, what else? Money. I heard ya'll been tipping outta the park," Phill said.

"We'll get the money we owe you a little later on," Slim said.

"It ain't even been a whole week," Double J said.

"So what? I want my money ya'll been tipping," Phill said.

"A'ight we got you," Double J said.

"How much you'll sell us twenty-five grams of dope for?" Slim asked.

"Three thousand," Phill said.

"That's kinda high, ain't it?" Double J said.

"Naw, that's low. Anybody else I charge one fifty a gram. I'm only charging ya'll like one twenty-five a gram. At one twenty-five a gram, twenty-five grams suppose to come out to thirty-one twenty-five, but I just said an even three stacks. I ain't tripping over a hundred and twenty-five dollars. Look, right, I got shit I gotta do. Is ya'll gone need that twenty-five grams or not?" Phill asked.

"Yeah, we need it now," Double J said.

"I can't get it for ya'll right now, but I'll have somebody get it for ya'll later," Phill said.

"We gone have the g we owe you when you sell us the twenty-five grams, so we'll bring the whole four thousand with us," Slim said.

"I gotta go. I'll holla at ya'll later on," Phill said.

"Make sure we get them twenty-five grams today. Our joint is outta work," Slim said.

"I got ya'll. Don't worry about it," Phill said.

"A'ight, we'll holla at you," Slim said.

Later on that day, they were sitting in Double J's crib, chilling, when they got a call from Phill telling them that he was going to send his guy John over with the twenty-five grams, and that they needed to make sure the four stacks was counted up right before they gave it to John.

Once John delivered the twenty-five grams, they went straight to Double J's kitchen table and started bagging up.

"How many pills we gone use?" Double J asked.

"We gone use three first, to see how the dope fiends like it with three in it," Slim said.

Both of them began opening up the seventy-five capsules and dumping the inside of the dorms on the table, on top of the twenty-five grams.

"Lord, if this dope is any good, we finna be getting money like never before. Fuck spending our money. We need to stack our shit and get into some real estate, then we can leave the dope game alone," Slim said.

"Yeah, I agree with you on that. You know all these other niggas be spending their shit, then when it comes time for bound money, they can't even bound out for ten or fifteen stacks," Double J said.

As they continued mixing up the dope, they both imagined of riches.

They next day, they put the dope on their joint, and to their surprise, the dope fiends loved it.

They finished that twenty-five grams in one day, and was right back at Phill's buying fifty grams this time. Phill was a player who liked to see niggas doing good getting money, so he sold them fifty grams for fifty-five hundred.

Once they put that fifty grams out, their they thought it would slow down some because the dope fiends would know from the last twenty-five grams that they ain't selling the same dope they had originally when they first opened up.

Double J and Slim sat back at the end of the park, admiring the view of the customers swarming to buy dope. It was as if every time the pack worker would bring out a new pack, the dope fiends would swarm on him like flies to shit.

"How the hell is our joint tipping like this with Phill's dope, and his joint ain't putting up numbers like ours?" Double J asked.

"That 'cuz Phill and a lot of these other niggas be putting that crazy shit on they dope. That's why I told you we ain't gone use nothing but dorms. Phill nam still checking a bag, but their turnover rate is slower," Slim said.

Within a month, Double J and Slim were the men. Their joint was putting up numbers. They bought new Cadillacs, new sports cars, and all. Their team of workers constantly grew. Hos coming from everywhere were trying to get with them. Throughout it all, they continued to buy dope from Phill.

Chapter 3

One hot sunny day, Double J was simply bending blocks in the hood, listening to Al Green, puffing on joints that weren't laced with cocaine when he saw her from the back in those jeans.

Damn, this ho thick as hell, Double J thought.

He pulled up to her. Once he saw her face, he became disappointed. Aw, this Cynthia dope fiend ass, he thought.

Cynthia immediately opened the passenger-side door and just jumped in his car.

"Take me to your spot to get some dope," she said.

"I got a few bags in my pocket," Double J said.

"What are you doing, riding around with dope in your pocket?" Cynthia asked.

"What else am I doing with dope in my pocket?" Double J said sarcastically.

"I didn't know you shoot dope," Cynthia said.

"Tell somebody, and I'll kill you," Double J said.

They drove to a quiet block on the outskirts of the hood, pulled over, and parked.

Double J gave Cynthia the dope to hook it up and put in the needle.

Once she hooked the dope up and put it in the needle, she tried handing the needle to Double J.

"Naw, you go ahead. Ladies first," Double J said.

With her right hand, she shot dope into the veins of her left arm. As her eyes rolled in the back of her head, her entire body felt as if it were taken to a whole other planet. Afterward, she passed the needle to Double J.

With his right hand, he shot dope into the veins of his left arm. As Barry White's song "I'm Never Gone Leave Your Love" played on the radio, Double J felt as if he was soaring above the clouds.

Afterward, Double J dropped Cynthia off at home and went and met Slim at his crib to shake up some dope.

"I bought a hundred grams instead of fifty," Slim said.

"That's cool," Double J said.

"Start busting the dorms down. I gotta go use the bathroom. My stomach fucked up from smoking all them lace joints," Slim said.

Slim came out the bathroom and saw Double J sitting at the table, nodding and scratching.

"Damn, nigga, you look like you done had a dope," Slim said.

"Naw, man, I'm just sleepy," Double J said.

So they both began busting the dorms down.

Double J kept scratching and nodding at the table.

This nigga fucking around with dope, Slim thought.

"Lord, tell the truth. Ain't you getting high?" Slim asked.

"Nigga, you know damn well I been getting high ever since you've known me," Double J said.

"Nigga, you know what I'm talking about. Is you fucking with dope?" Slim said.

Double J paused for a little while. "Yeah, I fuck around with the dope a little," Double J said.

"What made you turn into a dope fiend?" Slim asked.

"I use to be seeing how dope fiends look after they get high. Some of them looked like it's the best feeling in the world. Some of them be looking like they're walking on the clouds or some shit. Then I start to see how the dope fiends do whatever it takes to get money for dope. That made me want to try some even more, 'cuz I knew it had to be some good shit. Once I tried it, it felt like heaven on Earth. No lie, I'ma be a dope fiend forever. I'ma get high 'til I die," Double J said.

Slim looked at Double J with a smirk on his face, thinking, This nigga done lost his mind.

189

"Niggas always trying to belittle dope fiends, when they get high they motherfucking self off all types of shit. A drug addict is a drug addict. It don't matter if you smoke weed, lace weed, toot cocaine, toot dope, or shoot dope—you still a drug addict," Double J said.

"I can agree with you on that 'cuz I smoke more lace joints than some people use dope," Slim said.

"We gone have to start paying somebody to bag up this dope. This shit a headache," Slim said.

"Straight up," Double J said.

In the days that followed, Slim began to admire how suave Double J was as he was high off dope. As he walked, talked, drove, ate, smoked cigarettes, every way he maneuvered was super cool when he was drunk off dope.

Before long, Slim began asking Double J a gang of questions on how it felt to be high off dope.

"You steady asking me about how it feels to be high off dope. My best answer is you won't know how it feels until you try it," Double J said.

"I'm scared of needles," Slim said.

"You ain't gotta shot it. You can toot it. But it ain't nothing look shooting it. As that dope run up your veins, it's the best high you'll ever experience," Double J said.

Slim was still hesitant to try dope. He let his pride get in the way. He knew certain people looked down on dope fiends.

A couple of days later at a club, with these two lesbian chicks he dated and paid for sex, he began wanting to try some dope again. The lesbian chicks Tricey and Reese did it all besides dope. They snorted lines of cocaine, smoked lace joints and regular weed, and smoked leaf.

After downing a few drinks at the club. The girls sat at the table, snorting line after line of cocaine secretly, not in the public's eye.

"Damn, ya'll gone fuck around and OD," Slim said.

"That's only if you use dope. You ain't gonna find to many people OD'ing off cocaine, although you can OD off cocaine," Reese said.

"Have ya'll ever fucked around with dope before?" Slim asked.

"Hell naw, we ain't no motherfucking dope fiends," Tricey said.

"Shiiit, ya'll get high off everything else," Slim said.

"Everything besides dope," Tricey said.

"I heard that dope is the best high known to mankind," Slim said.

"Yeah, me too. But it takes control over your body. You gotta have it or your body won't be able to function right. And I heard the sickness is a motherfucker," Tricey said.

"I wanna snort a line or two to see how it feels," Slim said.

"So you wanna be a dope fiend?" Reese said sarcastically.

"Naw, I just wanna snort just one bag of dope to see how it feels. I want ya'll to snort it with me," Slim said.

"Hell naw," Reese said.

"Let's all three of us try it together," Slim said.

For almost an hour at the club, Slim tried convincing the girls to snort a bag of dope with him, and it worked. Slim pulled up to his dope spot.

"Tyrone, who working, Lord?" Slim asked.

"Ush working," Tyrone said.

"Why don't I see nobody shopping?" Slim asked.

"It's kinda slow right now, but you can best believe it'll be a gang of customers in line in no time," Tyrone said.

"Go get me three bags of dope, and hurry up, Lord," Slim said.

Tyrone rushed to go get three bags from Ush and brought it right back to the car. Slim took the dope and smashed off.

Slim parked a few blocks over from his joint. He tore open a bag of dope with his teeth and laid it on one of the girls' cigarette box. He tore a piece of the paper off his matchbox. He scooped up half the dope and snorted it like a pro. He sat the Newport box on the dash and leaned back in his seat to feel the total effect of the dope.

Within seconds, Slim had his door opened as he bent over, throwing up his guts.

If that shit gone have me throwing up like that, I don't even want none, Tricey thought.

After Slim finished throwing up, he snorted the other half of the dope off of the Newport box. He lay back in his seat and relaxed for minutes and began to feel the effect of being drunk off dope. The girls then snorted their bags.

As they lay there, high, they all thought within their own silent minds that dope was the best drug known to man.

Slim and both women wound up in a motel room. Slim's dick stayed on hard all the while. Slim had heard of the dope dick but didn't know that it was this intense.

For the entire week that followed, Slim snorted dope and smoked laced joints each day.

One morning as Slim went home, he got into it with his main girlfriend. She was tired of him spending nights out and cheating on her. She threw some hot coffee on him and swung at him a few times, leaving him with a few minor scars on his face. Slim stormed out the house and went to his joint.

Slim pulled on the joint, got two bags of dope, and pulled around the corner to blow them. He pulled back around to his joint sat on the hood of his car smoking a lace joint, thinking of all the good times, and the bad times he had, had with his girlfriend. He was still a little pissed off 'cuz she put her hands on him.

Double J pulled off, laughing.

"So I see you having problems with your girl," Double J said.

"How you know?" Slim asked.

"'Cuz I see you sitting there, faced all scratched up, looking crazy. I know you ain't let no nigga do it to you, because we'll be in war right now," Double J said.

Slim tossed the duck of the joint on the ground, bailed in with Double J, and Double J pulled off.

"Man this ho crazy. As soon as I walked through the door, she got to throwing shit, hollering, screaming, and swinging," Slim said.

"We all go through problems with women. That's been going on since the beginning of time," Double J said.

"Pull over for a minute. I need to take care of some business," Slim said.

Double J pulled over and put the car in park.

"What, you gotta piss or something?" Double J asked.

"Naw, I need to take care of something else," Slim said.

Slim pulled out his pack of cigarettes, then pulled out a bag of dope, opened it with his teeth, and poured it on the cigarette box. Double J remained silent. He couldn't believe what he was seeing. Slim then pulled out a small piece of a straw and snorted the entire bag of dope. Double J just sat there, looking at him like he was crazy.

Slim fired up a cigarette, looked at Double J, and asked, "Is my nose clean?"

"Yes, it's clean," Double J said.

"I can't believe you sat there and snorted a bag of dope after you been getting down on me after you found out I was getting high," Double J said.

"I been seeing how good you been looking when you high off dope. It be like you be walking on clouds or some shit, and I wanted that feeling. So I tried it, and I love it," Slim said.

"I told you it was a bomb, especially if you shoot it," Double J said.

Double J began smiling and pulled off, listening to Barry White's song "Ecstasy" as they drove to the mall.

Once they made it inside the mall, Slim became so happy at seeing all the hos there that he forgot all about what he and his girl had gone through earlier.

Slim wound up getting a gang of numbers from ho's.

When they entered this one shoe store, Slim couldn't take his eyes off this white chick. She was raw as hell. She was about five feet six, 140 pounds, a redhead, with black eyeliner around her hazel blue eyes, and red lipstick. She looked like a model or some shit. Slim decided to walk over and strike up a conversation with her.

Slim came to find out that her name was Angie. She lived on the north side of town. Twenty years of age with no boyfriend, no kids, or none of that. They exchanged numbers and went their separate ways.

All the rest of the day, Slim couldn't stop thinking of Angie. She just looked so good to him.

Slim went home that night and made up with his girl, and they got down from break-up to make-up sex.

Slim had never been with a white woman before but always wanted one. The next day, Slim wound up giving Angie a call. He thought she was gonna be on some phony shit, but he was wrong. She was real cool.

Slim and Angie starting hanging out together damn near every day. One of the things Slim liked about Angie was that she genuinely liked him for him. She wasn't like the other women that he'd fucked around with. They were only interested in money one way or the other. Angie wasn't.

Within a couple months, Slim left his main girl for Angie and moved in with her.

Within several months, Double J and Slim found their dope habits increasing. Having to spend more money to support their habits, for guns, for money on bonding their guys outta jail, and for having to pay more bills. This fortune and fame wasn't all what it seemed.

Chapter 4

"Roxanne you need a ride?" Slim asked.

"Naw, no, thank you. Here come my bus now," Roxanne said.

"Girl, get in. You ain't gotta wait on no bus," Slim said.

"No, it's okay. Thanks anyway," Roxanne said.

"Get in I insist," Slim said.

She wound up getting in. She looked around inside his Cadillac and noticed that it was super clean. The upholstery looked as if it was brand-new from the manufacturing place.

He put on some Teddy Pendergrass, "Turn off The Lights," as he pulled off. She immediately made herself comfortable.

"Where do you need me to take you to?" Slim asked.

"I need you to drop me off at the Cook County hospital," she said.

"What's wrong with you?" he asked.

"Ain't nothing wrong with me. I'm going to see my friend. She just had a baby," she said.

"Do you have any kids?" he asked.

"I don't have no kids, nor a boyfriend," she said.

Roxanne was one of Slim's grammar school friends that he'd only see every once in a while. On the rest of the short ride there, they began to reminisce about grammar school. They both admitted that they had been liking each other since grammar school.

As he pulled up in front of the hospital, he tried to park.

"Naw, you ain't gotta park. Just let me out in the front," she said.

"You need me to come back and pick you up when you get finished seeing your friend?" he asked.

"Naw, I'm straight," she said.

"What's up with later on? Let's go somewhere and fuck," Slim said as they both began laughing. "Naw, I'm just joking about fucking, but serious, let's get together and kick it later on," he said.

She reached into her purse and pulled out a little card with her phone number on it and handed it to him. "Well, here go my number just call me later on tonight," she said.

As she walked into the hospital, Slim just sat there, watching her in a daze, imagining what she'd look like naked.

Later on that day, Slim called her. The phone rang seven times. He didn't get any answer. He called her three more times, periodically, but still didn't get any answer. After calling her for the fifth time, he finally got an answer.

"Hello," she said.

"Hello, can I speak to Roxanne?" Slim said.

"Yes, this is me," she said.

"This Slim. Let me come through and pick you up," he said.

"Why you wait so late?" she asked.

"I been calling you all day. Ain't nobody answer the phone," he said.

"I been running errands for my granny. I been in and out the house all day. You got bad timing, you must been calling the times when I was out. Fuck it, come on over and pick me up. We'll kick it for a little while," she said.

He went over and picked her up. They rode around seeing the sights and reminiscing for about thirty minutes. Then he took her back home.

In the days that followed, he began sneaking off from Angie to hang with Roxanne almost every day for about two weeks straight. Each time they were together, she refused to give the pussy up.

One night, Slim was drunk off dope and liquor and had been smoking lace joints. He had his mind set on fucking the shit outta Roxanne this particular night. He went to her house unannounced. She got dressed and decided to kick it with him anyway. As she entered his car, she smelled the smoke from lace joints.

"Why do you gotta smoke that stuff?" she asked.

"'Cuz it makes me feel good. You need to try it," he said.

"Never that. I'll never use drugs. I don't need drugs to make me feel good. I get high off life," she said.

"Getting high off life. I liked that. That sounded slick," he said.

As they cruised down the street, listening to Al Green's "Let's Stay Together," both of them became relaxed. She began slowly taking off her shoes to get comfortable. Outta the corner of his eyes, he looked at her, admiring her beauty.

"Let's go somewhere and chill out," he said.

"We already chilling out," she said.

"Naw, let's get a room or something," he said.

"Hell naw, we ain't getting no room or none of that until you get rid of her and let me become your main girl," she said.

"Who is her?" he asked.

"You know who she is. The woman that you go home to every night when you drop me off. The one you share your love and life with, the one you live with," she said.

He paused, trying to think of some good game to pop back at her but couldn't because he knew she was speaking the truth.

"But I been with her for a long time now and I just can't up and leave her," he said.

"Well, whenever you do decide to leave her, I'm willing to fill in her position and take on all responsibilities. And when I say all responsibilities, that's exactly what I mean," she said as she looked him in his eyes seductively.

As he cruised the streets, they peacefully listened to Al Green as thoughts of her in pornographic positions raced through his mind. He'd visualize his dick in and out her pussy, ass, and mouth.

He pulled up at a liquor store and parked. "Do you want me to get you something to drink?" he asked.

"A pink lemonade," she said.

As he exited the car, thoughts of him and herself walking down the aisle and getting married raced through her mind. She really liked him, but the only way he was going to get between her legs was if she was his main girl and only girl.

He came back into the car with two bottles of champagne, two cups, the pink lemonade, and a few bags of chips. He instantly popped open a bottle and poured some champagne in a cup. He handed her the other cup.

"Naw, I'm straight. You know I don't drink," she said.

"Try it out just for tonight. Just for me?" he asked.

"Thanks, but no thanks. I don't drink," she said.

She grabbed the pink lemonade, opened it, and began sipping on it like it was the best lemonade she ever had as they pulled off and began cruising through the town.

Roxanne reached into her purse and pulled out a pickle. She took the pickle out of its wrapper and began sucking on it like it was a dick. For a long time, she pulled the pickle in and out her mouth, sucking on it like she was trying to suck out all the juices from it.

Her reasoning for sucking on the pickle like that was to tease and entice him to wanna be with her and only her.

After cruising for a little, while Slim pulled into this vacant lot right next to this body shop where he use to get his cars spray painted at. The shop was closed because it was so late at night. As they began listening to Stevie Wonder's "Ribbon in the Sky" they started reminiscing about past times and began talking about things they'd like to do in the future. Slim began to roll a joint.

"Uhhhh, you ain't finna smoke that while I'm in here," she boldly said.

"Don't worry. I ain't gone lace it," he said.

"It don't matter if you lace it or not. You ain't finna smoke that while I'm in here," she said.

"I'ma crack the window," he said.

"You gone have my clothes smelling like weed," she said.

"I told you, I'ma crack the window," he said.

"Fuck it. Gone head," she said.

He finished rolling up the joint and set fire to it. He inhaled and exhaled the smoke harshly, which instantly boosted his dope high.

This shit a bomb, he thought.

He began to try to convince her for sex. She still wasn't interested. After he finished the joint, he downed a half bottle of champagne. As he was downing the champagne, he visualized her and him fucking and sucking each other. He began rubbing on her titties.

"Stop, boy! Don't put you hands on my titties. I ain't no ho. I don't get down like that," she said.

He then grabbed her left titty.

She snatched his hand away from her titties. "Drop me off! Drop me off!" she said.

In a frustrated, sex-craving rage, he locked his car doors and ripped off her shirt as she began yelling, kicking, and screaming.

He upped a .38 outta his jacket pocket and told her, "Bitch, shut the fuck up."

She immediately shut the fuck up.

Tears began to roll down her face as he snatched off the rest of her clothes then her panties in a storming rage. Craving for her pussy, he forced her to bend over the front seat and swiftly unbutton his pants and pull them down to his knees. He tried to force-feed her pussy his dick, but it didn't work because her pussy was too tight. His dick was too big to get in.

She continued silently crying and pleading inside her heart and mind for him to stop, but he didn't.

With the gun in his left hand, he spat in his right hand and rubbed it on the tip of his dick for lubrication. He worked on getting his dick in her pussy. After a minute, the tip of his dick finally slipped in. As he slowly worked his dick in and out her pussy to get it wet, he began thinking, Damn, this ho pussy tight as hell. Once her inner juices began flowing within, he commenced to slamming his dick in and out her pussy in a furious rage as she continued crying. To him it seemed as if every stroke, her pussy got wetter and wetter.

After the eighth pump, he put the gun in his jacket pocket and squeezed her waist, stopped pumping, and held his dick in her pussy until his entire nut was released in her guts. He took his dick out, grabbed her by the shoulders, and turned her body around to face him.

"Please, please, please stop," she cried out to him.

He backhanded her with his left hand.

"Shut up, bitch," he said.

She did exactly what he said. He pulled the gun back outta his jacket and put it to her head.

"Bitch, suck this dick," he said.

"Please, please, don't do this," she cried out.

"Bitch, suck this dick before I kill you," he said.

She began crying even harder and pouting like a little kid as her life flashed before her eyes. She wrapped her lips around his dick. She began to suck his dick like never before. The wetness of her mouth combined with her deep throat and his high made it feel so good that he instantly unleashed a glob of nut down her throat as she swallowed it all.

"Bitch, get in the backseat," he said.

"Please, please let me leave," she cried out.

He slapped her, busting her bottom lip.

She jumped into the backseat, frightened of what he'd do if she didn't do what he told her to do. She got on the backseat facedown, crying, lying flat on her stomach as he began raping her in the ass. She'd never felt so much pain in her life.

He never felt so much pleasure in his life. As he began nutting, he visualized the skies filled with fireworks similar to the Fourth of July.

He pushed her outta the car and threw her clothes on top of her. He smashed off, listening to "I'm Never Gone Leave Your Love" by Barry White.

At that very moment, Slim felt as if he ruled the world. He loved the power he achieved from raping her.

As Roxanne sat in the lot, scared to death and putting on her clothes, a car drove past slowly. There were two individuals in the car, an old lady and her daughter coming from church.

"Mom, it's a lady in that lot, naked," the little girl said.

"Hush up now. It ain't nobody in no lot, naked," the old lady said.

"It is, it is! We need to go back and help her," the little girl said.

Her mother looked at her, saw the sincerity in her words, and pulled over.

"Girl, if you have me to go back and it's not a naked woman there, Lord knows what I'ma do to you when we get home," the old lady said.

She made a U-turn and went back to see if there really was a naked woman. As she pulled up to the lot, Roxanne ran to her car with no shoes or shirt on—nothing but her skirt, with her hands over her titties—crying, "Please help me. Please help me." She jumped into the backseat of the four-door car.

"Oh my god, what happened to you?" the old lady said historically.

"He raped me!" Roxanne cried out in a loud voice.

The old lady immediately drove off. She and her daughter were in shock. They'd never experienced being in a situation like that before.

Nervous, scared, unfocused, and not being able to drive right, the old lady told Roxanne, "We gotta get you some clothes and take you to the hospital and report this to the police."

"No, no police," Roxanne said with authority.

Roxanne didn't wanna get the police involved 'cuz she knew Slim was a ViceLord, and she knew what ViceLords would do to her if they found out she told the police on one of their members.

"Please just take me home," Roxanne said frantically.

"You sure you don't want me to take you to my home and get you cleaned up first?" the old lady asked.

"Naw, please just take me home," Roxanne said.

"Where do you live?" the old lady asked.

Roxanne gave her her address.

The rest of the ride, all three of their minds were filled with sick satanic thoughts as each individual remained silent.

Once the old lady pulled up in front of Roxanne's house, she looked at her, feeling sorry and sad for her. "You sure you'll be okay?" the old lady asked.

"I'm going to be all right," Roxanne said with tears running down her face.

Roxanne got out the car with her hands over her breasts, running to her doorstep. She rang the doorbell twice, then her grandmother let her in as she fell to floor crying out, "He raped me!"

The old lady and her daughter rode home, crying and mentally thanking God that they'd never been attacked or raped before.

Roxanne's grandmother and the rest of the family pleaded with her to tell the cops, but she never did. Roxanne didn't want to jeopardize the safety of herself and her family. A couple of days later, Roxanne's family sent her to live in Atlanta with her aunt Rachel.

A few days later, Phill pulled up to Slim and Double J's joint, parked in the middle of the street, and bailed outta the car.

"You's a stupid motherfucker. You done went and raped that girl. Do you know how much time rapes carry? Nigga, ain't no ViceLord gotta rape no hos. Shiit, we got hos throwing us the pussy," Phill said as he ran back to his car and smashed off, burning rubber.

Double J looked at Slim with a frown on his face, with curiosity running through his head.

"Man, what the fuck is Phill talking about?" Double J asked.

"I don't know what that nigga tripping about," Slim said.

"What the fuck he talking about somebody got raped?" Double J said.

"I told you, I don't know what the fuck that nigga talking about," Slim said.

Later on that day, Phill came through and politely closed Double J and Slim down. He took their joint and gave it to one of the universal elites. Phill was tired of Double J and Slim's bullshit. They weren't paying him his g a week. They were leaving their workers in jail, weren't bonding them out. Nor were they standing on nation business. Then this nigga Slim went and raped a ho.

Phill found out about the rape through Roxanne's little cousins who were Renegade ViceLords. Roxanne's cousins were shorties. They weren't experienced in gunslinging yet, so they hollered at Phill to see if Phill would violate Slim. Phill lied and told them he'd violate them if they made sure she didn't press charges. Roxanne never pressed charges.

Now Slim and Double J didn't have a joint to sell their dope from. Slim was mad at Double J for the money he fucked up in the past. Double J was mad at Slim for committing that rape. Both of them were mad at Phill for taking their joint. Slim and Double J didn't talk to each other for almost a week.

Slim ended up going over Double J's crib to get back some of his belongings. Double J and Slim ended up making back up. They went to this dope spot on the low end that was supposed to have some good dope.

For the first time in life, Slim shot dope into his veins. The rush felt better than sex, snorting dope, smoking lace joints, or any other thing he'd experienced in life. From that day forth, Slim felt the true meaning of "High 'til I die," because Slim knew he'd forever be a dope fiend.

Chapter 5

Months later, January 1972

Slim and Double J had become straight up dope fiends. The majority of their cars was confiscated by the repo man. All their jewelry, leathers, and almost everything else they owned were either sold or pawned.

They had been accustomed to making fast money and spending it fast. They had an expensive cost of living. But by them steadily spending fast and not making it fast anymore, the money they did possess started to become extinct.

They had resorted to doing whatever it took to get high. They was on some straight dope fiend shit.

Slim had begun doing a little pimping to get money to buy dope. Double J was against soliciting women. Although Double J was true dope fiend, he still respected women.

One night, Double J and Slim had finished doing some petty hustling. Double J decided to spend a night at Slim's crib. Double J usually didn't spend nights out—he'd go home to his wife each night—but not this night.

The next morning, Double J woke up outta his sleep as the sun shone on his face.

Double J went into the bathroom to take a piss and then went to Slim's room with one thing on his mind: getting some dope. As he walked to Slim's bedroom, he noticed that the bedroom door was partially opened.

He didn't want to knock just in case they were asleep. So he looked in to see if they were awake, and yes, they were wide awake.

To Double J's surprise, there were Slim; Slim's white chick, Angie; and two black women, Reese and Tricey.

There Slim stood with his shirt off, face and head looking like he ain't shaved in years, nodding and shooting dope into his veins.

The three women were on the bed, doing the nasty. Angie was on all fours while Reese tortured her pussy from the back with this big black strap-on dildo as Tricey was on her knees holding Angie's head to her pussy. It was as if she was forcing her to eat her pussy.

"Bitch, stop acting like you ain't up with it and perform for the customers," Slim said.

Slim had turned innocent Angie into a drug fiend and a prostitute.

Double J burst into the room.

"Lord, what the fuck is you on? You done turned your main girl into a ho," Double J said.

"She's my bottom bitch," Slim said.

"But that damn girl is four months pregnant and you got her selling pussy to other women," Double J said.

The three ladies kept doing what they were doing as if Slim or Double J wasn't even there.

"Nigga, do you want to fuck her?" Slim asked.

"Naw, man! You know I'm married, but let me get some of that dope," Double J said.

Slim gave Double J the needle. As he watched the girls sexing, he shot dope into his veins.

Chapter 6

Slim started robbing solo. Sometimes Slim would stick people up by himself 'cuz he didn't want to share the profit with Double J or anybody else.

Slim was from the west side, so he'd go to the south side and rob 'cuz nobody really knew him out south. Late at night, he'd catch women walking by themselves on streets where there wasn't very much traffic and rob them for everything.

One time, he robbed this young Mexican lady who didn't speak very much English on a dark street at the back of a high school. After robbing her, she began cursing him out in Spanish. He didn't speak any Spanish but he could tell that she was saying some foul shit 'cuz of her body language.

In rage, he forced her into his car at gunpoint and pulled her into the nearest alley. He began punching her in her face like they were in a heavyweight professional boxers' match until she was knocked unconscious. He undressed her slowly with ease as if she were his actual girlfriend and as if he was getting ready for lovemaking.

Once undressed, while she was sprawled out over the front seats unconscious, he paused for a second, checking out her flawless body, which made his dick get hard as a brick. Violently, sexually crazed, with a frustrated, erotic craving, he took the pussy.

After nutting in the pussy, he turned her over and took her booty. Afterward, he dressed her and easily laid her in the alley, behind a big garbage can.

Six o'clock the next morning, she awoke from the barking of dogs. Slowly she stood up, feeling the pain of her battered face and the tissues in her pussy and ass that were torn. As she slowly began limping up the alley, she saw this man pulling out his garage. He was a police officer on his way to work.

She flagged him down, and after seeing her bloody face, he immediately put the car in park, got out and helped her get into the passenger seat of his car. Once she was in, he showed her his badge. She let out a great sigh of relief.

He then drove her to the county hospital to be examined by a doctor. On the way there, she told him the horrifying story about what had happened to her last night. Well, at least the part she'd remember before actually going unconscious. The officer was so pissed off that he said if he ever caught the individual who did that to her, the criminal wouldn't have to worry about going to jail. He'd probably shoot and kill the guy on sight.

The doctor's examination showed that she'd been beaten and raped in her vagina and anus. The doctor gave her twelve stitches in three different parts of her face.

The officer then took her to the police station to file a report. Once they made it within the police station, all the other officers stared at her in silence. The officer wound up filing a police report and taking pictures of her bruises.

She told the truth in the report. The report stated that she'd been robbed, abducted into a red Chevy Impala, taken into an alley, beaten unconscious, and left within that alley. All these things were done by a masked gunman.

Slim wasn't a dummy. The same night, he burned up that red Chevy Impala. He didn't give a fuck about that car. It was stolen steamer.

After that night, over the course of a month, Slim had committed four more rapes—three masked and one unmasked. So now the authorities had a sketch of what he looked like. But a sketch wasn't the same as an actual picture. As a matter of fact, the individual who did the sketching didn't do a good job of making it look like Slim.

Slim continued hanging out with Double J, robbing, thieving, pimping Angie, and doing whatever else it took to support his dope habit. Slim lived a double life that no one knew of. No one ever knew that Slim had secretly turned into a rapist.

Slim started to go up to the University of Chicago late at night to prey on the women coming from night school. At first, Slim couldn't rob or rape any of the women because the university's security cops would patrol the university frequently. Before long, Slim studied and learned the time the university security cops would patrol certain areas of the university.

One night after the students exited the first entrance of the school (which was on a side street), Slim saw her. A redhead stood almost six feet, makeup was flawless, and she walked like she was auditioning for a beauty pageant that she would definitely win.

Slim couldn't do anything to her because there were too many other students around.

He ended up stalking her for a few days until, one night, he caught her walking up the street by herself. He walked up to her unmasked. She saw him coming toward her. She thought he was getting ready to strike up a conversation in order to get a date or something. She was interested, because Slim wasn't a bad-looking guy although he was a dope fiend.

As Slim made it to her, he upped a chrome .44. "Bitch, you bet not say a word or I'ma kill your ass," he said fiercely and sincerely.

"Oh my gosh, oh my gosh, take whatever you want," she said as she handed him her purse. "Just please don't hurt me."

"Bitch, shut up and follow me. I ain't gone hurt you," Slim said. Slim walked her to his car at gunpoint and forced her in.

Once they got into the car and he drove off, she pleaded for him not to hurt her.

"I told you I ain't gone hurt you," he said.

In the back of her mind, she knew he was lying. What else would an individual abduct someone at gunpoint for in the nighttime? I hope the police pulls on the side of us or pull us over for a traffic violation, she thought.

Once they were far away from the campus, he pulled over and duct-taped her mouth, handcuffed her hands together at the back the same exact way the police do it, and blindfolded her.

He drove her to the other side of town, to his grandfather's home. Once he made it to his grandfather's home, he pulled up in the garage, which was in the back of the house. He escorted her from the garage and took her to the basement. The neighbors couldn't see what was going on because of the wooden fences that surrounded the garage and the back of the house.

In her heart and mind, she cried out for him to let her free.

Once he got her in the basement, he made her get on her knees as he uncuffed her hands then tied up her hands and feet with cords, leaving the blindfold on her eyes and the duct tape around her mouth. She'd never been so scared in her life.

Slim then went upstairs to the second floor to check on his grandfather who was sound asleep.

His grandfather was eighty-eight years old. He caught a disease when he was eighty that made him blind. His grandfather didn't have very much company besides the nurses who would come to check on him each morning, bathe him, feed him, and do other things of that nature. He'd even bribe a few nurses into having sex with him. His grandfather lived in and owned a two-flat building.

Slim figured that his grandfather's basement would be a good place to keep the female he kidnapped. Slim knew that he was the only one who had keys to the basement, that his grandfather didn't have company besides the nurses, and that his grandfather couldn't get up and move around on his own, so therefore nobody would be coming into the basement.

Even if Slim's grandfather did have lots of company, his grandmother wouldn't let nobody in the basement, 'cuz his grandfather used to be a gangster back in his younger days and kept a lot of guns he had from back in the day in the basement.

For years, his grandfather stopped renting out the first floor to tenants, because some tenants didn't pay their rent on time.

After Slim saw that his grandfather was sound asleep, he went back into the basement and stared at this hot pretty young white lady he kidnapped. He couldn't stop staring at her. Although she was tied up, blindfolded, and her mouth was duct-taped he still enjoyed watching her beautiful features.

Slim began to slowly undress his victim.

She began crying. As tears ran down her face, she was thinking like, Damn, he finna rape me.

She tried to move her body, struggling for him not to rape her, but it was like a mission impossible.

As he slowly undressed her, his dick got hard at the sight of her freshly shaved pussy. As he upped his dick and entered her pussy with force, it was like heaven on earth for him. To her it was like a living hell. As he began taking the pussy from her, he started slapping on her ass cheeks, calling her every disrespectful name in the book. In a sick, sexual, perverted way, he was really enjoying himself.

All night, he did almost every sexual act known to man, from fingering her pussy and ass and sucking her titties to sticking his dick in her pussy and ass. And for the first time in life, he stuck his tongue up a woman's ass.

A couple of days later, on a cold winter's night, Slim and Double J was sitting in a car in Garfield Park, finishing shooting and snorting dope and smoking lace joints, wondering to themselves what they could do to make some more money to get high.

"Lord, what we gone do to get some more dope?" Slim asked Double J.

"I don't know. That's a good question," Double J said.

Both men remained silent for a brief moment, enjoying their highs and trying to figure out how they was gonna get some more dope.

"Let's steal some cars," Double J said.

"Hell naw, man, that's a headache. First we gotta find some cars to steal, then we gotta find somebody to buy the parts off it," Slim said.

"Well, when you come up with something better, then let me know," Double J said.

"I'm tired of stealing cars, boosting clothes, and pimping. All that shit takes too long. I be needing instant money. I love to get high," Slim said.

"Yeah, I feel you, 'cuz I'm tired of the same shit. I like robbing dope spots 'cuz you get money and dope right then and there. But we done robbed damn near every spot out west. And the ones we didn't rob was because they had guns on it or they was patting us down," Double J said.

"Let's order a pizza," Slim said.

Double J turned his head, directly facing Slim, looking at him like he was crazy. "Damn, you went from trying to figure out how to get some money to ordering a pizza," Double J said sarcastically.

"I'm talking about robbing the pizza man," Slim said.

"Robbing the pizza man is burned up. Everybody's been doing it. Majority of the pizza men don't even have that much money on them, just in case they do get robbed," Double J said.

"They gone have some money on them. Whatever he have, it'll be enough to get some dope, and we gone get something to eat, all for free," Slim said.

Double J began laughing and thinking *This nigga Slim is silly.*

"The average pizza man ain't gone come to certain hoods," Double J said.

"Yeah, I know. We gone go to one of them nice-ass hoods and call him and give him one of the addresses. Once he makes it to the address, before he even gets a chance to knock on the door, here comes me to take his shit," Slim said.

"Sounds like a good plan to me, so, uhhh, what we waiting on?" Double J said.

Slim pulled off and rode for about twenty minutes to a hood that wasn't ghetto.

He pulled on a super-quiet block and got the address from the house that was on the corner. They then went to the pay phone and ordered two large cheese pizzas with most of the toppings.

As they went back, they parked in front of the house with the address they gave. It was as if both of them could actually taste and smell the pizza. They couldn't wait to get paid and wrap their lips around them pizzas.

In no time flat, the pizza man was pulling up and parking right behind them. They saw a Hispanic-looking dude get out the car with two big pizzas in his hands.

Slim jumped out the driver's side of the car with gun in hand. "Bitch, give me them motherfucking pizzas and empty your pockets," Slim said.

The pizza man did exactly what Slim said with no hesitation, scared to death.

"Bitch, get in the car and drive off," Slim said after robbing him.

The pizza man got in his car and pulled off, damn near causing a car collision once he made it to the intersection.

Slim got into the car and pulled off, going in the opposite direction from the pizza man.

Once they made it back to the hood, they parked and began eating pizza and counting the money.

"Damn, Lord, this pizza is a bomb," Double J said.

"It came from Home Run Inn," Slim said. Slim continued counting the money. "We got two hundred and eighty dollars," Slim said.

"Give me my half," Double J said.

Slim counted out a hundred and forty and passed it to Double J. What Double J didn't know was that Slim only pulled out some of the money outta his pocket. He played for the rest.

They continued eating pizza on their way to the dope spot. They spent majority of that two-eighty getting high that night.

Two days later, while Slim was asleep, he had a dream that two midget women—one was black, one was white—were taking turns sucking on his dick. When he was about to unleash a load of nut, he awoke to the reality of his girl Angie lying there asshole-naked, sucking on his dick, and it felt so good to him. As he unleashed his nut down Angie's throat, he began rubbing on her titties and pregnant belly.

Afterward they both stood up as he looked her straight in the eyes and told her, "See, that's why I love you so." Then he kissed her on her left cheek and hugged her tightly.

They ended up getting high then getting dressed and going to a breakfast joint. While they sat at the table eating breakfast, a glimpse of the woman's face he had tied up in his grandfather's basement flashed in his mind.

Damn, I done left that lady tied up in the basement for two days with nothing to eat, Slim thought.

Slim and Angie ate, and then Slim immediately dropped her off at home. On his way to his grandfather's home, he stopped at McDonalds to buy the lady he'd kidnapped something to eat.

Once he made it to his grandfather's basement, his victim could hear his footsteps and began yelling and crying, but no one could hear her cries because of the duct tape around her mouth. She surely thought that eventually he'd kill her.

For the last two days, she'd been living a nonfiction horror story. She'd tried to get loose, to escape, but always came up unsuccessful.

Slim took the blindfold off and said, "How are you doing sleeping beauty?"

Her eyes got wide as she became more scared than ever by this maniac.

"I'm going to take this tape off your mouth to feed you. If you start to make any noise, I'm putting the tape back on your mouth and you won't eat," he said.

She nodded her head up and down in agreement. He put the blindfold back on. As soon as he took the tape off her mouth, she began yelling at the top of her lungs, "Somebody, please help me! Somebody, please!"

Before she could finish yelling, he put the tape back around her mouth. "I guess you don't wanna eat," he said sinisterly.

He pulled off his pants, got on his knees, and began rubbing her clitoris with his left hand and fondling his own dick with his right hand. As Slim began to get erect and the moisture of her pussy started to be felt on his hand, he got behind her and shoved his dick in her pussy. The tightness combined with the moisture and him being high felt great. He slammed his dick in and out her pussy showing no remorse for it.

Afterward he went up to the second floor and checked on his grandfather. His grandfather was doing okay.

He went back to the basement.

He began whispering in his victims ear, "I'm going to ask you one more time, do you want to eat something?"

She began shaking her head up and down.

"If I take this tape off your mouth and you start hollering and shit, I'ma make sure you don't eat for a long-ass time," he said.

He took the tape off her mouth. She didn't say a word. She was starving, and she knew that no matter how loud she'd holler, no one would probably hear her.

As she opened her mouth wide, all Slim could do was visualize his dick going in and out her mouth.

With a split-second decision, he decided to use some type of tool to feed her 'cuz if he used his hands, she might try to bite off some of his fingers. He looked over at the barbecue grill, walked over, and opened it up. There sat a tool used to grip and flip meat. He went to the sink, rinsed the tool, and went back over and began feeding her the cold McDonalds.

She ate the food like she was a starving little kid from one of them third-world countries.

After she finished eating, she began to cry out to him, "Please, please let me go. I'll give you anything. My family is rich. They'll make sure you get compensated for letting me free."

He put the tape back over her mouth, thinking about the compensation money. If I let this ho go and try to get compensated, my ass gone be in jail forever, he thought.

He forced her to the floor, lying flat on her stomach, and dived into her pussy full force, slamming his dope fiend dick in and out of her tight pussy as hard as he possibly could while admiring the view of the way her ass cheeks would jiggle each time he'd bounce up and down on her.

Slim and Double J's dope habits had started as a monkey on their back and turned into a real live silverback gorilla.

They began robbing any- and everybody, from cab drivers, pizza men, corner stores, hood restaurants, and dope dealers to old people and all. Every single day, they'd rob many different people, just to get high.

A month after the robbing spree began, Chicago police were on the hunt for Double J and Slim 'cuz they'd robbed so many people. Some of the corner stores and hood restaurants, they'd robbed more than once, and witnesses had positively indentified Double J and Slim.

Now Double J and Slim were on the run.

Double J's wife had filed for a divorce. She didn't wanna be with no dope fiend–ass nigga. So Double J was living from house to house. A majority of the people he lived with was some of his dope fiend buddies.

Slim, on the other hand, had told Angie to move in with one of her friends, and he himself stayed in his grandfather's building. Slim assumed that no one from the hood knew where his grandfather lived, so he figured his grandfather's home would be a good place to hide out in.

A couple of weeks went by. Slim had just finished shooting up some dope and went back to his grandfather's basement. He fed his victim. After she finished eating, he put the tape back over her mouth. He got naked and took off her blindfold to finally let her see his full body naked.

He laid her flat on her stomach and went off in her ass for the first time. She yelled, screamed, and cried tears. Slim couldn't hear her yells, screams, or cries because of the tape around her mouth.

In the midst of Slim having his way with her ass, the basement door flew open.

"Freeze! Police!" Almost thirty police officers flooded the room. The police immediately snatched Slim off his victim, handcuffed him, and told him that he was being charged with twenty separate counts of armed robbery.

They untied the kidnapped woman. To the police, she seemed to be almost lifeless, with her booty bleeding as if she were stabbed in it. Once they took the duct tape off her mouth, she jumped up, crying, "Oh my gosh, thank you for rescuing me," she said.

They wrapped a blanket around her as she told her nonfiction horror story.

As the police searched the basement, they found all seven of the old guns his grandfather had and put them on Slim. Now Slim had twenty counts of robbery, a kidnapping, a sexual assault, and seven unlawful use of weapons. He was never getting outta jail. And when and if he did, he'd be an old man.

They came to find out that the lady he'd kidnapped and raped repeatedly was Suzan Armstrong, a twenty-seven-year-old English teacher.

On the ride to the police station, the police beat his ass. They gave him two black eyes, a busted nose, and knocked out two of his teeth.

Once he made it to the police station, they ended up putting him in a lineup. Five more business owners picked him out of the lineup for robbing their businesses. One other woman picked him out of a lineup for raping her. She was the one he raped with no mask on.

Once he made it to the Cook County jail, he felt the full effect of being dope sick. He sat in the bull pen, crying out to Allah, Father of the Universe, as he threw up his guts. It was as if twenty maniacs were all poking away at his stomach with small sharp objects. He'd never felt so much pain in his life.

Once he finally made it to the dec the guys screened him to see if he was gang affiliated. Once they found out he was a ViceLord, they checked to see if he had any status. Once they found out he wasn't a universal elite, they showed him the ropes and introduced him to all the brothers.

They next day, they gave him a knife and put him on the ViceLords' security.

A few days later, Slim got in touch with his grandfather and Angie. His grandfather started sending money, and Angie began visiting on his visiting days.

After a few weeks of being in the county jail, Slim began to notice the ViceLords and everybody else on the dec start straying away from him.

One morning Slim didn't wake for breakfast. He overslept. While asleep, three big dudes came into his dark cell and began beating the shit out of him with man-made weapons. Slim didn't stand a chance of fighting back.

One man took his pants off and took his booty. Slim's screams were like horrifying echoes as the tissue in his booty hole got torn.

The ViceLords and all other gangs under the fin were against homosexuality; therefore, a ViceLord or any other gang under the fin wouldn't rape another man or women. But other gangs didn't give a fuck about homosexuality, especially if a man let another man rape him. The other gangs that weren't fin ball looked at it as, if a nigga let another nigga rape him, then he needed to be raped. A majority—if not all—gangs in Chicago was against raping women. That's why they raped him—so he could see how it felt to be raped.

Afterward Slim ran to the ViceLords, body filled with pain, barely able to see because of his eyes being covered with blood, crying out for the ViceLords' assistance.

The ViceLord and everybody on the dec laughed at him as if he were a comedian on stage and they were the audience.

Slim looked around, crying out for help. As they laughed, he couldn't believe what was going on. The dramatization was that of a horror flick for Slim.

One ViceLord shouted out, "We don't fuck with no raper man."

Slim then ran to the COs. The COs called 10-10 and within seconds, a gang of COs flew on the dec, whupping the inmates' asses and putting the dec on lockdown and escorted Slim to the jail's hospital.

Slim received seventeen stitches and ten staples. The staples were in his head. The stitches were in various places in his body, including his ass. He got fucked up real bad. Slim told the COs he didn't know what happen. He didn't know who did that to him. Slim didn't believe in telling the police shit.

Slim was escorted back to the dec, which was still on lockdown, to get his things. Slim went to the cells of a few of the ViceLords who were universal elites. "Lord, ya'll gone let them niggas get down on me like that," Slim said.

"You know we don't get down like that," one of the universal elites said through the cell door.

"Like what?" Slim asked.

"We heard you was locked up for raping hos. We against that, Lord. We ain't ever honoring you as no ViceLord no more. Shiiit, since you been raped, you're a faggot now. Wherever you go in jail, you ain't gone get no respect for letting them niggas rape you."

Slim went to other ViceLords' cells, and they didn't even wanna talk to him, disgusted by him being a raper man and letting niggas rape him.

Once Slim made it to PC, right then and there, he saw two of his homies from the streets. They had fucked up some people's drugs and commissary and checked into PC 'cuz they couldn't pay them.

Slim immediately noticed there were a lot of faggots in PC. He didn't like being around the faggots.

After a couple of months in jail, Slim's grandfather died. That was so fucked up for him. His grandfather was the only family he ever really had. He never knew his real dad. His mom had been dead for many years. She was killed in a car accident when he was a kid. The rest of his family lived down south, and the little family he had that lived in Chicago was phony as hell.

He couldn't even attend his grandfather's funeral 'cuz it cost $1,500 for the county jail to escort inmates to funerals.

A couple months after Slim's grandfather's death, Double J was found in an abandon building, dead, with a needle stuck in his arm. He died of an overdose of dope.

Slim came to find out that his girl Angie was fucking around with a nigga from the hood.

It was as if Slim and his entire world were beginning to fall apart.

Chapter 7

A ngie began feeling labor pains. "My water just broke. I'm going into labor," Angie told her lover, Todd.

Todd's eyes got wide. Todd immediately drove her to the hospital.

After seven hours of labor, Angie gave birth. Once the baby was released from Angie, the female doctor stated, "It's a beautiful little girl. She's beautiful enough to be a queen." The baby weighed six pounds and two ounces.

Angie had stop getting high when she was seven months pregnant so the baby wouldn't have any drugs in her system so DCFS wouldn't take the baby from her. Therefore, the baby came out healthy.

Angie looked in her beautiful little baby's eyes, and it was as if she could see the queen her daughter was destined to be, so she named her Queeny.

Queeny had gray eyes. Usually when a baby is born with gray eyes, they don't remain that color. They change to hazel, green, brown, even blue, as the baby gets older. Queeny had brown hair and high yellow skin. You could look at her and tell she was mixed with white and black.

A couple weeks after the baby was born, Angie took Queeny to the county jail to see her dad.

Slim came out to the visiting room and saw the baby in her hands. He didn't even know that she had given birth.

"Here is your daughter," Angie said through the tiny holes in the glass.

Slim instantly began smiling, looking through the glass of the visiting cage as Angie took the blanket off the baby's face. "She so cute. What is her name?" Slim asked.

"I named her Queeny because she's destined to be a queen," Angie said.

"I didn't even know you had the baby. When did you have her?" Slim asked.

"A couple weeks ago," Angie said.

"She's so cute. She looks just like you," he said.

"She looks more like you to me," Angie said.

As the baby opened her eyes, it was as if he could see the sunrise. Reality started to set in. Slim began thinking like, Damn, I'm never getting outta jail. My child is going to be a bastard.

The visit didn't last long 'cuz Slim couldn't stand to be around Angie and Queeny knowing he'd never see the streets again in order to actually be a part of their lives.

Angie and her boyfriend Todd began living in this studio apartment on the north side of Chicago.

Angie had stopped getting high when she was seven months pregnant, but once she had Queeny, she started right back, getting high at an all-time high. She always had regrets for letting Slim turn her into an addict 'cuz she knew drugs were her downfall, but she loved to get high.

Todd and Angie had devoted their lives to the usage of drugs.

One late night, Todd was coming back home from the twenty-four-hour liquor store.

As Todd opened the door, someone pushed him into their apartment.

Todd turned around, on the verge of laying hands on whoever pushed him, but turned around and saw that big-ass gun.

"Nigga, step back," the gunman said fiercely in a Jamaican accent.

Once Todd stepped all the way into the apartment, Angie saw the gunman step in behind Todd, and she yelled out, "We finna die."

The gunman immediately shut the door, leaving it unlocked. He then put his index finger over his mouth, shushing Angie. "Be cool and be quiet. I ain't gone hurt ya'll. I'm just gone rob ya'll and leave ya'll here tied up so ya'll can't call the police once I leave," the gunman said sincerely.

Rob us? We ain't got shit, Todd thought.

The robber took off his hoodie. He was black as hell, with Jamaican dreads in his head.

Aw shit! This is one of those crazy-ass Jamaicans, Todd thought.

Todd instantly began sizing him up. Just in case the guy slipped up, he'd try to knock the gun outta the Jamaican's hand and take it.

The gunman stood about five feet seven, and Todd could tell that he had been to the joint before 'cuz he was swole to death.

Within seconds, another man dressed in black came in. He looked as if he could be the other guy's big brother. The second man came right in and blindfolded Todd and Angie. He then made them get on their knees, duct tape their hands behind their backs, duct tape their legs together, and put duct tape around their mouths.

Angie and Todd weren't worried about what the robbers would do to them because they honestly believed that the robbers would only rob them and then leave. Todd and Angie were more worried about how they was going to get free from that duct tape.

The first robber began to notice Queeny sitting in her rocking chair asleep. As he stepped closer to her, she awoke, opening her beautiful eyes.

She's so cute, the robber thought.

Both men upped knives and began stabbing away at Todd and Angie's flesh as Queeny watched emotionlessly because she was only a baby and didn't know or understand what was going on.

Outside, it began to rain and thunder as the so-called robbers continued stabbing Todd and Angie up over thirty times apiece, leaving them for dead.

Within minutes, the killers left the two bodies there, laid out in their own puddles of blood that filled the carpet.

They left Queeny lying there in her rocking chair, smiling and listening to a Fisher-Price toy that played baby music.

As they left, they didn't bother to take anything because they weren't robbers. They were sent to kill. They ran out, leaving the door open.

A few years earlier, Todd used to buy dope from some Jamaicans up north but wound up having them front him some dope, and he fuck the money up. He thought he'd never see the Jamaicans again.

But he was wrong. One of the Jamaicans saw him coming out of their apartment building and sent killers.

The next morning, one of the neighbors had been in and out her apartment all that morning for various reasons and noticed that their door had been open all that morning.

The first time she saw the door open, it really wasn't any concern to her. But after seeing it open for hours, she knocked on it to see if everything was all right. After not getting a response from her hard knocks, she opened it and saw the bleeding dead bodies and began screaming. It was as if the screams echoed for blocks and blocks.

She ran to her apartment, scared to death, as if a killer were actually after her. She went into her apartment, locked the door, and put the chain on it. Ran to the phone and dialed 911.

After the fourth ring, the dispatcher answered. "Hello, this Chicago police dispatcher. May I help you?"

"It's two dead people. It's two dead people," she said, breathing heavy, crying, scared nervous.

"Calm down, ma'am. Now can you repeat yourself?" the dispatcher said.

"Two of my neighbors are lying in their front room, dead. Somebody killed them," the lady said.

"Ma'am, give me the address, and I'll send help over immediately," the dispatcher said.

"1170 N. Jarvis," the lady said.

"What apartment or floor?" the dispatcher asked.

"Apartment 2B," she said.

"Help will be over shortly," the dispatcher said. "Did you see who did these murders?"

"No, damnit! I don't want to talk. Send the police over here," the lady said.

Before the dispatcher could say another word, she'd hung up the phone.

This was a prominently white neighborhood; therefore, the police were there in no time.

Two rookie cops entered the apartment first and became sick to their stomachs. As all the other police entered and saw the dead bodies, it was nothing to them. They seen dead bodies many times before.

One of the rookie cops, who was a white woman in her midtwenties, began crying "Why, why, why would somebody do this?" as tears ran down her face.

They took Queeny to the hospital to see if everything was all right with her. Queeny was okay. The authorities tried to find Queeny's family and came up unsuccessful.

Angie's family mainly lived in other states and didn't even know a child existed. Those who lived in Chicago or near Chicago didn't want to have anything to do with the baby because she was partially black. They were racist as hell. They even disowned Angie when she first began fucking around with Slim. They felt like Angie had disgraced their family name.

Once Slim found out about Angie being killed, he felt like he had nothing else worth living for.

The next morning, after Slim found out about Angie, a female officer came through, doing the 11:00 a.m. count. She immediately noticed that some of the two-man cells only had one inmate in, which was fucking up her count, 'cuz she was used to counting by twos.

Slim was in the cell by himself. He had no celly. His last celly had gone home a couple of days ago.

The woman CO came to count Slim, looked through his cell door, and there Slim was, asshole-naked, hanging from a homemade rope he made from bed sheets.

The CO began instantly screaming. She started screaming so loud that she woke up everybody on the dec. All the inmates began looking outta the chuckhole of their cell doors as the other COs rushed in to see what was going on.

Once the COs made it to her, she said in a loud screeching voice, "He hung himself."

The COs instantly keyed the door open and took him down from the rope.

One CO knew how to check his pulse. The CO checked his pulse, looked at the other officers with water in his eyes, and said, "He's dead."

The other CO got on his walkie-talkie and called for doctors to come and attend to Slim's body.

One of the other COs grabbed the big piece of paper that was taped to his stomach and read it out loud: "That's one thing about life is that at the end of it, we must all die, and I chose my own time to die. I'll see you in hell where my sinful soul will dwell."

The room got silent, as his handwritten words were a reality check for the CO's. They knew that one day we must all die.

Police ended up turning Queeny over to the custody of DCFS.

Within weeks, this elderly lady, who was a landlord in one of the buildings that Angie and Slim lived in together before, attended both Angie's and Slim's funerals and found out Queeny was with DCFS. The elderly lady tried to locate Slim's and Angie's families, and she came to find out that neither Slim's nor Angie's family gave a fuck about Queeny. The elderly lady, Christine, took it upon herself to obtain custody of Queeny.

At first, DCFS didn't want to give Christine custody of Queeny 'cuz she was old and because she wasn't married. One of Christine's grandkids was lovers with the twenty-seventh ward alderman, and he helped Christine obtain custody of Queeny.

Queeny brought joy and sunshine to Christine's life. Christine had never been happier than she'd been in her entire sixty-five years of living.

Christine died at the age of seventy when Queeny was only five. When Christine died, it was as if a piece of Queeny died inside. Although she was really young, she still felt the pain of losing Christine. Queeny never knew her mom and dad or any of their family. All she knew was Christine. Christine treated her as if she was her very own daughter.

After Christine's death, none of her family members wanted to adopt Queeny. One of Christine's daughters, Roseline, ended up taking custody of Queeny. Roseline was Christine's only daughter who turned out bad. Roseline was an alcoholic and tooted raw cocaine.

Inside Roseline's home, it smelled like a dead body was there. Roseline didn't know or understand what clean meant. Roseline's house wasn't even fit for wild animals to live in.

Daily, Roseline would beat Queeny for petty reasons. Queeny cried from Roseline's beatings. They would literally haunt her in her sleep. Some nights, she couldn't sleep, constantly awaking from nightmares of Roseline's beatings. Queeny always promised herself that if she ever had kids, she'd show nothing but love and would never put her hands on them under any circumstances.

Chapter 8

A few years later, although Queeny was still experiencing difficulties with Roseline, she had no other choice because this was all the family she really had.

Queeny maintained good grades in school. She was a real smart kid. The only problem she had was that she got into many fights in school because they assumed she was white. The school she went to was all populated by blacks. Although she was mixed with white and black, she mainly looked white. The immature kids would make racial slurs and continue picking on her.

She got tired of going through bullshit at home with Roseline, and at school, with the kids bullying her, she began starting fights, becoming the bully herself. If anyone at school would create any problems, she'd instantly start a fistfight with anybody, releasing all her anger and frustration on them. In no time, she began to get respect from the kids at school.

King Phill would see Queeny walking to school some mornings. Phill would look at Queeny and feel sorry for her. Phill knew her story. He knew her mom and dad was dead, and that Roseline was a drug addict.

Queeny knew Phill as well. Ever since she could remember, within her young life, Phill always helped her out with Christmas gifts and school supplies among other things.

One day, while Queeny was walking to school alone, he decided to walk her to school. "Queeny, slow down. I'ma walk you to school," Phill said.

"Why don't you drop me off in your car?" Queeny said.

"Somebody in my car. I'm just gone walk you to school," he said.

Phill began to pour his heart out to her and give her a little game. "I like seeing you go to school, go to college and do something with your life. You're destined for fortune and fame. Never settle for anything less than the best. Don't never let a man rule or ruin your life. Live your life like the queen of all queens," Phill said.

When Queeny was twelve, Roseline became a prostitute.

One night, Roseline went out on the ho stroll to sell some pussy and never came back. People in the neighborhood assumed she was killed by a trick, but her dead body was never found and no one witnessed her being killed. There were only assumptions.

King Phill had his sister Rachel get custody of Queeny.

Rachel was an alcoholic, but she didn't use drugs and she took care of her business, doing the best she could to raise her own kids. Rachel had five kids of her own. Rachel's two teenage boys were eighteen and seventeen years old, and her other three kids' (who were girls) ages were fifteen, thirteen, and eleven.

Queeny began smoking weed with Tom and Paul, Rachel's two sons, and hanging on the streets a little, seeing the actions and transactions of the ViceLords. She began being infatuated with the ViceLord nation. The ViceLords showed out as far as selling dope and getting money. Most women are attracted to money. She was intrigued by the mass amount of men who was representing VL. They wore their hats to the left and dressed in the slickest gear. There were many other gangs in Chicago, but the ViceLords were mostly adored by the women.

Queeny didn't need any finances because Phill and Rochelle made sure she was straight financially. But with her being young and dumb, she began to get involved in criminal activities, not only for the extra money, but for the excitement as well.

At age fourteen, Queeny and some of the niggas she went to high school with would go to clothing stores and steal. They'd do the thieving while Queeny would be talking to the store workers for long periods as a distraction method. They'd take the clothing and sell them to dope dealers. The money was cool, but Queeny was full of greed and wanted more. She became victim to the fast life and fast money.

Before long, she began selling dope with Tom and Paul. Tom, Paul, and Queeny knew that if Phill found out, they'd be in deep shit. King Phill didn't want any of his family members using or selling drugs, but he didn't attempt to stop the men in his family from using or selling drugs, although he didn't like it. As far as the women were concerned, he'd go crazy if he'd found out they were selling or using dope.

One day, Phill noticed that Queeny was hanging on one of the spots in the hood during school hours. Phill began snapping at Queeny. He told her that every time school hours were in process, she'd better be in school. And when she got outta school, she still couldn't hang out at any dope spots.

The same week, he caught her hanging at one of the hood's dope spots—this time, after school hours.

She made up an excuse, claiming that she was passing by and began talking to a nigga she went to school with. Phill told her that if she didn't get her act together, he'd stop giving her money. That was his way and other street niggas' way of punishing people—ceasing to provide them with finances—but that didn't work. She continued to hang at the dope spots and continued selling dope.

At this time, within Chicago, a majority of the dope spots were behind closed doors. But Tom and Paul's dope house continued to get raided by the police; therefore, they decided to start selling their dope on the corners. Therefore, they wanted Queeny to work, because the police wouldn't suspect her as the one selling the dope. The only problem is that she was a candidate for a stickup. She got robbed twice in one week.

Tom and Paul came to the realization that she was still a little girl, and there was no need for her to be out there. Tom and Paul knew that she could get shot by the stickup man, catch a juvenile case, and a lot of other bad shit could happen.

Tom and Paul started telling her that she didn't have to sell dope, because they'd give her money and Phill would too, only if she behaved herself.

She'd told them that she enjoyed selling dope, which was the truth. She was selling dope partially for the money and partially for the thrill and art of it. The boys told her that the streets were cold and unfair. She then told them that if they didn't want her to work for them, there'll be others who would let her work.

The boys knew in the back of their minds that she was right. They both became upset that they even introduced her to this aspect of the street life.

So she wouldn't be on the spot, they then started letting her go to the table to bag up dope. Sometimes they'd be at the table with her. Sometimes she'd do it by herself. The pay was greater for her, and there was less risk of her getting robbed or catching a case. And Phill would never find out about her going to the table.

One day, Queeny was walking home from school through a dope spot that wasn't indoors. It was out on the corner, and she saw a member of the ViceLords shooting at a rival gang. This was her first time seeing a gun being shot. She liked the excitement.

The night before, at a party, the ViceLords and GDs got into a fight over one guy who felt a female's ass. The two men ended up fighting. One man was a ViceLord and the other one was a GD. It led to a mass amount of both gangs fighting in the club.

The club had metal detectors; therefore, they couldn't get in with their guns or any other weapons. Once the crowd dispersed out of the club and went to their cars, one of the ViceLords opened fire and wounded one of the GDs. He didn't die, but he was seriously injured, which led to a street war against the ViceLords and GDs.

During this war, she heard so much gunfire it became like music to her ears.

During this particular war, she started carrying guns, not for her personal use, but to only transport them for Tom and Paul or other members of the ViceLords. By her being a female, it was less chance for the police to harass her than they would a man.

She liked carrying guns, she craved for the day she'd be able to squeeze the trigger of one.

One time, one of the guys who worked for her brothers purchased a fully loaded .32 revolver from a dope fiend for forty dollars. Normally when an individual from the streets buys a gun, they immediately shot it to see if it'll shoot with no defects, but he didn't. He wanted to wait until nightfall.

Queeny was there when he bought the gun. She wanted to hear how it would sound. She adored the sound of gunfire. He told her to wait to tonight, and he'd let her shoot it.

Her eyes opened with amazement, thinking I can't wait until tonight.

Later on that night, he let her shoot it. She thought it would be difficult to shoot. All along, it was like chewing bubble gum.

The first shot felt and sounded so good to her that she unloaded all six shots into the sky.

Chapter 9

After months progressed along, the ViceLords and the GDs' war had long ceased. Now the ViceLords were into it with each other. The Insanes were into it with the Renegade ViceLords. This was unusual because all branches of ViceLords worked together. But one of the Insanes robbed one of the Renegades for ten thousand in drugs.

Queeny wanted to be involved and do some shootings, but they wouldn't let her because she was a female, and so young. In reality, they didn't take her seriously as far as doing any shootings. More and more, Queeny would gaze at the skies viciously, lusting for the day she could unload a gun. Not in the skies like she once did before but in a human being this time.

Although Queeny was so young, still in her own heart and mind, she felt as a queen over all. Queeny knew the meaning of power, and she wanted it in abundance.

Once Queeny initially started bagging up dope for Tom and Paul, she stopped hustling directly on the dope spot for a little while.

One day, Queeny started back hustling on Tom and Paul's joint just to get a little extra money and was robbed for the third time.

Once her brothers Tom and Paul found out about it, they told her once again to stay away from the dope spots. She didn't listen.

Tom and Paul got tired of their dope spots getting robbed, so they started paying a man two hundred each day to stand on security with a gun just in case the stickup man came by. The security man shift would consist of twelve hours.

By this time, Tom and Paul had all sorts of people in play to run their dope spot. Tom and Paul basically didn't do shit but collect money.

One day, Queeny decided to get up with Tom and Paul's workers to take the security position of holding the gun just in case the stickup man came by.

She took this position for two reasons: To be in possession of the gun so she could bust it if the stickup man ever came by—she could shoot the shit outta him or them. Also, so she could show the guys that she had more heart than them. While standing on security, she prayed that the stickup man would come by.

She took this security position on a saturday. She knew that if Phill caught her on the spot on a saturday she'd think of some lame excuse of why she was hanging on the spot and knew she'd have less problems from Phill, being that it wasn't a school day.

The security hours revolved around her curfew. The security hours were twelve hours a day. Usually 8:00 a.m. to 8:00 p.m. then 8:00 p.m. to 8:00 a.m. Her curfew was at 10:00 p.m., so she'd work the shift from 8:00 a.m. to 8:00 p.m.

She ended up working security on saturday and sunday.

Sunday morning, a stickup a man robbed the workers. With her being on security, she was supposed to make sure the stickup man didn't even get a chance to rob the workers, but he did.

As the stickup man ran to his car after robbing the workers, she saw him running with his gun in hand as the workers yelled, "He just robbed me!"

She unloaded a .38 into the back window of his car. She didn't hit him although she was really trying.

When this incident occurred, it was broad daylight. Everyone saw it.

She immediately went to a house in the hood to stash the weapon and went home.

Although she didn't hit the stickup man, she didn't find this out 'til later on.

She sat at home, traumatized, thinking that she'd shot and killed him and that she'd be going to jail for a long-ass time.

The entire day, it was the talk of the hood, how Queeny's young ass popped that pistol.

In this day and age, in the 1990s, you didn't have too many females shooting guns like the females in the 1980s. The women in the 1990s were more caught up in being pretty girls, mainly dressing fresh, partying, and having fun.

Once Tom and Paul heard about it, they went home snapping on her.

"Girl, we give you money and momma and Phill give you money and we let you go to the table for us. What the fuck was you even doing out there on security for a funky two hundred dollars?" Tom said.

"I wasn't doing it for the money. I was out there just in case the stickup man came through," Queeny said.

"Why the fuck is you worried about the stickup man for?" Paul asked.

"Because I'ma queen, and I got my own ways of doing things," Queeny said.

"Girl, you done lost your motherfucking mind. A queen, my ass! You betta hope that guy ain't get shot or killed. If he did, your ass gone be the queen of jail," Paul said.

The next morning, King Phill heard what she'd done. Phill knew it was Tom and Paul's dope spot; therefore, King Phill was intelligent enough to know that the Tom and Paul had something to do with it, one way or the other.

Phill confronted Tom and Paul and didn't even give them a chance to explain. Phill had both Tom and Paul violated by other members of the ViceLord nation.

Phill wanted to beat Queeny's ass, but he didn't because she was a girl. He was against putting his hands on females, especially a little girl whom he considered to be a part of his family.

The next day, Phill told Queeny to pack her shit—she was moving. He took her to the house of one of his other sisters who lived on the south side of town.

After several weeks, Queeny ran away from the crib of Phill's sister Sheila. Sheila was rude and disrespectful at the mouth and too controlling. She knew if she didn't leave from Phill's sister Sheila's crib they would end up fighting.

Queeny went back to the West Side to live with one of the girls she went to school with, Susan.

Queeny didn't have too many girlfriends because she was the true essence of a tomboy and mainly hung around with the guys. But she and Susan were real cool. She knew her since grammar school. In grammar

ALAN HINES

school, she spent a lot of time with Susan and her family. Once she got to high school, she didn't hang out with her a lot. She'd mostly kicked it with her in school.

She knew she couldn't stay with Susan's family for too long. It'd only be temporarily—maybe for a few weeks or a couple months at the most.

It was cool for Queeny to live with Susan because Susan lived close to the school and they had some of the same classes together.

Once King Phill found out that Queeny was missing, the first thing that came to his mind was that something bad had happen to her. Not once did it cross his mind that she'd run away from home.

King Phill began looking for Queeny relentlessly. He also told everyone he knew that if someone had any information of her whereabouts, he'd pay heavily for that information.

A couple of days later, one of Phill's tightest homies saw her going to school and went and told Phill. Phill sat in his car outside of Queeny's high school, waiting for her to depart.

Once school was over, he saw Queeny exit the door among a gang of other students. When he first saw her, he couldn't believe it.

Queeny began walking past his car and didn't even notice it. Phill lowered his window. "Queeny, get your ass in this car," Phill said.

She jumped right in the passenger seat.

"Girl, where the fuck you been? I've been worried about you, thinking something bad happened to you," Phill said.

"I've been over my friend Susan's house. Me and your sister weren't getting along. Your sister don't know how to treat people," Queeny said.

Phill wanted to curse her out, but he knew that it'd only make matters worse. Phill drove her around for hours, talking to her on a civilized level, telling her that she was a queen and a beautiful human being and that she deserved better than being some hood rat or some low-life drug addict.

Phill knew that on the route she was going, she was destined for self-destruction.

"Your momma and daddy's demise came from them running the streets and using drugs, and I know you ain't ready to die. And I ain't ready to bury you in a casket. I love you as you're my very own. I always cared about you even when you were a little girl. I want for you the same things I'd want for my very own daughter if I had one," Phill said.

"I know in a few more years you're gonna be grown and you'll have to make your own decisions, but I hope that I can inspire you to be a great woman instead of a nobody. You're destined to be a queen in your own mind in time," Phill said.

She ended up moving back into Rochelle's home. She stopped selling dope and getting into trouble for the time being. Although she continued to smoke weed, she stayed away from the streets.

Chapter 10

Queeny stayed out of trouble for a couple of years. Phill would spend lots of time with Queeny because he loved her and wanted her to be a success story of being an honest working citizen and a respected businesswoman.

By the time Queeny was sixteen, Phill's prince Black was checking her out, but Black knew if he got involved with her, Phill would be pissed off. Prince was a snake in the flesh of a human, a dope-fiend killer-slash-stickup-man. King Phill made him the prince for one main reason. Phill knew that Black would run the ViceLord mob with an iron fist and wouldn't take any bullshit.

Black even started hanging out with Queeny. Phill didn't mind. He figured Queeny was like Black's goddaughter or younger sister. Although Phill knew Black was a snake, he didn't think he'd ever snake him.

When Black and Queeny would hang out together, they'd smoke weed and do average shit like going to the show, shopping, or just riding around bending blocks.

Around this time, Queeny's grades began to excel. She began to get a higher learning, with plans of being a college student.

Around the time Queeny was seventeen, she was riding in the car with Phill. Phill was going to pick up some money that a nigga owed him. He usually had someone to take care of his drug business. The reason why he went this time to take care of this transaction himself was because he was only collecting money.

The reason he took Queeny with him was because she was already in the car.

Phill had been sweating this nigga to pay him some money he owed him. He'd fronted him four and a half ounces of raw cocaine. But the nigga who owed him had been bullshitting on paying him. The nigga finally beeped him, and Phill called him as they made arrangements for Phill to come pick up the money he owed him.

Once Phill made it to his destination, he parked in front of the building the nigga gave him the address to.

As soon as he finished parking, the nigga who owed Phill the money ran up to the car in a madman rage, shooting and hitting Phill in the head three times.

At first, the triggerman was unaware that Queeny was in the car until he start shooting up Phill. After he shot Phill in the head, at the third shot, Queeny frantically tried to open the door and get out of the car but didn't make it out. The triggerman shot her twice in the neck as she fell out the door, onto the ground. He then shot her once in the back and fled the scene of the crime. In the back of his mind, he was positive that he had killed Phill and Queeny.

Silky Mac was the killer. Silky Mac was one of Phill's long-term homies. Phill knew Silky Mac almost all his life and would've never thought he'd cross him, especially not for something small as a four and a half.

Silky Mac began using more cocaine than selling and ended up fucking up Phill's money. Usually, when Silky Mac would pay Phill, he'd be short. This time, Silky Mac had fucked up more than half of the money. Silky Mac knew that if he didn't pay Phill, Phill would have his joint robbed repeatedly or possibly have him shot or killed. Silky Mac had clout for the ViceLords but not like Phill.

Silky Mac figured that if he killed Phill and no one knew about it, he would get away with the murder and paying Phill, and he wouldn't have to worry about anyone doing anything to him.

Phill had so many people attending the funeral that it was as if a celebrity had died. Silky Mac was one of the pallbearers.

After Phill got killed, Phill's followers and Silky Mac and his guys walked the streets like zombies day and night, night and day, trying to find out any information on who killed Phill.

If they'd ever found out who killed Phill, that individual or anyone else who was related or even affiliated with him would have to die. Unfortunately, the only witness was Queeny, who was in critical condition.

Silky Mac heard that Queeny survived. Silky Mac was only a little worried, although he assumed she didn't know him. He also figured that it happened so quickly that she wouldn't recognize it was him even if she did see him again.

Several days after the funeral, everyone was still sad. Although Phill was a gang chief, he did a lot of good things for people: paid people's ways through college, helped people with bills, even stopped people from getting killed or being endangered by his own ViceLord members. He even forced some people to rehab to stop their addiction. Phill had some bad ways, but he had some good ways as well.

For the next past couple weeks, Phill's followers among others including Homicide had been visiting Queeny daily anxious to know who the killer was, but she was still in critical condition.

By a twist of fate of luck, this particular day and time, Prince Black came to the hospital shortly after her recovery. Black was the first one who saw her after her recovery. This first thing that came out of Black's mouth was "Who did this to you and Phill?"

"Silky Mac," Queeny said.

"Silky Mac," Black said in disbelief, surprised. "Which Silky Mac?" Black asked.

"Conservative Silky Mac," Queeny said.

"You sure it was Silky Mac?" Black asked in disbelief.

As Queeny attempted to tell him she was sure it was Silky Mac, Black mentally blocked Queeny out and paused, thinking I only know one Silky Mac and Why would he kill Phill?

Queeny began to vividly tell Black the horrifying story, and Black was focused, listening attentively. As she talked, it was as if Black could visualize the ordeal as if he was actually there.

"Phill had got a beep, looked at his beeper, and told me to grab the cellular phone outta his glove compartment. He dialed the number off his beeper. Once the person on the other line answered, Phill asked him 'Who is this?' Then Phill was like, 'Silky Mac, what the fuck took you so long to get up with me?' I don't know what Silky Mac said. Then Phill asked him, did he have all the money he owed him? Phill then hung up and drove to where Silky Mac was. We drove to this big brown building and parked, and then Silky Mac came outta nowhere, shooting."

Black paused as his mind went blank for a few seconds and closed his eyes, visualizing the bullets ripping through Phill's flesh, putting him to death.

Black then opened his eyes.

"You sure it was Silky Mac? How do you know Silky Mac?" Black asked.

"I know it was Silky Mac because I heard Phill say his name over the phone, and I know Silky Mac personally 'cuz he fucks with my friend Susan's mother," she said.

"Did you tell anybody about what happened?" Black asked.

"Naw, I'm just waking up after I got shot," Queeny said.

"Don't tell nobody, you hear me, girl? Don't tell nobody," Black said.

"A'ight," Queeny said.

Black immediately left the hospital, filled with rage. Once he entered his car, he remembered that he had pictures of Silky Mac from the past that they took at a club.

He went and got the pictures and went right back to the hospital.

Once he made it back to the hospital, he noticed that Rochelle and her daughters were there. Black sat down and chilled out, impatiently waiting for Rochelle and her daughters to leave in order to show Queeny the pictures to see if she could positively ID Silky Mac.

Once Rochelle and her daughters left, Black showed her the pictures and told her to pick out which individual was Silky Mac. Each picture displayed a group of niggas on it. Black had already had it on his mind that if she could pick out Silky Mac outta the groups, then she was right in knowing who exactly took Phill's life from him.

With no hesitation, she picked out Silky Mac on each and every picture. "You bet not tell nobody about Silky Mac killing Phill. If they ask who killed Phill and shot you, tell them you don't know 'cuz it happened so fast," Black told her.

"I know how this shit go. He took Phill's life. Now you'll take his—eye for an eye," Queeny said.

Black slightly smiled, thinking, This girl got a little game under her belt.

"I gotta go. I gotta run some errands," Black said.

As Black sat in his car outside the hospital, he tried to put all the puzzle pieces together. He remembered what Quenny said, that he owed Phill some money.

But Phill's a good nigga. He would've given him some work or fronted him some shit to get on. Aw, this nigga must've been fucking up the money and couldn't pay Phill back. So he told Phill to meet him outside the hood to collect, and once Phill came to collect, he killed him, not knowing that Queeny would be with him. This pussy-ass nigga came to the funeral, was even one of the pallbearers, and roamed the streets with us, looking for the one who killed Phill, and all along he was the one who did it. He did all this shit so he wouldn't be suspect as the killer, Black thought.

Black yelled out, "Bitch-ass nigga!"

At first, Silky Mac wasn't hiding out because he assumed Queeny didn't see him when the shooting occurred, and if she did see him during the shooting, she didn't know who he was. But now Silky Mac was hiding out. He started to get nervous about if Queeny would recognize him or not.

What Silky Mac didn't know was Queeny already knew exactly who he was.

Silky Mac was the chief of the Conservative ViceLords, which was a branch of ViceLords that didn't have a large number of members.

Black told all the IVL to kill any CVL they see and that anyone who killed Silky Mac will be granted fifty thousand. Once people heard about that fifty thousand, everybody and their momma was looking for Silky Mac. Most people didn't give a fuck about avenging Phill's death. They were only interested in that fifty thousand.

Less than an hour later, there were casualties of street wars. The Insanes went everywhere the Cs hung out at and caused bloodshed. What made this war different was that the CVLs didn't know they were in war at first. Therefore, they'd be somewhere chilling. Seeing members of the Insanes walk up, the Cs would assume that they were just coming to kick it or buy some drugs. All along, they were coming to commit bloody murder.

The streets were filled with madness. There was no peace or sleep, nothing but continuous gunfire, death, and destruction. It was like something out of a religious book. How the creator brought certain villages and towns to an end. Even the police were nervous to patrol the streets.

The next day after Black gave word to the IVL to slay Silky Mac or any other CVL they came across, the CVLs began to retaliate. The CVLs still didn't know what the war was about. The only thing they knew was that the Insanes were coming through, fucking them up, and that they must battle. The Cs didn't stand a chance. The Insanes were deeper and had more heartless killers.

Usually, when two different branches of ViceLords had a problem, they'd resolve it by putting someone in violation. It was rare that it resulted in gunfire, and when it did, it didn't last long. The chiefs would squash the problem. But this war would be a never-ending bloodshed because a king was killed. Never in the history of ViceLord existence was a king killed. Usually the worst that would happen to a king was he'd get lots of time in the state or federal prison or die of a disease or even natural causes.

At this point, Silky Mac had gone to a family reunion a day before the war kicked off.

A day after the war, he called one of his homies' house in Chicago for nothing more than to tell him that the family reunion in Memphis was fun. When he called his homey Tim's house, before he could get a chance to explain how good the reunion was, Tim began snapping out.

"Lord, we warring with the Insanes. It's like Vietnam in the streets. I ain't never heard this much gunfire," Tim said.

"What ya'll warring with the Insanes for?" Silky Mac asked.

"I don't know, man. They just been coming through, shooting motherfuckers in broad daylight as if they don't even give a fuck."

"Make sure all the brothers are secure with guns and shit. I'll investigate to see what the problem is," Silky Mac said.

Silky Mac called one of his hos from the hood and asked her why was it war in the streets between the Cs and the Insanes. He knew she'd know 'cuz she was the hoods' spy and detective. She stayed in everybody's business. Coincidentally, she knew what the war was about 'cuz her little brother was an Insane.

"They warrring 'cuz they think you is the one that killed Phill," she said.

"I ain't kill Phill," Silky Mac said.

"That's what they think. Black told the Insanes to kill any CVL they see on sight, and he got a price on your head for fifty g's," she said.

"Why would they think I killed Phill? I got love for Phill. Phill was my guy," Silky Mac said.

"I don't know, but I know that they think you were the one that killed Phill," she said.

Silky Mac immediately hung up the phone without even saying bye.

Silky Mac sat for hours, trying to figure out who told Black that, because no one was around to witness the murder. Silky Mac knew that he was in for a world of trouble and figured that he'd better stay properly placed away from Chicago, in Memphis.

Weeks passed along, and Silky Mac was still nowhere to be found.

Now not only was Black and the Insanes looking for him, Homicide was too. They came to find out that an old lady and her granddaughter had witnessed the entire murder of Phill and the attempted murder of Queeny. At first they didn't wanna tell anyone because they were too scared that Silky Mac would kill them if he found out they'd told the police on him. But both the mother's and granddaughter's consciences got the best of them. Feeling guilty, they decided to inform the authorities of what they'd witnessed. After Homicide found out Silky Mac was the killer, they went out on an all-out manhunt.

Homicide began repeatedly questioning Queeny, was Silky Mac the one who killed Phill and shot her? They'd continue to show her mugshots and other photos of Silky Mac. She continued to tell them that she didn't actually see who shot her. Homicide could get a conviction with just the old lady and her granddaughter as witnesses. But they knew that with Queeny, the old lady, and her granddaughter as witnesses, Silky Mac would get found guilty beyond reasonable doubt.

Queeny still never told anyone but Black that Silky Mac was the one who did it. Black didn't want Silky Mac to go to prison. Black wanted to take his life as he took Phill's life. Black believed in the old-school rule that under no circumstances were you to work with the police. Other people believed that if you testified on someone as far as witnessing to family member or friend being shot, then you weren't actually snitching, because they shot a loved one. But in reality, if an individual worked with the police in any shape, form, or fashion, you're still a stool pigeon.

Through it all, Queeny told no one of Silky Mac being the one. The only reason that people in the streets knew that Silky Mac was the one who killed Phill was because Black told everybody. Black never told anybody that Queeny told him that. The only reason Black told people was so that they'd avenge Phill's death. Black couldn't just tell people to shoot up the Cs without telling them that Silky Mac killed Phill.

Approximately one month after Black gave word to have all the Cs and Silky Mac whacked, Silky Mac was still nowhere to be found. The CVLs, on the other hand, were mostly dead, killed by the Insanes. And those Cs who weren't killed got fucked up so bad that they wished they were dead. The CVLs who were still alive, they were hiding out. Some even relocated to other states. During this war, many Insanes and some Cs were caught in cases of violence, such as murders, attempted murders, arsons, and gun cases, among other shit.

One day, Queeny asked Black, "Did you find Silky Mac yet?" That was her indirect way of asking Black, did he kill Silky Mac bitch ass yet? She knew that if Black ever caught Silky Mac, he'd be in the history books.

Black told her, "No, I can't seem to find him."

"Did you check on their spot out south?" Queeny said.

Black paused, looking at Queeny, clueless.

"What spot out south?" Black asked.

"The Cs got a block out south," Queeny said.

Black looked at Queeny angrily, as if he'd wanted to bite her head off.

"Why didn't you tell me about this block out south?" Black said.

"I assumed you'd find Silky on your own," she said.

"Where is this spot out south, and how do you know about it?" Black asked.

"It's around Seventy-Third and Green," she said.

"Ain't no ViceLords around there. That's all GDs and BDs," Black said.

"The Cs got one block around there. I know about this block. Years ago, Phill sent me to live with his sister out south for a little while. When I used to walk to the store, I remember seeing Silky Mac standing on Green," she said.

"How do know if it's one of the Cs' blocks? He could've knew some people around there and was, rotating, with them," Black said.

"I could tell, because everybody had their hats to the left. And Silky used to be standing around dictating things."

Black immediately left Queeny to his destination at Seventy-Third and Green. Black went by himself in an unmarked car.

All the while, driving over there, he assumed that Queeny didn't know what she was talking about, because that area was filled with GDs and BDs who hated ViceLords.

Once he finally made it to Seventy-Third and Green, he noticed that all the niggas on that block wore their hats to the left. Then he noticed two of Silky Mac's guys who were from out west on the block as well.

Damn! Queeny knew what she was talking about, Black thought.

As he drove back to the hood, he wondered how they get a block in the heart of the GD's. He then figured it out. He'd saw Silky Mac at a club one time with some guys who had their hats to the right. Black could tell that the niggas were ballers as far as getting money from the way they dressed; Silky Mac walked over to Black, introduced his cousins to him. Black shook their hands, and they went their separate ways.

Black figured out that Silky Mac's family were GDs who had juice for the GDs, and let Silky get a block in their hood.

Later on that night, Black and eleven of his guys went through Seventy-Third and Green with fully loaded semiautomatic weapons, killed ten men, and wounded seven others. This incident had the Chicago Police Department leery because they'd never seen that amount of casualties and injuries all at once in over forty years within Chicago since Al Capone's Saint Valentine's Day Massacre. After that day, the CVLs on Seventy-Third and Green were no more. Those who weren't out there to witness the mass bloodshed were glad and decided to do other things with their lives after all the killings and imprisonments of other CVLs throughout the city in this short period. Some even flipped to join other gangs. Others left the street life alone. Some even became Christians.

Approximately six months later, Homicide found Silky Mac in Memphis, Tennessee, at a family member's house. He was brought back to Chicago's Cook County Jail, eventually convicted of the murder of Phill and attempted murder of Queeny, and sentenced to fifty-five years in prison.

Queeny never testified against him in court, but the other two witnesses did. Silky Mac didn't last long in prison. He was stabbed to death by some of King Phill's loyal followers. 'Til this very day, you'll never see too many CVLs in the streets of Chicago or in the Illinois prison system due to Silky Mac's rat play and slaying of King Phill.